Sheltering Naomi

Ruby James

To all the animal lovers out there.

Contents

Animals of Hawkins Ridge

As a sanctuary ran by a family who loves animals, many will play side characters in the series. For Shelting Naomi, you will meet the following dogs. You can use this as a reference.

Shorty—Naomi's long-haired Dachshund
Scout—Caden's German Shepherd therapy dog
Rosebud, Tulip and Bluebell—Pug sisters and Fiona's pets
Mika and Tam—Terrier mix sisters and Naomi's foster fails
Vader—Harold Smith
Brutus—Ophelia Norris Newfoundland
Cinnamon—Fiona's horse

Chapter 1

The early afternoon sunbeam bounced off the painted charcoal gray concrete floor as Logan Beckett sat across from a large wire crate which held his patient coming out of anesthesia. The Pitbull mix was a recent addition to the Hawkins Ridge pack and had needed to be neutered. While the tan, muscular beauty hadn't shown aggression in the two weeks he'd been on the property, Logan didn't want to take any chances if the dog woke up irritable from surgery. Even with the flexible cone around his head.

Logan moved the syringe, holding a sedative closer to him when the Pitbull's slightly unfocused eyes slowly opened.

"Do I really need to be here?" Caden, Logan's younger brother by eighteen months, said from behind him. "He's not your first patient or neuter."

"What if he rips a chunk out of my leg? You'd feel guilty you weren't here to help."

Caden blinked a few times before pulling off his cap and scratching his short spiky hair. A former Marine, his brother came home after serving five years with PTSD, impaired hearing and a bitter divorce. He was also Logan's best friend, and the two relied on each other after their marriages ended around the same time.

"Wow. At least we know where Fiona gets her dramatic flair from."

Fiona, Logan's eleven-year-old daughter, was their resident drama queen. She loved to play the 'only grandchild' card when she didn't always get her way. But everyone adored her. Besides being the veterinarian for his family's rescue, which included tending to the horses they boarded, the goats on their small farm and their employees' pets, Logan was also a single father.

All the Beckett boys were practically clones of their father. Though Jace had their mother's dark blond hair, the chiseled jawline, dimples, straight noses, and height were all Thomas. At six feet, three inches, Logan wore his thick barreled chest with pride.

Though Caden gave him a hard time, they'd grown up around animals and knew never to assume things would go smoothly. Stress and uncertainty could make any animal act out of the norm. The mixed breed lifted his head and looked around, rising to his feet. Once the dog had its legs under him, Logan eased his hand close to the opening. After a good sniff, he rewarded Logan with a hearty lick.

"See, you didn't need me." Caden placed a bowl of water next to the crate's opening and squatted beside him. "How did your visit go this morning?"

Logan raked his fingers through his dark hair once the dog started drinking. He thought of the best way to answer the question. Growing up, Logan had always wanted to follow in his father's footsteps and become a veterinarian. Everyone at the sanctuary had expected him to take over for Thomas when the time came. Not because he was the oldest of the three boys, but for his ability to ease the worries of scared owners. They've been easing Logan taking over the rescue in the next year. It wasn't a hardship for Logan. He would do what he loved, stay in his hometown and help grow the family business.

What he hadn't expected was for the old timers on the neighboring generational farms to continue to compare him to his father each time he went out to check on their animals.

"About the same. Mr. Stephenson looked over my shoulder the entire time I gave the calf an exam. Comments about how dad would do it differently. His son kept trying to get him to go back inside." Logan chuckled. "I guess it doesn't matter when the kids take over for the parents."

"Mom said she went through the same thing when grandpa stepped back. It's going to be the same way when Fiona takes over for you."

"That's a scary thought." Logan's daughter had a way with animals. Even better than him or their father.

Hawkins Ridge Animal Sanctuary rested on five hundred and fifty acres. It had been in his mother's family since the founding of the town, over one hundred years. Once his mother, Josephine—Josie to everyone in Oak Mountain —had inherited the land, she and his father had expanded the number of horses boarding, the number of cat and dog rescues, and crops. They'd also added chickens and goats shortly after his youngest brother, Jace, was born.

Logan quietly checked for any complications from the anesthesia as he slowly led the dog around the decompress room they used for new rescue arrivals.

"So what are you going to do with the farmers being difficult?" Caden asked as he returned to his chair near the corner and crossed his ankles.

"It's not like they're making it hard to do my job. I just want to be recognized for my work, not compared to dad." He paused when the dog stopped on a disposable pad to relieve himself. "It took you how long before people stopped saying you were giving the horses more apples than Mom?"

Caden rolled his eyes, causing Logan to laugh. "They still ask where she is when they come to take the horses out for rides. She hasn't dealt with the horses in five years."

Logan understood. They'd grown up with the town, revering their parents. Thomas and Josie Beckett were the people you called if you needed help. From organizing volunteers to help repair a neighbor's fence to putting together food for a shut in, people had their parents' number on speed dial. Logan, Caden and Jace, had big shoes to fill now that their parents had taken a step back from the day-to-day operations. Though Josie had no plans to give up her cat rescue.

The dog made one lap around the room and headed to a large, overstuffed bed and curled up for a nap. Logan caught a bottle of water Caden tossed his way before unfolding a chair and taking a seat. The cold liquid coated his dry mouth before speaking.

"I got a call from Harold Smith five minutes after I finished the surgery."

Caden had a knowing grin on his face. "Let me guess. His dog got into the prickly patch?"

He nodded. "I told him I'd be over before I pick up Fiona."

"You're there every week."

"Yep. Considering he's responsible for a few of our horse boarders, I can't say no." Logan liked the older man and didn't mind pulling the thorns out of the dog's paw once in a while. But he suspected the man let his dog in the patch because he was lonely.

"Get dad to talk to him," Caden offered before putting the bottle to his lips.

"Doesn't that defeat the purpose of making a name for myself? Besides, at thirty-eight, I'm not complaining to our parents."

"Just a thought."

Logan shook his head when his phone rang. His brows furrowed when he saw the name of Fiona's best friend's mother pop up on the display. He placed the call on speaker.

"Afternoon, Tiffany."

"Hey, Logan."

He shrugged at the question look on his brother's face. "Fiona asked for permission to hang out with Megan for a bit after school. Is everything okay?"

"Well, I found out Megan and Fiona had plans to go to Kyle's house to study with two other boys. Now I know you wouldn't allow her to go without a parent being home."

Logan blew out a calming breath. "You're right, I wouldn't. Plus, Kyle's parents are working today, so I know they wouldn't be home."

Kyle's parents worked with his family for fifteen years; his father oversaw the stables with Caden while his mother was the manager of the greenhouse.. Logan felt comfortable saying they wouldn't agree with mixed company hanging out at their house while they were at work.

"I didn't think so," Tiffany said. The woman did medical coding from home and that was the only reason he'd said it was okay for the girls to go there after school. "Is it okay if I bring Fiona home? Megan's grounded for the night."

Logan stood, already pulling his keys from his pocket. "No need to make a trip. I'll come get her. Thank you for calling."

They said their goodbyes, and he growled in frustration. Caden clapped his brother on the shoulder. "I'll watch over the dog until Claire is done with the goats. Don't forget about Old Man Smith."

Logan thanked his brother and scrolled to the contact and pressed send. Mr. Smith answered on the second ring without a proper hello.

"You on your way?"

"I'm going to be late. An emergency with my daughter came up."

The man sniffed. "That's fine. I'll take her to that vet in town. Talk to you later."

Smith disconnected the call before Logan could say goodbye. He closed his eyes and counted to ten. People assumed even though he was a single father, he came from a close family and had a list of people he could ask to help with Fiona. Yes, everyone in his family would drop what they were doing if she needed a ride. But in situations such as this, it was his responsibility. Not his parents or brothers.

"You want me to mention something to Kyle's father when I head back?" Caden offered as he walked Logan to the front door.

"If you could. Tell him I'll stop by after I get the full story."

Logan jogged to his truck parked on the side of his house, just steps away from the sanctuary's clinic. Climbing into the driver's seat, he thanked the powers that be Megan's mother was home and aware of what her daughter had planned.

It's times like this the thought of having a special someone in his life crossed his mind. A partner to help him carry the load and be there to listen when he battled doubts he'd live up to his father's reputation. Or give him support to make his own. A woman he could encourage to best she wanted to be and would spoil with flowers and quiet picnics. Logan snorted as he steered onto the main road. The single women in town had been champing at the bit to catch his or his brothers' eyes since they all became single. They wanted the Beckett name; most weren't willing to do the work that came with it.

No, if anyone were ever to turn his head, she would have to not care about him being the eldest Beckett, have her own career, but see Hawkins Ridge as something they could build for their future. More importantly, willing to put up with a boy crazy teenager.

CHAPTER 2

Naomi Hendrix stretched her arms over her head after she exited the dictation program. Lifting her last patient, a pregnant Maine Coon cat, had wrenched her shoulders. The mother and embryos were doing well, and Naomi didn't foresee any complications down the road.

Her stomach growled, forcing her to glance at the clock. She'd let her vet tech Isabella—Izzy to her friends—leave for an early lunch with her husband. Normally, Naomi would bring lunch even though her home was mere yards away from her veterinarian practice, but she needed to go grocery shopping. Time was already a rare commodity. She could ask her mother, Maeve, whom she lived with, but the woman already did enough for her.

As the new vet in Oak Mountain, Maryland, Naomi's focus was building the trust of the small foothills town. At thirty-five, her long-term plans hadn't included moving from her home state of Oklahoma to a town over a thousand miles east. After her divorce from her ex-husband, John, he demanded a share of profits from her old practice. He subsequently ruined her reputation as a vet when she, along with the judge, unequivocally denied his request. John's revenge forced her back to her family home, living with her mother for two years, lost, depressed, and desperate to figure out her next step. And, being a Black female veterinarian in rural Oklahoma, job offers weren't exactly rolling in.

When Walter, her friend and the man who'd introduced her to John in the first place, offered to sell his practice, Naomi had jumped at the chance to start over.

Maeve had agreed to come with her, and Naomi was thankful. They'd spent a month making the converted post office more ADA compliant by widening the doorways, lowering the front desk, and installing a ramp. Naomi opened the doors to her first patient five months ago.

Oak Mountain had been slow to welcome her, but people gradually began trusting her with the care of their pets. She had Izzy to thank for that when she had her family bring their animals in for exams and word spread. Naomi slipped her phone into the pocket of her scrubs and made her way to the front desk. Maeve sat behind the computer talking to Naomi's long-haired dachshund, Shorty. After her divorce, she adopted Shorty, a rescue and the most laid back dog ever. Her little man scampered down from his perch behind the front desk and hurried to greet her. Naomi scooped him up and nuzzled her face against his soft coat. Maeve shook her head at the two.

"He wanted to come back and see you when your last patient left."

Naomi lowered herself into the extra desk chair. At five feet, one inch, she had curves for days. She'd only recently regained her self-esteem after the damage her ex-husband had done and was now a healthy size sixteen. Naomi had inherited her medium brown complexion and hips from her mother.

"You could have let him. I was just dictating." She sat Shorty on the floor and pulled the menu from the diner out from the side drawer. It was also where her vet tech had gone to lunch. "I was thinking about ordering a salad. Think Izzy would bring it back for me?"

"You know she would. Please tell me you aren't trying a new diet." Maeve narrowed her eyes. "You're fine the way you are."

It took everything Naomi had *not* to roll her eyes. "No, it's not a new diet. I planned on ordering a pizza for dinner since we have hardly anything in the house. I figured we could go grocery shopping tomorrow."

"If that's the case, order me one, too." Maeve gave her a wink and snuck a dog biscuit to Shorty.

After her mother received a pre–diabetic diagnosis three years ago, the two of them worked hard to find a balance in their diet and started walking in the morning. Naomi placed the order and sent a text to Izzy. After receiving confirmation she would bring their food back, Naomi returned the phone to her pocket.

Maeve busied herself straightening the stationery when she spoke. "I've been thinking. There's a lady down at the senior center has a single grandson…" Naomi was already shaking her head before her mother could finish.

"I don't need to be set up with someone. I want to get settled a little more."

"You're settled and need to venture out into the town.

"You can't live your life in the few yards between home and the office. Izzy has offered to introduce you to some people. Why don't you take her up on that?"

"I am meeting the owners of my patients. Right now, I think that's all I can handle."

Maeve snorted. "You aren't happy, baby. The only time I see you light up is when you're at the office or have your head in a book. Stop listening to ghosts and people trying to keep you down. This move is to be a new beginning. It's time you act like it is."

Naomi slouched further in the chair. Her mother was right, as always. They'd moved to Oak Mountain at the end of October. Between setting up the house and the practice to her liking, the snowy winter, Naomi didn't venture out. But it was now spring; she could no longer use the bad weather as an excuse. Of course, her social butterfly mother had made friends as soon as they'd settled in, starting with Izzy's mom, Winnie.

No, it was the fear of getting close to people and having them turn on her. John's negative words played in her mind that she wasn't good enough, farmers giving her a chance as a favor to him. In her heart, she knew it was a lie. Being an introvert made it hard to be the first to introduce herself to people. As her mother said, drowning out the ghosts of the past was the first step.

Before she could respond, the front door opened, revealing an older, light brown-skinned man. In his arms, he held a medium mixed breed whose sole focus was to shower his owner with kisses. Naomi hurried over to help take the dog from the man. The plant needles on the dog's face and his front paw were obvious.

"Are you the new vet?" he asked, before moving his eyes to Maeve. A grin Naomi could only describe as comical graced the man's face. "Maeve, right?"

Her mother batted her lashes and came from around the desk. "Mr. Smith?"

"Please, call me Harold." He took Maeve's hand and brought it to his lips.

Naomi glanced between the two for a moment, then cleared her throat. Shorty took that as his cue to come greet the man and the new patient. Maeve daintily lifted her boy up to say hello. Naomi tried to get a handle on the situation. Mr. Smith's dog was *not* light.

"What can I help you with?" She nodded her head towards the dog, who was eagerly trying to sniff Shorty. The older man had the decency to look abashed.

"My apologies. I briefly met your mother last week at the seed swap they held at the community center. Vader here got into my prickly pear patch chasing a squirrel. Came out covered in this." Harold waved his hand towards the dog's face. "Logan Beckett, not sure if you know him or not, was supposed to come over and take a look at him. Ended up canceling at the last minute. His father would never do something like that."

Logan Beckett. Walter did not have kind words to say about the man and his family. Logan was the other vet in town who ran the Hawkins Ridge Animal Sanctuary and took care of the local farm animals. The man didn't take on the townspeople's pets, nor had he bothered to introduce himself to Naomi. You know, professional courtesy. "I'm sorry you had to drive out here, Mr. Smith. Let me take Vader in the back and get him settled while my mother checks you in. She can walk you back when you're done.

Harold's chuckle was deep and throaty. "My daughter used to babysit little Izzy. Girl always has a smile on her face. Walter never treated her with any respect. Surprised she didn't up and quit on him."

Naomi kept her mouth shut but didn't miss the "told you so" look from her mother. Now that Naomi found herself in closer proximity to Walter, she was seeing him in a new light. It wasn't a good one. And while she appreciated him selling her the practice and that it came with a house on the property, that was where it ended..

Naomi left the two to get the paperwork, purposely ignoring the sly looks the two gave each other. Her father had passed over ten years ago. Maeve was fifty-nine and considered young. No one expected her to mourn the rest of her life.

In the exam room, Naomi rested the dog on the padded table, careful of his front paw. She still couldn't get over Logan leaving the man in a lurch. What if something was seriously wrong with the dog or the thorns became infected? Yes, Harold said the man had an emergency and truly couldn't make it. It wasn't her place to judge, but she found it hard not to.

Naomi snapped a pair of gloves on and ripped the plastic on a disposable pair of tweezers. "Okay boy. Let's start with your paw." Vader's response was a soft lick on her cheek.

Naomi quickly removed ten small thorns from the dog's paw and wiped it clean with an antibiotic cream. Maeve led Harold to the exam room just as Naomi started on Vader's muzzle. Her mother gave a parting wave before going back to the front desk. Harold gave a lingering look, then positioned himself on the other side of the table and gently stroked his furry friend to soothe him.

Harold cleared his throat. "Thank you for giving discounts to senior citizens. Lot of people in town are on a fixed income but have pets to keep their company."

Naomi stayed focused on her patient while she answered. "I've known people back home that would sacrifice food to keep their pets fed. Animals have a special place in our hearts. If I can offer something simple in order to keep the owner and pet thriving, I'll do it."

"That right there will have people coming to you. Shows you care and not just about the money."

The kind words warmed her heart. While moving to Vader's other side, the original reason for having the dog resurfaced. "You said that Logan Beckett canceled at the last minute."

Harold nodded. "He had an emergency. I can't really be upset with him. He's a nice boy with a lot on his plate."

"I guess there are some things that we can't avoid."

Naomi considered her statement. Running your own business is not as easy as it seems. Having to keep a family business going had to be time consuming. Naomi respected that about the man she didn't know. She would call her patients if something came up. Logan did that, and some of the animosity towards the man diminished.

"That's true. His parents raised all three of them right and taught them the meaning of hard work." Harold patted his dog's side. "You're good with him. He'd let me know if he wasn't comfortable with you."

Naomi placed a kiss on the mixed breed's forehead. "He is a good boy." She removed the last thorn and ran her fingers slowly across his face. "Looks like I got them all. You're going to want to keep his paws and face clean. If you notice swelling or redness, call me."

"Yes, ma'am."

Harold lifted the dog to the floor. Naomi watched for any discomfort as the dog tested his paw. Realizing there wasn't any pain, he trotted out the door, causing them both to laugh. She casually gave the man a once over. Gray stubble covered his chin, offsetting his freshly shaven bald head. Not overly tall, with a lean frame. His calloused hands showed he was not afraid of hard work. They caught up with Vader at the front desk. He and Shorty were giving each other a serious sniff. Naomi distracted them with organic dog biscuits so Harold could slip a lead around his neck. Maeve passed the receipt in front of the man and faced her daughter.

"Izzy texted to say she's on her way back and asked if we needed anything else. I told her no."

Naomi nodded in agreement. She pulled a business card from the holder and jotted her cell phone number on the back. "If you need to reach me over the weekend, call me."

"Will do, but I'm sure he'll be fine." Harold slipped the card in the pocket of his overalls and returned with his keys. "Thank you again for taking the time to see us. Not sure Walter would have done that. Maeve, it was a pleasure seeing you again."

Her mother gave a finger wave as the man and his companion strolled out the door. Naomi tilted an eyebrow, crossing her arms.

"You two seem friendly."

Maeve stapled the receipt to his paperwork. "As he said, we met last week briefly. He had bags of sunflower seeds for swapping. I'm sure I'll see him around town."

"He seems nice. He talked a little about the Becketts." Naomi tossed the ball Shorty dropped at her feet. Maeve turned to Naomi with an incredulous look..

"Are you going to ignore what he said about Walter? I don't understand why you're loyal to a man that suggested you consider John's offer of sharing the profits after he cheated on you with his assistant."

Naomi sighed. This conversation had been in the making for the past month. "It's not loyalty. Obligation is closer, but still isn't the right word. He found a buyer for my practice in Oklahoma and set me up with a lifeline here by selling me his. I recognize Walter isn't a positive influence and that's why I've limited my time with him."

"You know his wife is the reason they're banned from the senior center. At least that's what Josie Beckett said."

Naomi hadn't known that. She supposed if she was more involved with the town, as her mother suggested, she would've known.

"I plan on having a conversation with Walter soon. His negative energy isn't helping me heal." She lowered her gaze. "Honestly, I have a fear he would do the same thing here that John did back in Oklahoma. These people only know me by the kind things Izzy has said."

"And whose fault is that? The difference between here and your old town is that you and Izzy have built your patient base. Back in Oklahoma, it was John that told the farms to give you a chance. It gave them a valid reason to listen to him when he spread those lies." Maeve rested her hand on Naomi's arm, drawing her eyes to her. "People are coming to you because you're an excellent vet. Not one person has said they are coming to the practice because of Walter's recommendations. It's word of mouth from other patients. That's why I said it's time for you to be seen in town. Let them get to know you. Then, if Walter wants to ruin your friendship and badmouth you around town, it won't do any good because they will know you as the amazing, capable veterinarian that you are."

Naomi took her mother's words to heart and swallowed the lump in her throat, giving Maeve a soft smile. It didn't kill the fear she harbored, but it eased slightly. Coming out of her shell wouldn't happen until she remembered who she was. Naomi Hendrix, veterinarian, who graduated at the top of her class. Every good thing that has happened was because she was strong.

"Thank you." Naomi stood and hugged her mother over the back of the chair. "I needed to hear that. Let me get through this weekend and the storm next week, then I'll talk to Izzy about doing an open house for the practice. I'll even invite the Beckett family, personally."

"That's my baby." Maeve patted her hand and stood. "Izzy will be here any minute with lunch. Go get started on your notes so you can eat before your next appointment."

Naomi whistled for Shorty to follow her to her office. As she turned on the computer, her mood brightened. Oak

Mountain was her new home. It was time she eased her way out of her normal rut and get to know her neighbors.

CHAPTER 3

Logan loved this time of year when the bright green leaves popped from their winter cocoon on the oak trees along the two-lane road.

The carrots and kale grown in his family's greenhouse would be ready for harvest in a couple of weeks. His mother's green thumb had skipped him and his brothers, and he was okay with that.

"You're being completely unfair," Fiona said from the passenger seat. While she'd inherited her long black hair and piercing blue eyes from him, the death glare she shot him was all his ex-wife

Logan pulled on a strand of hair sticking out from his baseball cap.

"Tell me how I'm being unfair?"

"We were just going to study," she whined.

"Fi, spring break just started. No twelve-year-old boy wants to study on a Friday night when he doesn't have school for an entire week."

"We have a report due when we come back."

"I offered to bring Kyle to the house so Nana and Pop Pop can keep an eye on you, but you shot that down. Your exact words were, I quote, *'we'll embarrass you'.*" Logan smiled, because they certainly would. Thomas's unnecessary knife sharpening and Josie's invasive questioning would mortify his daughter.

He made a left onto the packed gravel driveway. The Hawkins Ridge Animal Sanctuary and Farms wooden sign stood proudly. They passed the climate controlled greenhouse to the left and the pumpkin patch and apple grove to the right. Noah Garrison, Logan's brother from another mother, directed workers in the parking lot of the small store on the property. Their goat milk products, canned produce, and fresh baked goods were a staple to their income.

"Other people were going to be there," Fiona crossed her slender arms.

Logan couldn't believe she was still on this. "Two girls, three boys in a house with no supervision is not happening."

"Kyle's older brother is home from college."

"You are only proving my point even more. Let's pull over and ask Kyle's mother if she's okay with that. She's talking to Noah."

Fiona hissed. "Don't you dare."

"Are you sure? We can clear this up right now." He slowed the truck, preparing to pull over if she called his bluff.

"Why are you being difficult?" Fiona huffed and kept her eyes on the passing scenery. "We're friends. We've hung out before."

"With supervision." Logan made a right towards the animal rescue and the family homes. He pressed the button for the gate, which swung silently open. "I'm sorry, sweetheart. If an adult, a mature adult, was there, I wouldn't mind. Don't forget, it was Megan that told on you."

He drove past the main house. It was where he and his brothers gathered for either breakfast or dinner daily. His parents still lived there and where the cat nursery was located.

Logan pulled into the open parking area in the middle of the three structures. Fiona was out of the car before he could put it in park. He blew out a breath, shaking his head. As the only grandchild, Fiona had the men in the family wrapped around her little finger. It made raising her hard sometimes. Whenever Logan would say no to something she wanted, Fiona would go tell her uncles who would come to Logan and argue on her behalf. However, in this case, he didn't think she'd get much sympathy.

Logan clomped up the front stairs as he stepped into his living and dining area. His four bedroom cabin had belonged to his two uncles before they'd retired to Florida. He'd worked on remodeling the place during his breaks from college and had turned the front of the house into a large open space. Kaylee had liked the house, but it hadn't been enough to keep her happy. Now that it was just him and Fiona, it had become a second place for his brothers to hang out and watch sports. Case in point, the muscular, hulking man lounging on his couch, channel surfing.

"Why are you in my house, Jace?" Logan asked, pulling off his boots.

"What's wrong with Fi? She came storming through, said she wanted a new family and slammed her bedroom door."

Logan padded to the other side of the couch, dropped onto the cushion, tossing his cap onto the coffee table. Logan pulled on the ends of his graying hair and propped his feet on the solid cherry wood coffee table. He glanced at his brother.

"She's having a pre-teen moment." Logan told Jace about her spoiled study date and wanted to punch his brother when he laughed.

"You're right, Mom and Dad would purposely try to embarrass her." Jace shook his head. "Isn't she too young to date?"

Logan slouched further into the couch. "I don't even want to think about it. She used to think I was her hero. Now she's ashamed to be seen with me around her friends."

"That's because she sees how half the mothers flirt with you." Jace slapped him on the thigh. "It's the Beckett curse. Mom and Dad shouldn't have made such handsome boys."

"Yeah, I don't think that's the reason. She'll get over it. I'll let her stay at the main house tonight to help with the kittens." Logan's gaze went to his brother. "You never said why you're in my house."

"I just wanted to spend time with my big brother."

"Lie." Jace let himself into Logan's house whenever he wanted something, had gossip or was bored.

Jace flashed a smile. "Mom is making fried chicken, mashed potatoes and kale for dinner."

Logan's stomach growled. Normally Owen, Noah's father and Thomas' best friend, did the cooking as the chief of staff. He'd moved into the main house after selling his consulting company five years ago, and supervised the staff that weren't family. But he and his husband, Sam, were currently out-of-town caring for a family member which had their mother cooking more often.

"That sounds good. But what else is going on?"

"There's a shelter in Frederick that has three dogs they can't adopt. They're eight-year-old pugs from the same litter. The owners got a job overseas and couldn't take them. Says they have a great temperament, but no one will take all three." Jace scratched his dark blond five o'clock shadow. "Obviously they're bonded. I can head out first thing to pick them up."

That was Jace's position. He was the face of the sanctuary—he handled contracts, did the pickups of strays, and kept in touch with the shelters for dogs and cats who've shown no sign of adoption. When he wasn't helping around the farm, he was also a volunteer firefighter.

"If they're bonded and seniors, we may have to see about an employee taking them. We'll make a judgement call when they're here."

Jace gave him a goofy thumbs up. "Oh, Old Man Smith may have called dad."

Logan rolled his eyes. "I need to apologize again. Was there anything else wrong with Vader besides the thorns?"

"Not that he said. Said he'd be going to the town vet from now on because she's pretty, and her mother is right up his alley. His words."

"If he's interested in her mother, he's going to have his dog in the prickly pear patch every day." Logan stood and ran his hands down his jeans. "Have you met the new vet?"

Jace shook his head. "Not yet. I ran into Izzy last week. She said the new doc is a breath of fresh air and a pleasure to work for. People are bringing their pets back."

Logan had wanted their childhood friend to work for him as his vet tech, but she'd taken time off to start a family. That had been around the time Walter Holloway had put feelers out for his business.

"Anyone's a pleasure after that ornery, evil man." Logan snorted.

"You shouldn't talk about people," Fiona said, strolling into the room. She'd changed into her work jeans, a pink long sleeve T-shirt, and cowboy boots. She'd pulled her hair into a ponytail. "Uncle Caden said I can help him feed the horses."

"That's fine. See if he can give you a ride over. Nana said she could use some help tonight with the kittens, if you're interested." Logan pretended not to notice the small smile on his daughter's lips.

"Sure. Whatever."

His daughter walked out of the house, softly closing the door behind her. Logan looked at his brother. "Kittens are her weak spot. I'm gonna hang with the dogs before dinner. You coming?"

"Why not? I'll call the shelter to let them know I'll be there in the morning." Jace pulled out his phone. "You know you should introduce yourself to the new vet."

"Maybe."

Logan led the way outside after slipping his boots back on. The late afternoon sun had dropped behind the tree line, leaving the sky a soft pink color.

"It's the least you could do. She's new in town and may need your help with patients and vice versa," Jace added.

His brother was right. Though Logan may not have met the new doctor, he'd heard good things about her. And it made no sense that he hadn't reached out to his own town's vet when he had a working relationship with vets from the surrounding towns. He blamed it on the rumor she was Walter's mentee. She'd surely inherited the man's hatred of him.

Logan flipped the hinge lock on the gate, and dogs of all ages, shapes and sizes, immediately surrounded him. He took his time and gave each a scratch behind their ears before they went to Jace.

"Do you know anything about her other than Izzy's biased opinion?" Logan squatted in front of one of their blind dogs, letting him sniff his hand before wrapping him in a hug.

Jace picked up a thick rope to play tug with a mastiff. "Only that she brings her dog to work. You can't judge her based on your interactions with Walter. You wouldn't want her doing the same thing with you."

"When did you become the smart one?"

"I've always been the smart one." Jace flashed a toothy grin.

Logan rose to his feet and walked towards the pond. Walter spent four decades spreading false information to anyone who would listen, claiming that Logan's grandfather hired Thomas as the sanctuary veterinarian because he was dating his mother. It was an imagined slight Walter never got over. Then Logan married Kaylee, his goddaughter. Walter tried to keep them apart when they dated, saying Logan didn't appreciate her and her rodeo career. It was Walter who encouraged Kaylee to give up on their marriage and go back on the road. Could he be using his past with Walter as an excuse not to welcome her? That was a question he couldn't answer at the moment. It was time for him to bond with the pack.

Chapter 4

A strand of hair fell from Izzy's ponytail as she struggled with a vicious chihuahua, who nipped her and Naomi during his exam. They chuckled when Naomi wrapped a too large cone around his neck. They'd both be happy to give him back to his owner after they finished drawing his blood sample..

"We should have sedated him," Isabella commented.

"He's our last patient. I had no desire to stay late while he came around." Naomi capped the vial and grabbed the lead from the chair. "I will suggest to the owner to make an earlier appointment next time so we can, if he acts this bad."

"Or suggest they take him to the vet in the next town over."

Izzy removed the cone once Naomi had attached the woven hemp leash and the terror immediately went for her hand.

Naomi had always loved animals and had never met one she didn't like. It was why she'd gone into the field. Animals didn't care that she didn't have the body of a model, had more curves than was socially acceptable, and hadn't grown out of her introvert stage. No, animals just wanted love and someone who understood them.

The little yapping pooch was an alien, not an animal.

"I'll walk him out if you don't mind sanitizing the table."

Naomi opened the door and led him to the lobby. It was truly frightening how the dog's personality changed once he saw his barely twenty-one-year-old owner..

"Thank you so much, Dr. Hendrix. Titus rarely likes strangers." The owner gave him lots of cuddles and love before slipping the dog into her purse. "Do you want me to set an appointment now for his next visit?"

Naomi rested her hand on Maeve's shoulder before she spoke. "We'll send you a reminder card. We are only scheduling a month out. I'll call you if there are any abnormalities with the blood work."

The young woman paid her bill and left with an enthusiastic wave over her shoulder. Naomi followed and locked the door before leaning her back against it. Shorty eased his way from behind the desk with a whimper, scanning the lobby for threats before asking for treats.

"Shorty did not like that dog," Maeve commented as she straighten the reception desk. "Shivered the entire time."

Naomi scooped Shorty up and buried her face in his tri-color coat. She set him back on the floor and met her mother's gaze.

"That dog was aggressive and I'm seriously debating telling the owner to contact Logan Beckett to handle its care going forward." Naomi tugged on the bottom of her African print scarf, holding her twisted locs in a high bun.

"I told you to stop listening to the hatred Walter has been spewing," Isabella said, coming down the hall, purse in hand. "I've known the Becketts my entire life. If Logan couldn't help Mr. Smith, there had to be a reason."

"I understand that," Naomi commented.

"There's more to Walter's feelings towards the family than he's letting you know." Isabella bent over to say goodbye to Shorty before holding Naomi's gaze. "Not once in my life have the Becketts been anything but kind to me and my family. Heck, Jace Beckett is a volunteer firefighter with my father and brother. I've told you to ask Walter why he harbors hard feelings for the Becketts, especially Logan. If he isn't telling you, stop and ask yourself why." She gave Naomi's arm a squeeze before turning it into a side hug. "On that note, ladies have a wonderful weekend. I'll see you on Monday."

Naomi stood by the door as she watched her tech climb into the passenger side of her husband's police cruiser. Izzy offered a last wave, and Naomi locked the door and lowered the blinds.

"You know she's not wrong," Maeve commented, pushing the chair under the desk. "You've already passed judgement on a person because of someone else's feelings. Mr. Smith told you Logan called instead of standing him up. We already talked about you taking the step to introduce yourself. For now, keep an open mind about the Becketts."

"I know." Naomi's thoughts were all over the place. She accepted she was being hypocritical. If she ventured out like Maeve, she would have probably met Logan's mother, and this wouldn't be an issue. Not that she didn't believe Izzy—she valued her opinion. She was just struggling to rationalize Walter's behavior since they'd moved to Oak Mountain.

"You were worried that people would not accept a black veterinarian in a small rural town before we moved here. You assumed they would think that you didn't know what you were doing. But Oak Mountain is diverse, and they have accepted you. We've had new patients each week, the few months we've been here." Maeve pulled her purse from the bottom drawer. "You're a thirty-five-year-old woman, but you're acting like a five-year-old."

Maeve and Shorty strolled down the hall, leaving Naomi to make sure all the lights were off. On her way to her office, she checked the two exam rooms, and the chihuahua sample was in the refrigerator for the lab to pick up on Monday.

Maybe she was overreacting, but she knew firsthand about gossip. It was the reason she left Oklahoma. The words from her past rushed forward in her mind. John telling farmers she cheated on her board exams or the reason she did so well in school was because of inappropriate actions. Disgust and sneers marred the faces of her former neighbors and friends. Words and looks, Naomi didn't think she'd ever bury for good.

Naomi met her mother in the office, Shorty scurrying at her feet. She shut down her computer and grabbed her bag before finishing the conversation.

"I know what you're saying is true, and Mr. Smith spoke highly of the family. I've also explained my plan for the open house to Izzy, who said is a good idea.. I'm working on opening up to the town and that includes the Becketts and keeping Walter at arms' length in order to thrive here. Just be patient with me."

Maeve sighed and pulled her daughter in for a hug. "I'm sorry if you think I'm pushing you. That's the last thing I want. You're still shell-shocked after Oklahoma and your hesitation is normal. But you have me and Izzy to help get you through this. Don't worry about it now, and we'll tackle it after that terrible storm next week."

Naomi gave a soft smile in thanks and took a step back. She set the alarm at the back door and locked the deadbolt.

The two-bedroom house Naomi shared with her mother sat yards from the practice and included in the sale.. Naomi mumbled a groan upon seeing the familiar expensive SUV parked behind her Subaru. A man with thinning gray hair poking out from underneath a cowboy hat stood next to the driver's side door, glancing at the dense tree line. Naomi fought the urge to roll her eyes. She didn't appreciate Walter's random drop-ins and told him on more than one occasion.

Shorty kept his nose to the ground, making sure no unfamiliar smells were in his territory before marking again. He scampered around the older man and darted through the doggy door.

"Walter, we weren't expecting you," Maeve said in greeting. "You should have called so we could make sure there was enough for you to have dinner."

Naomi stopped beside her mother, resting an arm on her shoulder. Maeve didn't hide her feelings towards Walter, who flashed a smile that didn't reach his eyes.

"A pleasure, as always, Maeve. I was driving by and saw the empty parking lot. Just wanted to see how business was going."

His constant concern about her business bothered Naomi. At the initial onset, the question came up once a week and Naomi chalked it up to a friend asking to see how things were going. Now it was up to three times and the questions became more invasive regarding profit and who her patients were. Naomi would never answer and diverted the conversation. Only two people knew the financial stability of her business—her mother and the accountant.

"Business is fine, as I mentioned earlier in the week. My mother is right, you should have called. We have a quiet evening planned."

"Right." Walter twirled his keys around his fingers. "With the storm planned for next week, I wanted to invite you both to stay with us. They are calling for days of measurable rain and damaging winds."

Naomi and Maeve shared a look, keeping their expressions neutral. Based on the meteorologist, the storm coming through would have them holed up in the house for days.

"Thank you for the offer, but I think we'll ride it out here."

Maeve nodded in agreement. "Naomi needs to be near the clinic. I don't want her to have to drive from the other side of town in the high standing water."

Walter's eyes briefly darted towards the house before shoving his hands in his pockets. "The town is prone to flooding. Without someone to take care of you who is used to this weather, I worry something may happen. It's not like you two have met many people you can call on," he said, condescension obvious.

Naomi had to snort. "We've survived tornadoes and torrential storms in Oklahoma. Mom and I know what to do. Regarding meeting people, we have met a few. Now, if you don't mind, I'm tired and need to give Shorty his dinner." She meant it as a dismissal and prayed he took the hint.

With one last look towards the top of the house, Walter gave a quick nod. "I'll leave you to it. I'll check on you over the weekend. Have a pleasant night."

Naomi and Maeve watched their unexpected visitor turn around and head back down their driveway. Naomi's shoulders dropped as they stepped into the warm living room. She and Maeve's decorating styles complimented each other with creamy ivory walls that held family photos, abstract painting and the flat screen TV over the fireplace. Rich navy blue couch and recliner anchored the living area and brushed up against the family heirloom dining table. Fond memories of doing her homework at the same table while her mother cooked soothed Naomi's nerves.

"Are you still up for exploring tomorrow?" Naomi asked, setting her water bottle in the sink.

On Saturday, they opened from nine to noon, just in case there was an emergency. For the past two weekends, they had taken advantage of the nice weather to explore and visit the surrounding towns. It was a way for Naomi to decompress.

"That sounds nice." Maeve pulled Shorty's food from the fridge. The four-legged ham started his dinner dance. "You go take a shower, then we'll order pizza."

Naomi gave her mother a kiss on the cheek. "Thanks."

Maeve nodded, setting the food bowl in the holder next to Shorty's water dish.

Naomi padded into the first bedroom on the right, closing the door. She tossed her scrubs into the special hamper next to the queen-sized bed to take to the cleaners. Shorty's wooden stairs were a weekend project she did with her mother so he could climb onto the bed with ease.

Closing her eyes, Naomi raised her hands over her head. With a deep cleansing breath, she pushed Walter, the difficult chihuahua and Logan Beckett from her mind. Ideas of how she could move forward with her open house came to mind as she exhaled. It was out of her comfort zone, that's for sure. But she would deal with that next week.

Now she looked forward to an evening of pizza and a good book.

Chapter 5

Logan inhaled the fresh mountain air as he stepped off his porch, nodding a good morning to the two workers filling the water pails they kept in the fenced dog run. He smiled when he heard the harmonious bleats and cheerful barks from the goats and dogs.

The glorious aroma of bacon greeted him when he entered the main house mudroom. Nostalgia overwhelmed him as he took in the large farmhouse kitchen. Wood shelves displayed their family pottery and ceramic serving dishes, while the sage cabinets with window doors hung above recently installed granite countertops. The six-burner stainless steel stove—along with the double-door refrigerator—had been him and his brothers' forty-year anniversary gift to his parents.

"Good morning!" he called out to the empty kitchen.

The oven buzzed just as his mother and father strolled into the room. Josephine Beckett was a beautiful woman. Her long, gray hair hung over one shoulder in a thick braid, and her perfectly applied makeup accented the blue eyes she'd given Logan. She looked ready to tackle the world dressed in a Hawkins Ridge long-sleeve shirt and jeans.

Logan poured himself a cup of coffee and leaned against the counter while his mother pulled out a large casserole dish from the oven. Crispy hash browns surrounded the fluffy eggs and gooey melted cheddar cheese. It was one of Logan's favorite breakfasts.

Thomas set a platter of bacon on the butcher block style kitchen table. "Your mother and Fiona were up with the kittens. She thinks the calico is going to go into labor today because it's making a nest."

"I was wondering what Fi mumbled as she stumbled past me when she came in. She'll be asleep for the rest of the morning."

"Fiona said she wanted to be here this evening, if that's okay?" Josie commented, easing a serving spoon into the dish. "You know my grandchild is going to be a better vet than you or your father."

"Now, dear, why would you disparage your husband like that?" Thomas Beckett joked, giving Josie a loving tap on her rear. Logan swore Josie's cheeks pinked.

He silently agreed with his mother. Fiona became fascinated with animals at an early age with cat as her first word. Dada was a close second.

"If she wants to stay, that's fine. Depending on what time Jace and Caden return with the dogs, I'm sure I'll be busy with the new arrivals. Fi and I have plans for lunch and a movie tomorrow."

"Are you sure you don't want to come to the home and garden show with us?" Thomas asked, resting his black Stetson on the corner of a chair.

"Positive," Logan replied. He made his way back to the coffeepot for another refill. "I need to head into town to pick up a few things." He hesitated before his next statement, but decided he wanted his family's feedback, that he was making the right decision. "I was thinking about stopping by the clinic to introduce myself to the new vet."

"You should have done that a while ago," Josie fussed, resting her hands on her hips. "I know I raised you better than that."

"I know. There's no excuse." Every mental argument he had held little merit.

"I met her mother. Lovely woman. Little Isabella just loves going to work now." Josephine pointed a manicured finger at him. "Take a peace offering."

A confused look must have been on his face, because Josie continued.

"The last thing you want is to go in there empty-handed. This is an apology for not going by earlier." She held up a hand to stop his protest. "I know she could have introduced herself first, but she's new in town and we always welcome new residents. Now, I'll grab some of the canned preserves before we leave. Noah got a fresh supply of summer sausage from the butcher at the store. See if Claire or Noah can set up a basket for you. Lord knows what yours would look like if you did it yourself."

His parents doubled over in laughter at the thought, and Logan had to smile, because he definitely sucked at wrapping. Gift bags were more his speed. Thomas set a container of biscuits and butter on the table and took a seat before stilling Logan with a look.

"You apologized to Smith, didn't you? We can't lose his business boarding his horses."

Though they only boarded three of his horses, Mr. Smith was influential in getting the rest of their boarding customers. If he wasn't happy, he could nudge others to find a new stable.

Logan nodded, taking a couple of biscuits. "I called him again last night and explained I had to pick up Fi. He said he understood. I offered to bring over a trailer of mulch next week when I check his filly."

Thomas nodded. "That's an excellent offer."

Logan thanked his father and dug into his breakfast. The conversation was light as they talked about plans for the following week. With Fiona on spring break, he would need to keep her busy. Logan knew his family, especially his mother, would volunteer to watch her while he went to appointments, but he planned to check his schedule to see which ones he could bring her along. Logan wanted to do more around the sanctuary during the break so they could spend more time together. Even if it's just giving the pack baths.

When they finished eating breakfast, Logan got to cleaning the kitchen. Josie pulled together jars of apple, pear, and blueberry preserves, along with a new deep rectangle basket.

"Make sure you were your best shirt."

Logan glanced down at his gray Henley. He thought he looked okay enough to run errands. "Why?"

"Rumor has it the vet is single, voluptuous, and easy on the eyes."

"So you want me to warn her away from Jace?" Logan teased, causing his father to chuckle.

"That might be smart, but I was thinking it might be time for you to get back out there."

It didn't come as a shock to Logan when Kaylee left to chase her dreams on the rodeo circuit. Their relationship had evolved from friendship to dating, and then, unexpectedly, a surprise pregnancy caught them off guard. And while Logan had embraced fatherhood and loved his baby girl, he'd known him and Fiona's mother weren't true loves.

Kaylee had dreamed of being a rodeo star and had wanted to leave having children for later in life. She'd put her career on pause because of the pregnancy. When Fiona turned two, Kaylee had eased her way back into regional competition. And by the time Fiona had turned seven, she'd gone back full time after filing for divorce and signing over custody.

Now, Fiona and her mother did a few video chats and shared cards during holidays and birthdays, but it was not a mother and daughter relationship.

"I'm not sure I'm looking to date but, thank you."

"Ready, honey?" Thomas called from the front of the house.

Josie patted Logan on the shoulder. "Don't deny yourself another chance at happiness because of the past. We're probably going to eat in the city, so you're on your own for dinner."

Logan said his goodbyes and headed back to his house to grab his keys and leave a note for Fiona. He had no intention of changing his shirt and thought what he had on was fine.

This was an introduction visit and nothing more. He'd deal with his dating life at another time. Maybe after Fiona went to college. For now, his focus was on being a good father, building his reputation separate from his father's and growing the family business the way he and his brothers wanted.

CHAPTER 6

Naomi smiled as she heard the distinct sound of the motorized ball launcher echo in the quiet lobby. Shorty bounced as he waited for his special green ball to sail to the other side of the room. A quick bark was the only warning before scampering across the floor. Shorty ran back and dropped the ball into the top opening, and started his dance all over again.

Best purchase ever, Naomi thought as she finished her paperwork.

Like most Saturdays, business was typically slow. She'd only had one patient who needed their vaccinations, but no one had crossed the threshold for the last two hours. Naomi had even sent her mother back to the house to get a snack bag ready for their relaxing drive. The Appalachian Mountain Range made for picturesque views and they enjoyed weaving their way along the road through the majestic trees. As soon as she sent the invoices to the accountant, she would close early and get started on the rest of her weekend.

A series of barks had Naomi looking out the front window as a large, dark, four-door pickup pulled into the lot.

"Be good, Shorty. Use your spidey senses to tell me if they're good or evil." Naomi giggled at her joke. She closed her laptop and rose to her feet. Naomi wouldn't turn away an animal needing help.

Sunlight, no longer filtered by the tinted glass, formed a halo around a mountain of a body as a man who didn't seem to have a pet with him opened the door to the practice.. Maybe she shouldn't have sent her mother home. As he stepped forward, allowing the door to close, Naomi's mouth went dry.

"Sweet butter biscuit," she mumbled.

Every male model in her romance books paled compared to the man. Broad shoulders, accented by a henley shirt tucked into a pair of well-worn jeans, clung to muscular legs. Inky black hair with strands of gray brushed against a hint of morning stubble that dotted his square jaw. Above his dimples, a scar deepened when he smiled to greet Shorty.

"Aren't you a gorgeous thing? Yes, you are. Who's a good boy?"

From the way Shorty pranced under the man's attention, Naomi assumed the stranger wasn't a foe.

"He's supposed to be a guard dog," Naomi lovingly smiled at her pooch. It was then she noticed the basket in the man's hands. "Are you looking for someone?"

After giving Shorty another scratch behind the ear, the man rose to an impressive height. He turned his smile to her and let his gaze trace her five feet one inch height before closing the distance to the reception desk in one step.

"My apologies, Darlin'. I should have greeted you first. I'm looking for Dr. Hendrix."

Naomi blinked. Being from Oklahoma, she'd heard country twang her entire life—heck, she still fought hers from time to time—but hearing her name along with the word "darlin'" turned her insides to mush.

"Thank you." She reached for the basket, but the delivery man moved it out of her reach.

"Sorry. I'd like to give them to her myself." His gaze glanced down the hall.

Naomi's frown disappeared, and she flashed him a kind smile of understanding. "I'm sorry. I'm Dr. Hendrix."

"Oh." The stranger ran his fingers through his hair in that sexy way men do. "My apologies. I didn't know you were the doctor. I was expecting someone else."

Naomi looked down at herself. Since they were only open for three hours, she hadn't bothered with her usual scrubs, but had dressed in nice jeans and a flattering spring sweater. "What were you expecting? Someone older?"

"No. I—"

"Someone other than a black woman?" Back home, people had assumed she was the assistant instead of the vet because her tech was a man.

The stranger shook his head. "Not at all. It's just…you don't look like a veterinarian."

Naomi stormed around the desk and glared up at him. "And what is a vet supposed to look like?"

"Are you okay, sweetie?" Maeve asked as she strolled in from the back door and stood beside Naomi.

"Ma'am.' He nodded to her mother. "I'm trying to take my foot out of my mouth, but she won't let me."

Naomi wanted to slap the mirth out of his twinkling blue eyes. "You said that you didn't think I looked like a vet. So I'm trying to figure out why someone who is making a delivery would think that a short, fat, black woman can't be a vet."

Maeve stepped forward and peeked into the basket. "Baby, give the man a chance to eat crow."

Her mother had the nerve to wink.

"Thank you." He actually chuckled. What I was trying to say is that I was expecting someone older, not as attractive. He held out his hand. "I'm Logan Beckett, and the basket was a peace offering for not introducing myself earlier and to thank you for helping Mr. Smith yesterday."

"*You're* Logan Beckett?" Naomi wished for the floor to open up and swallow her.

"Nice to meet you, Mr. Beckett," Maeve stepped forward and shook Logan's still outstretched hand. "Maeve Hendrix."

"Ma'am. Please call me Logan."

Naomi would not let herself get lulled by his handsome face, deep voice, or the delicious-looking basket. Though the summer sausage was tempting. "Why did you leave Mr. Smith in a lurch? He was worried sick about his dog, and you waited until the last minute to call. Thorns covered Vader's poor muzzle.

"Naomi," Maeve hissed. "You're being rude."

A muscle in Logan's neck twitched as he exhaled. "It's good to see Walter has already poisoned your mind without you ever meeting me. To answer your accusatory question, I did not leave Smith in a lurch. Every other week, his dog chases rabbits or squirrels into his prickly pear patch that he keeps on his land, which he makes moonshine with. But I'm guessing he didn't tell you I offered to stop by a little later, or that he dismissed my offer and hung up on me without saying goodbye? Despite that, I still called him to make sure the dog was okay." Logan took a breath and continued. "I had to pick up my eleven-year-old daughter after I got a call from her friend's mother that my child was going to be alone in a house with three boys to *study*." Logan used air quotes around the last word. Before Naomi could respond, he pressed on.

"Forgive me for being more concerned about my only child than a dog who I've taken care of for the past few years. The same dog that could have waited another hour or two while I dealt with a sullen teenager who thinks her father was overreacting." He turned his attention to Maeve. "Raising a child on my own while trying to step out of the shadow of my father is hard enough. All I wanted was to come here, finally introduce myself and tell you thanks for stepping in with Smith. Maybe I should have taken my mother's advice and changed my shirt."

"I don't think my daughter—" Maeve started, but Logan cut her off.

"Ma'am, my mother had nothing but wonderful things to say about you. I hope you enjoy the basket." He glared at Naomi. "Welcome to Oak Mountain."

Logan spun on the heel of his scuffed cowboy boots and stormed out of the office. Naomi dropped her head in shame.

"I messed up."

"That is an understatement, young lady." Maeve locked the front door and lowered the blinds. "I know I raised you better than to act the way you just did to a man that was kind enough to say thank you for helping him with a patient he couldn't get to because of an emergency. Believe me, if I got a call that you were going to be spending time with a group of boys, I would have done the same thing."

"I'm sorry. My reaction was uncalled for."

Maeve shook her head. "Uncalled for is putting it mildly."

Naomi threw up her hands and walked back behind the desk. "What do you want me to do?"

"I want you to act like a grown woman and make your own conclusions. Then, apologize to that man once he's calmed down."

Maeve snatched her laptop from the desk and walked down the hall, Shorty on her heels. Naomi couldn't believe what she'd said to Logan. Maybe his good looks, kind smile and the attention he'd given Shorty had jumbled her thoughts. Naomi used to have to fight to be taken seriously by her colleagues back home.. All the veterinarians in the tri-county area were men over the age of forty who thought women ran the office, not care for a common foot-and-mouth disease in cows. While she could have moved to a larger city after school, she was a small-town girl at heart. Naomi thought she'd proven herself, but she'd been wrong. Once the lie saying she'd cheated on her boards had spread like wildfire, her career there was over.

Naomi, not introducing herself properly, had led to Logan's initial assumption she wasn't the doctor. Did she allow Walter's comments to worsen the accidental misunderstanding? She didn't miss the hypocrisy. She was doing the same thing she'd fought so hard against.

"Are you ready to go?" Maeve asked, carrying Shorty's ball launcher and the basket.

Naomi scooped the items from her arms. "Yes. I'm sorry I embarrassed you."

"You embarrassed yourself more than me, but I understand. You should still apologize."

"I will. Promise. I'll check the schedule and see when I can drive out there next week." Maybe she could put together her own basket or bake something. Perhaps wear that purple top that looks good on her.

Maeve squeezed her arm. "That's my baby."

Naomi nodded and grabbed her things. It would take a few days for her to gather enough nerves and humble herself to eat crow.

CHAPTER 7

Logan used his arm to wipe the sweat dripping off his forehead. He'd been mucking out the stalls for the past hour and giving the horses fresh hay. Hard labor helped him with the build up energy coursing under his skin.

Naomi Hendrix confused and frustrated him. He replayed the events from earlier on a loop in his mind. Logan could see the initial misunderstanding—he hadn't introduced himself because his brain had gone on vacation as soon as he focused on the woman..

Naomi was a natural beauty with a riot of dreadlocks held at the top of her head with a colorful scarf. Noah explained once that some people found the term to describe her hair offensive, but it was the word that popped into his head. Her makeup-free medium brown complexion had only highlighted those round, soulful dark eyes accented by the faintest of lines. And don't get him started on her body. Naomi called herself fat, and in today's judgmental society, he supposed, she would be. In Logan's eyes, her body was thick, shapely, and perfect. He and his brothers were big men. They preferred women who didn't raise a fear of squishing them.

Then there was the attitude. When she'd stomped from behind her desk, he'd had to swallow a chuckle. She barely cleared the middle of his body, but that hadn't stopped her from giving him a piece of her mind. And it had all gone downhill once she'd figured out who he was.

Logan shook his head, tossing a fresh bale of hay into the stall. Naomi had formed her opinion of him, assuming Logan had simply blown off Harold with no good reason to do so.. Maybe he should have asked his mother to pick up Fiona or agreed to let Tiffany bring her home. He growled, shoving the pitchfork into the dry grass. He shouldn't let a woman he barely knew make him doubt his decisions as a father. Picking up Fiona had been the right call. Being a good, available father was the most important thing to him. To give Fiona the stability she needed. He would have to forget how his pulse raced when Dr. Hendrix was close, and how her eyes had dilated when he'd called her Darlin'.

A nudge against the back of his knee made Logan jump. Scout, Caden's German Shepard therapy dog, sat on his haunches, gently panting.

"What are you doing in here?" Caden asked as he leaned against the gate. "They said you've been in here for a while."

"Just had to get some energy out." He leaned on the pitch-fork. "How did the pickup go? What's your take on the dogs?"

Caden pulled off his cowboy hat and scratched his scalp, his short hair matted in the pattern of his hat. "It went okay. We ended up bringing back a senior dog as well. Jace and I couldn't let him stay there. As far as the three sisters, by the way, the previous owner loved flowers, apparently. Their names are Bluebell, Tulip and Rosebud. Anyway, the shelter was right in saying the bond was too strong to separate them.

They have anxiety. I think it would be worse if they didn't have each other."

Logan blew out a breath, thinking of possible foster or forever homes for the bonded trio. "Do you think they will do well with the pack?"

"Over time, but for the next few weeks, we need to re-inforce that they're safe. They are starving for affection and came to Jace and I. Scout kept them calm on the ride."

"I'm glad. Tell me about the senior."

Logan walked out of the stall and handed the pitchfork to one of their workers to finish so he could check on the new arrivals. Caden and Scout followed.

"He's a ten-year-old hound mix in desperate need of a haircut and food. A stray that didn't mind the animal control person slipping a leash on it and placing it into the van. He didn't have a microchip and was likely abandoned." Caden climbed into the passenger seat of the ATV, with Scout taking the rear. The stables were on the back edge of the property and had their own entrance off the mountain road. It worked for the owners of horses so they wouldn't have to weave through the dips and curves of the property's gravel roads with their trailers.

"If it's cool with you, I'd like to take him tonight," Caden asked, reaching behind him to rest a hand on Scout's shoulder. "I'll bring him by the clinic tomorrow for a cut, bath, and exam,"

They zipped past the tiny homes for on-site employees, sticking to the trails that carved through the dense trees.

Logan considered his brother's request as they headed to-wards the clinic. Usually, Logan preferred to give all new arrivals a good once over, but Caden wouldn't ask to go against their procedure if he didn't think the hound would benefit from being with him. He nodded in approval.

"I'll focus on the sisters tonight."

"Cool. Jace said you were going to meet the new vet today. How'd that go?"

"Aces." Logan let the sarcasm coat his response before explaining what had happened as they continued their drive. He finished the story as they pulled in front of the clinic.

"So basically, you think the doctor is hot, but she felt you did Harold wrong and came to his defense. This was *after* you turned on the charm and flashed her your dimples. Is that about right?"

"I think she's attractive, but I said nothing about pursuing anything."

Logan hadn't asked a woman out since Kaylee. At first, he'd been adjusting to being a full-time single parent, but since his dad stepped back, Logan simply didn't have time to date.

Caden patted him on the shoulder. "Sure, sure."

"Shut up."

Caden cackled and climbed out of the ATV. "Please tell me you're going to change the Doc's opinion."

"How am I supposed to do that?" Logan had thought about how he would go about settling things with Naomi while he cleaned the stalls and came up with nothing.

"I don't know. Maybe mom could be your ticket in."

Logan stopped at the clinic door and stared at his brother. "You want me to tattle to Mommy that the new doctor was mean so she can arrange a play date?"

"You have any other ideas?"

He didn't, but asking his mother to play interference wasn't an option. He'd have to find his own way of making peace with Naomi if he wanted her to take him seriously.

"Why do I talk to you?"

Caden gave a toothy, cocky grin. "Sadly, because I'm the smartest."

They stepped into the bright, spacious room, where they brought new arrivals to help them decompress. Dog beds, water dishes, and toys littered the floor. Fiona sat cross-legged in the middle of the three dog sisters, giving them lovings. The pug trio were a mix of varying shades of black and beige.

"Daddy, can I stay with the dogs tonight?" The smile his daughter gave him was pure joy.

Logan strolled over and lowered himself beside her. The trio gave him a good sniff before resting their heads on his lap. He slowly ran his hands down their bodies, looking for any lumps.

"I thought you wanted to be with the cat in case she goes into labor."

Fiona nibbled her lip. "I do."

Logan tapped his chin with a twinkle in his eyes. "How about we bring Bluebell, Tulip and Rosebud to the house tonight and set them up in the quarantine room? Will have Nana call if the cat goes into labor. First, we have to give them a bath once they settle some more."

Fiona nodded. "I like their names." Logan met their wide, round eyes and thought the names fit.

"Where's the other new arrival?" Caden asked.

"Outside. Pop Pop wanted to let him walk around." Fiona shook a chew toy in front of one dog and giggled when she licked her hand.

"I'll catch up with you two later." Caden looked over his shoulder with this hand on the knob. "Thanks again."

"Uncle Jace told me to tell you he's headed to the firehouse." Fiona rested her head on his shoulder. "Do you think we could keep them as pets?"

While Logan considered the pack as theirs, he knew Fiona wanted companions that were just hers alone. He observed the trio go to the water dish as one unit. The pugs drank in unison, shoulder to shoulder.

"I think that may be a possibility." He pointed to the one in the middle. "See how they surround that one? Even when they were with us, she was the last one to rest her head on my leg. They're protecting her."

"Do you think she's pregnant?"

It was a good question. "I'm not sure, but I'll check tomorrow during their exam."

Thomas stepped through the back door, greeting them with a smile.

Logan rose to his feet, grimacing at the ache in his knees. "Thank you for being here when Jace and Caden got back."

Thomas dismissed the gratitude with a wave. "I actually was on my way to find you when they pulled up. That's when one of the guys said you were at the stables."

Logan pulled a shrink-wrapped bag of fresh, wet dog food from the fridge they kept in the clinic. Fiona had set three small bowls on the counter before Logan put them back and pulled out one larger one. Something told him they would eat from the same dish. He would ease them into using their own once they felt more comfortable.

"Did you need me for something?"

The sisters spun in circles while Logan dished out a small portion. Thomas added drops of vitamins on top.

"Austin called the house looking for you since you weren't answering your cell phone." Thomas leaned against the counter while Logan sat the bowl in front of the dogs. "A shelter in his town lost funding. They had a big adoption event. No problem with the cats. However, people passed over the large and older dogs. Of course, they're the ones that have been there the longest."

Logan copied his father's stance and leaned against the opposite counter, crossing his arms. Austin Harris ran a sanctuary in Virginia. They'd gone to veterinarian school together and Logan considered him a friend. "How many are we talking?"

"Twenty," Thomas replied. "That's after the ten he can take. His wife just had a baby and won't be able to help as much. He also has a call into the new vet to see if she can help with one or two."

Years ago, he'd seen the back of Naomi's clinic when Walter owned the practice. Unless she remodeled, she didn't have the space to board more than one or two animals.

"Did he say when?"

Thomas shook his head. "Maybe the middle of the week. He'd have to arrange transport, get a definitive answer from the vet once he knows what you want to do."

"We've got that storm coming in then. I'll check with Jace and Caden's schedule. Maybe we can drive out there and pick them up." Logan rubbed the back of his neck. "I'll call Austin. Once I talk with everyone, we'll go from there."

He would have to reach out to Naomi beforehand. But not tonight. He had three adorable dogs to get settled in his home.

Chapter 8

Picturesque beauty of the Appalachian Mountains settled Naomi's mind, bringing a smile to her lips. Maeve and Shorty had their eyes closed on the way home, and it gave Naomi time to get lost in her thoughts.

Logan Beckett had surprised her. From the moment he'd walked into the clinic until she'd defensively overreacted, he'd been nothing but nice and polite. Younger than she expected and a heck of a lot more handsome.

But then she'd heard Walter's words in the back of her mind, and it's like he'd taken over her mouth. In her mentor's eyes, Logan's only concern was the care of his precious pack and the farms that could help bring more money into his family's business. In the older man's opinion, the well-being of the local postal worker or grocer's pets was beneath Logan and his family. But wasn't that why Walter had his practice—for the forgotten townspeople? Wouldn't that make his practice as successful? Shouldn't he have been happy the Becketts supposedly pushed business to him? The questions slammed into her as she took the exit for their town.

The entire situation just made her question Walter's motive for bad-mouthing the Becketts. She'd passed judgement on the family without ever meeting them. Naomi had no right to question Logan—emergencies happen. It wasn't her business. Logan had the decency to call Mr. Smith instead of not showing. That was professional of him and something she would have done. Mr. Smith had said nothing about Vader's habit of getting into the thorns or that Logan was his regular doctor. Naomi also hadn't known he was a single father—something else Walter never mentioned.

The shrill tone of the phone startled Maeve, bringing Naomi out of her musing. She swallowed a groan before pressing the hands-free option.

"Hello?"

"Naomi? Are you okay?" Walter asked.

She fought the urge to roll her eyes. "Why? Did you try to call?"

"Yes. I left a message inviting you and Maeve to dinner. Then I received a call from Austin Harris when he couldn't reach you. When I couldn't get a hold of Maeve, we worried."

Naomi met Austin her first month in Oak Mountain when he came to visit friends. They kept in touch on social media.

"We went for a drive and didn't have cell service. I'm not sure about dinner, though. I had a long day." Maeve shook her head, clearly not up for visiting. "Can we take a raincheck?"

"Of course."

"What did Austin want?" Maeve asked Naomi's next question.

"Oh, yes. He wanted to ask if you could take in a couple of dogs. A shelter lost its funding and they don't have the space to take the unadoptable ones. He said the Becketts will handle the bulk of them since they have the room. I told him no because you didn't have space and Logan and his father wouldn't mind taking two more. Knowing the Becketts, they'll probably add them to their precious pack."

Naomi's gaze snapped to her mother's. No, they didn't have the space for two more dogs, but she'd be more than happy to foster them and see if any of the owners of her patients could take them in. She'd adopted Shorty from a shelter, for Pete's sake.

"Why would you do that? Maybe Austin asked because the Becketts *couldn't* handle any more. Perhaps they were at the limit allowed, or the two dogs needed specialized fostering. Did you even ask what breed they were? Smaller ones won't be a problem."

Walter snorted. "Austin only asked because he was desperate. He has the same type of sanctuary the Becketts have, just on a smaller scale. I'm sure he only reached out to you to take the ones knocking on death's door." She could hear the venom in her mentor's voice.

Naomi's blood boiled at his rude assumptions. "That's even more of a reason to say yes. I don't appreciate you speaking for me."

Naomi pulled into the driveway, circling around the clinic to park in front of their home.

"I was looking out for you. You don't have the time to deal with them. They probably wouldn't even compensate you for your time. You need to be available for paying clients, not charity. The practice is struggling as it is."

She made a point of never mentioning the clinic to Walter, regardless of his repeated inquiries. He *assumed* it wasn't doing well. But it was. There was a possibility that Naomi would include another tech later in the year. That did not cause her current fury.

Maeve made a sign of a cross, shaking her head. Naomi motioned to let Shorty out of his doggie seat, then turned back to the conversation.

"Payment is beside the point. These are animals that are scared and in need of a safe place. I will contact Austin and tell him you misspoke." She opened the car door. "We just got home. I'll talk to you next week."

"Naomi, I know the Becketts. They won't appreciate your help."

"If they don't, then that's on them, but it's my job to offer. Good night." She disconnected the call and counted to ten.

Shorty nudged her ankle with his nose before darting to the bush in front of the house. Maeve waited while Naomi grabbed their bags.

"Today's actions solidify my point about Walter," Maeve commented while Naomi unlocked the front door.

"I know. He knows I've fostered dogs in the past. Why dismiss the request right off the bat?"

"He overstepped today. This is your business and passion. Something tells me Austin would appreciate all the help he can get." Maeve toed off her sneakers. "I'm going to freshen up."

Naomi padded into the kitchen, eyeing the basket from Logan sitting on the counter, and unpacked their travel bag. After adding water to Shorty's bowl, she pulled out her phone, noticing three missed calls. Naomi pulled up Austin's number.

"Blue Sanctuary."

"Good evening. This is Naomi Hendrix. I received your message. I'm sorry it took a while to return your call."

"Doctor. Thank you for calling me back. I spoke to Walter—"

"He told me, but he doesn't speak for me," Naomi interrupted. Austin laughed.

"I didn't think so. That man has hated Thomas Beckett and has refused to help anyone who works with Hawkins Ridge. His dislike of them goes back way before Logan and his ex-wife. Anyway, will you be able to help with the animals?"

So this is a petty childhood squabble? What does Logan's ex-wife have to do with Walter? Naomi shook her head. "Yes, I'm more than happy to help."

"Great. I'm working on getting the dogs there before the storm. I'll send you pictures of the dogs we're rescuing shortly. Have an enjoyable night, Dr. Hendrix."

"Please, call me Naomi. Good night."

She pressed the end button and set the phone on the table. Why hadn't he told her his beef with the Becketts went back for decades? Was he worried she wouldn't take his side if she'd known?

Naomi couldn't answer those questions that night. But something told her she would need to eat more than crow the next time she saw Logan Beckett.

Chapter 9

Logan peered through the glass wall of the decompress room to study the thick gray clouds hanging low in the sky. The weather forecasted two days of heavy rain, flooding, and high wind for Oak Mountain, but Logan's family knew how to handle bad weather and even had a checklist. They'd placed sandbags around the stables, the chicken coop, goat housing, and in-ground crops. The high-capacity rain barrels were in place around the property while they had workers currently digging strategic ditches.

Fiona sat cross-legged in the middle of the floor, tearing open bags of dog toys despite the pair of scissors an arm's length away. Austin was due to arrive in a couple of hours with twenty new members for their sanctuary, which included dogs scheduled to be euthanized because of their age, health issues, or extended time at the closing shelter. Logan wanted to make sure they could relax comfortably in what would be a stressful situation.

It was also going to be the first time he would see Naomi since their initial meeting. To say he was nervous was an understatement. Austin told him Naomi had offered to foster two small terriers and would be by to pick them up. Logan wanted to volunteer to take them, but Austin insisted the dogs might not do well with a large pack right away. The last thing he wanted to do was to make it harder on the animals. If Naomi could ease them into socializing around other dogs, he was all for it.

His mother was the one who spoke to Naomi when she had called to schedule her visit. Logan had listened to his mother's side of the conversation while he examined the new kittens born to the calico. Within two minutes, Naomi had his mother laughing. Not a polite laugh, a legit guffaw. He still didn't know what the joke was. Once the call had ended, Josie had gushed about how she couldn't wait to meet her and how Naomi wanted to confirm Logan would be there. His mother had made it an order, even though he planned on it, anyway.

Logan had given more thought to their first meeting. They'd gotten off on the wrong foot and he hoped they could talk about it and move forward as colleagues, if not friends. Besides, just because her deep brown eyes had dilated when he'd called her Darlin', or she'd given him an appreciative once over when he'd first stepped into the clinic, didn't mean she was interested.

But until then, he had to deal with the two pregnant strays that animal control had dropped off an hour earlier,

"Can I take a few of these home to the pugs?" Fiona asked as she studied a bag that held a variety of plush vegetables. He'd already spent a tiny fortune on the three sisters because his daughter wanted them to feel loved.

"Sure. Make sure you clean up any plastic tags." Logan's phone rang just as his father stepped into the room. His brows knitted together when he saw Austin's name on the display. Maybe he was arriving early? "Hey Austin, are you close?"

"Sort of, but I got a problem. I just blew out two tires. The rain started about thirty minutes ago with a vengeance. Water flooded a pothole I didn't see until it was too late. I called roadside service and they're on their way, but it will be too late and dangerous to head there and then head home."

Logan motioned for his father to come closer and put the call on speaker. "Where are you?"

"On the old county highway about a mile past the fairgrounds."

"Hold on a sec." Logan pressed the mute button. He briefly explained the situation to his father. "We can't let him take the dogs back then have to load them up again in a few days." Thomas was already nodding.

"What do you want to do? There's a lot of activity going on now. We'll follow your lead."

It meant a lot that his father trusted him to take point. Logan knew if he needed his father to step and take over, he would, but he recognized this as another way to show him he was ready to run everything.

"Can you get Caden on the radio? Tell him to bring the van. If you don't mind, could you take a quick peek at the expectant mothers while I run over to the greenhouse and get the second van?" He unmuted the call and wrapped his arm around Fiona's shoulder. "We're going to head your way and get the dogs. We should be there in about ninety minutes."

"Sounds good. Be careful. I can see the small creek from here and it's slowly rising."

"If we can get there sooner, we will. Call if you see the road become impassable in the next hour, in case we need to take the long way to you. See you soon." He ended the call and walked his daughter to the supply cabinet. "I need you to stack up about twenty mats outside. While we're gone—"

"I want to go." Fiona pouted, but Logan couldn't give in.

"Sweetheart, I appreciate you wanting to help and if the weather was better, I'd take you with me. But it's dangerous and we still have a few things to do to get them ready."

Thomas slid his phone back into his pocket. "Your mother is on her way," "She'll help Fi finish everything. She wanted me to remind you that Doc Hendrix is on the way."

Logan would like to say that he hadn't forgotten, but it would be a lie. "We may not be here, and the clouds are getting dark. Getting the dogs is important now. Maybe she can check on the mothers. I'll ask Mom when I get back with the van."

He darted to his ATV and cranked the engine. He'd worry about getting it from the greenhouse later. Logan hoped they had time before the heavy rains closed the passageway. Living in the foothills near a creek that ran into a river, roads washed out quickly. If Naomi wasn't able to make it, he would take care of her fosters at his home until he could get them to her. Secretly, he hoped they had time to talk, but he wouldn't jeopardize her safety for an apology he hadn't formatted yet.

Maybe once the storm was over, they could talk over a cup of coffee. Logan was glad no one could see him smile at the thought.

Chapter 10

The GPS guided Naomi towards Hawkins Ridge. Deep, calming breaths were an attempt to settle her nerves. Maeve and Shorty were the perfect passengers enjoying the scenery.

Naomi had finally worked up the confidence to call Logan the day before to arrange a time to pick up her fosters. She hadn't expected for Josie to answer the phone. As her mother said, the woman was delightful and laughed when Naomi let it slip that she wanted to bathe in the preserves.

While she didn't want to assume Logan had shared what had happened with his mother, she'd made him some banana nut bread as an apology for her deplorable behavior. She prided herself on treating others the way she wanted to be treated. And Naomi could honestly say she didn't recognize the woman that had spoken that day. She'd embarrassed herself and her mother.

Her guilt over the whole interaction had plagued her for days. She didn't want to wait until the open house to repair the damage she'd caused. She wanted Logan to see her as a professional, mature colleague…and maybe as a woman. Hence the banana bread.

Maeve thought Naomi was using the baked good to flirt. While Naomi could lie to herself and say she'd dressed for her patients that morning, truthfully, she chose her outfit for Logan. His use of darlin' still echoed in her mind. His appreciative glances and compliments about her body made her heart race. So she'd paired her favorite jeans that hugged her curves to perfection with her purple V-neck sweater. And if that didn't work, she'd just apologize and they could move on as colleagues, maybe friends.

Naomi hoped that she and Maeve would make it back home before the rain started, as the dark clouds moved quickly.

"You didn't have to come with me," she said, her gaze sliding to her mother.

"Yes, I did. I need to make sure you don't say something you'll regret later. Also, I want to see what this property looks like." Maeve patted her arm. "Besides, sitting at home would be boring. Right, Shorty?"

Her fur baby gave a hearty bark and pressed his nose against the window. Naomi hadn't wanted to bring Shorty since he was unfamiliar with the fosters, but he did not do well with the rain. If it started while no one was home, his anxiety would take hours to calm down. Just to be on the safe side, she installed a temporary see-through metal partition to separate the back of her Subaru from the front.

Naomi second guessed her apology gift. "Do you think baking the banana nut bread was too much?" Maeve was already shaking her head.

"Not at all. I'll make sure they know I didn't help."

The first drop of rain hit as the tires crunched along the gravel when Naomi turned into the farm. People scurried placing covering over crops, knowing too much rain would damage their hard work. The relay line of workers placed sandbags along the driveway spoke of a people who had dealt with this before.

"It seems they are taking the weather report for flooding seriously," Maeve said as she leaned forward, her gaze on the sky. "We may want to make this quick."

They drove past a red barn with two tiny brick houses situated at the end of a shared lane. Three livestock guard dogs approached the fence, giving their car a close eye. Shorty barked hello in hopes they would hear him. They turned right, following the sign pointing to the sanctuary. Close to an eighth of a mile later, they pulled up to a stately white farm-house with navy blue shutters framing large pane windows. A wrap-around porch displayed hanging baskets and a few swings. A group of six people stood under a covered walkway between the house, a building with "Clinic" written on the roof, and a single-story cabin resting about a hundred yards away.

Shorty barked and bounced in his seat. Logan and an older version of him walked towards their car, scowls marring their faces. *Did Josie not tell them they were coming?* Naomi climbed out and met them at the bumper.

"Ma'am," the older gentleman said, clearly Logan's father. "Thomas Beckett."

"Naomi Hendrix and my mother Maeve." She looked between the two men. "Is everything okay? Is there a problem with the dogs?"

"There's been a situation." Thomas looked at his son to explain.

Maeve walked up beside her with Shorty in her arms. "What happened?"

Logan took off his worn baseball cap and ran his fingers through his hair. Naomi swallowed the drool threatening to escape when he held her gaze.

"Austin is stuck about an hour out. Blew out a tire when he hit a pothole. With the storm brewing, by the time he gets it fixed and makes his way here, it may be too rough for him to head back home. He didn't want to leave his wife by herself."

"So we're going to head out to meet him. The vans are ready," Thomas tilted his head towards two heavy-duty vehicles Naomi hadn't noticed.

She glanced at her mother. If Austin was an hour away, between traveling and transferring the dogs, it could take close to three hours for them to come back. The storm would be in full force. Could she afford to go with them? A stylish older woman with a warm smile on her face hurried over, pulling Maeve into a hug. The two women laughed as Shorty barked and wiggled from being in the middle, taking a step back. Josie's gaze turned towards Naomi and she saw where Logan got his piercing blue eyes from.

"You must be Naomi." She held out her hand. "Josie Beckett. Why don't you stay and wait for them to return? We have plenty of room and I can get this little guy some treats and a warm cup of coffee for you and your mother."

"We need to move," a man with a scar near his ear yelled. "The forecast says the heavy rains will hit Oak Mountain in forty-five minutes!"

Logan slipped his hat back on. "Mom will take good care of you and Maeve. My daughter is in the house taking care of our new litter of kittens."

"I want to go." Naomi surprised herself—and the men—with the words, but steadied her shoulders. Though the three men were probably capable, they could use more help. "You need the extra hands and I have experience dealing with moving animals in storms back in Oklahoma."

"Your call, son," Thomas said. "But it needs to be now."

Logan clenched his jaw. "Fine. We need the help since Jace is at the station and Sam and Owen are out of town. You're riding with me, Doc. Do we have an extra poncho?"

Another worker coming out of the clinic spun on his heels after hearing him and darted back inside. He ran back out a moment later with the yellow garment in his hands. Naomi turned to her mother, passing her car keys.

"I'll be okay. Make sure Shorty stays calm." She reached into the car and grabbed her cell phone and ID. "I'll text you if there's a problem."

She gave her mother a hug, then scurried towards the first van, slipping the poncho on as she went. Though it had a step rail, the van was still high off the ground. Naomi tried to reach the handle on the inside of the truck, but failed.

"You need help, Darlin'?"

Naomi startled at Logan's deep voice next to her ear. She fought the shiver racing up her spine and glanced over her shoulder. "Normally, I'd say no, but the step is slippery." And they didn't have time for her to figure out a dignified way to scramble into the van. Before she could comment further, Logan held her by the waist and lifted her into the vehicle.

Sweet baby corn. Why was it such a thrill to have him lift her? Her father had been the last man to sweep her off her feet literally, and she had been a teenager when it happened. Logan kept a firm hold on her until she'd safely placed her foot inside of the truck and grabbed the handle.

"You could have taken my arm," Naomi mumbled while settling herself on the heated seat.

"I could have, but that was more fun." He tugged on the seatbelt and held it out for her. "Buckle up."

He closed the door and jogged around to the driver's side. She'd have to reflect on how nice it felt to have Logan's large hands on her waist later that evening. The intoxicating scent of woodsy cologne mixed with his natural pheromones had Naomi inhale deeply and close her eyes as Logan pulled off.

Maybe she should have stayed with her mother and Shorty.

Chapter 11

The rain fell at a steady pace as the wind ticked up, blowing thin branches and debris across the road. Naomi couldn't imagine attempting this trip at night when the distances between the streetlamps would still leave a driver in pockets of darkness. Perhaps if she was more familiar with the area, it would be different, but she was thankful it was still afternoon. It did, however, add a wariness of visibility for her drive home once they were back at the sanctuary.

"I'm sorry for having to rush you today," Logan said as he turned onto the state road. "The weather just put a crunch on everything and the last thing I want is to be stuck where Austin is overnight."

She shook her head. "You didn't rush me. I understand. If the forecast is correct, there could be flooding."

He pointed to the landscape, where streams of mud and dry vegetation flowed through the trees. The rain had picked up in the ten minutes they were on the road. "As you know, the ground can only handle so much before puddles become washouts. The deluge is worse than a nice slow drizzle."

They drove for a mile or so in silence. Naomi bounced between figuring out how to start her apology and watching the low-hanging branches sway. Logan deftly handled the curves against the rapid beat of the windshield. When a stretch of road appeared, Naomi let her shoulders relax and spoke.

"Listen." She cleared her throat. "I wanted to apologize for the other day. My behavior was uncalled for. I admit I judged you based on someone else's opinion, which is wrong. I deal with that most of the time, so it wasn't right for me to turn around and do the same. Back home, it was hard to get people to trust me 'cause I wasn't part of the good old boys' club. Seeing your shock when you learned I was the doctor just triggered those memories, and I let Walter's words cloud my thinking."

Logan sighed and ran his fingers through his hair. "My strained relationship with Walter is *why* I hadn't been in to introduce myself. I thought you'd be a clone of him. That was wrong of me, so it's my turn to apologize."

"I've always wondered about that. Izzy, my mother and even Harold said positive opinions of you and your family, but no one ever came in to introduce themselves. So I thought Walter was right." Her gaze shifted slightly to the fast-moving water along the dip on the shoulder of the road. She wiped her hands along her jeans and turned back to their conversation. "When I first moved here, he was the only person I knew. It exposed me to his negativity my first month. Then, being around Izzy daily, talking to my patient's owners, opened up my eyes that I needed to do better. I'm not as outgoing as my mother, so taking that first step to meet people can be hard. I'm not making excuses, but I just wanted to let you know."

Naomi couldn't explain why she'd shared so much. It could be the nerves of the worsening weather, but she knew it was more than that. She had to be honest with Logan and herself. Her actions were inexcusable. She wanted to make Oak Mountain a home, to have the people see her as one of their own. It meant more than just showing owners she was a capable vet—she had to gain their trust. That started with Logan. She hoped her honesty, the banana nut bread, and her shirt did the trick.

"I hope we can start over."

Logan took his eyes off the road for a moment and flashed her those heart racing dimples. "Me too. There's a history I would like to share when we have time. It would be good for you to hear both sides."

"I'd like that."

Naomi gave herself a mental fist pump and focused on the beat of the wipers.

"How do you know Austin?" Logan broke the brief silence.

She adjusted in her seat to face him slightly. "He stopped by the office about a month after I took over. He said he was visiting friends. We keep in touch with email and social media."

The trees swayed harder as the winds picked up and the rain went sideways. Naomi gripped the door handle harder as she glanced in the side mirror to see the headlights from the second van falling behind. Logan slowed slightly as a sharp curve came into view. She sucked in a breath just as a branch dropped in front of a car coming towards them. Luckily, the water pushed the obstacle out of the way and the other motorist kept going. She didn't know how much further they had to go to reach Austin, but she hoped they got there soon. Her nerves had her talking, and she prayed it didn't bother Logan.

"Tell me about those delicious preserves you put in the basket."

"The jars were part of the family canning. It's different from the ones made with a small machine we sell at the farmer's market."

"So, those were by hand?"

Logan nodded, taking the exit he needed. "One weekend in October and November, we get together, either play music or movies, and can. We've been doing it for as long as I can remember. I hope Fiona keeps the tradition."

"How do you keep everything fresh until then?"

"Root cellar. There are a few items Mom and Owen, Noah's father and the chief of staff, will preserve earlier." He shrugged. "Even though we all live on the property and try to share at least one meal daily, getting together to do that is important for us to connect as a family."

"I used to can and bake with my grandmother before she passed. She would babysit me if dad was on a long-haul trip and my mom had to work. I made you some banana nut bread. I left it in the car with all the commotion, but I had planned to apologize with food as well."

"You didn't need to do that. Thank you. I'll have to share with my daughter, but my brothers are out of luck."

Naomi giggled, then let the comfortable silence fill the interior. A minute or two later, they maneuvered around the bend and saw a large cargo van with flashing lights on the side of the road. Naomi slowly exhaled when Logan pulled up beside the van. He flipped up the hood of his pullover and turned toward Naomi.

"Ready?"

She nodded and mimicked his move with her poncho. Thomas and Caden were already out of the car by the time they'd climbed out. Austin met them by the side door, his russet colored hair plastered to his head. Naomi thanked the stars she'd opted to wear her boots. She was itching to get the dogs transferred and get back on the road as quickly as possible.

"Sorry about this, guys," Austin said as he shook their hands. "Good to see you, Naomi."

She gave a warm smile in greeting. Thomas clapped Austin's shoulder and glanced at the tires. "Do you need for us to help get you up and running?"

Austin shook his head. "The tow truck left right before you pulled up. I'm good to go."

"Great. Then let's get these babies loaded and back to the sanctuary to dry off and decompress." Logan slid the door open. "Naomi, do you want to help the dogs get settled while we move them? The two you're fostering will be in our van, plus five of the bigger ones. The rest, we'll put in the other. It will give them space and allow them time to calm a little."

The plan sounded efficient. Wanting to lighten the stress, she gave him a playful stink eye. "Don't you dare lift me. I'll crawl in, so I'm at their level."

Everyone chuckled, and Logan gave a mock salute. Naomi flung the side doors open and crawled inside, appreciative of the layers of mats to cushion the hard flooring. She unfolded a towel from the stack behind the passenger seat as Thomas handed her a black and tan short hair dog. Naomi recognized her as one of her two fosters based on the picture Austin had emailed her. She ran the towel over the trembling pooch and greeted her with soft words. Logan quickly followed with the next, and Naomi repeated the same action.

As they moved their way through each dog, Naomi's heart swelled. This was why she'd became a veterinarian—to help animals that needed it the most. Despite the nerve wrecking trip, it was worth it because these babies were days away from their last, not given a second chance to know love. Watching Logan, his family, and Austin trying to keep the dogs as dry as possible and gently carry each dog had her mentally saying, aww. It only solidified what she now realized that everything Walter told her was a lie. It would be something she would need to talk through with her mother once they were home and over warm cups of tea.

Naomi greeted each dog, letting them get a good sniff of her. Twenty minutes later, they were saying goodbye to Austin.

"I wish I could take them all," Naomi commented as she made her way to the front of the van, stepping over a toolbox. Each dog had laid down but still shivered slightly.

Logan looked over his shoulder at their four-legged passengers and offered a smile. The hood on his poncho slid off at some point, revealing messy, wet hair. Naomi fought the urge to grab a towel and dry it for him. "I know. When we get calls from shelters to see if we have room for a cat or dog, we always end up with more than the one they called about." Logan made a U-turn and headed back home, letting Caden's van take the lead. "We had to stop letting my mother go to pick up animals. One time she went to get one senior cat and instead came home with four, plus three dogs."

"I didn't know you had both." Naomi held her hands in front of the vent to dry them.

"We have five barn cats, but the rest are in the main house. My folks converted the den to a feline sanctuary because there are large windows. The guest bedroom is the nursery for new mothers and orphan kittens. Except for five seniors, we prepare all the cats for a forever home."

"Wow. I hope I get to see it one day."

"You just name the day." Logan finished with a wink and warmth course through her veins.

They were on the road for twenty minutes when the radio crackled.

"Logan?" his father's voice came through clearly. Naomi picked up the walkie talkie and held it near his face, pressing the talk button.

"Yeah?"

"Jace called the house. They closed off the bottom of the mountain. It's already flooded, and a tree is threatening to fall."

What?! Naomi's thoughts of lodging for her and her mother raced through her mind. She hadn't seen a hotel on their way to meet Austin. Perhaps the Becketts could direct them to one or a bed-and-breakfast off the exit before the sanctuary.

Logan glanced at her. "Does Mom have clothes for Naomi and Maeve?"

"We can't stay," Naomi shook her head. "I need to open the clinic tomorrow and I don't have Shorty's food."

"I'm sure she does," Thomas answered Logan's question. "Call her."

"I will." He nodded to the satellite phone. "Can you dial the second programmed number and put it on speaker, please?"

"We don't want to be an imposition."

"Trust me, you won't." He pointed to the side of the road again, where the earlier streams of mud and debris were now borderline rapids. "Darlin', there's a reason they've already closed off access to town and the road to take you around the mountain is only going to be worse. There's a washer and dryer you can use and we'll find you clothes to wear until Jace lets us know when it's safe for you and Maeve to head home. It will probably be for a couple of days."

She hated his logical thinking. Naomi recognized staying with the Becketts was their only option. She wouldn't risk her mother, Shorty, or her new fosters' safety because being near Logan made her want to run her fingers through his hair. However, maybe Josie would give her a jar of preserves to eat in bed.

Pulling her mind from a decadent place, Naomi twisted her hands in her lap. "Shorty's teeth won't let him eat hard kibble."

He reached over and gave her wrist a gentle squeeze. "We feed our dogs fresh, wet food we prepare on site. I'll have my mom print the list of ingredients for you to review. You'll have Maeve and Shorty with you. Isabella can open the clinic or transfer the phones to her. Darlin', there's no excuse. You are sheltering in place with us for the next couple of days."

Naomi crossed her arms and kept her eyes straight ahead. "Fine, but there better be coffee in the morning."

Logan barked out a laugh and nodded for her to dial his mother.

Chapter 12

Logan draped a towel around his neck as he tried to see out of the front window of the sanctuary clinic. Rain fell in steady sheets while the fabric of the awning rippled in the wind. What he wouldn't give for two fingers of whiskey, a hot shower, and a solid eight hours of sleep. The shower was the only thing in his immediate future.

The worsening storm made the drive back to Hawkins Ridge longer. Logan white-knuckled the steering wheel the few times they drove through high standing water in dips in the road. It had him second guessing his decision to meet Austin, but hearing Naomi speak to the rescues in a soothing voice solidified that he made the right call.

Logan ran the towel over his hair and quietly chuckled when he insisted Naomi and Maeve stay in his home when they called his mother. Josie was adamant that their stay wouldn't be an inconvenience, even having Maeve hop on the line to tell her daughter it would be okay. It calmed Naomi, so her focus returned to the situation at hand—caring for the scared and nervous dogs. It didn't surprise Logan that his mother had everything ready to go when they pulled into the sanctuary, including a stack of clothes for Naomi and Maeve.

Everyone helped unload the dogs and get them settled into the bright decompress room. Pride swelled Logan's chest, watching Fiona pass out towels to everyone before turning her attention to the shivering animals. He kept a protective eye when Fiona lowered herself to the dogs' level and let them approach. He'd taught his daughter the value of hard work and to always lend a hand wherever it was necessary.

"How are you holding up?" Josie asked, coming to his side.

"Mentally exhausted. Thank you for having things ready."

"I've been doing this longer than you've been alive." She patted his cheek and stepped closer. "How'd Naomi take the news they were stuck?" Josie whispered.

Logan glanced to the other side of the lobby at Naomi and Maeve speaking in hushed tones.

"Better than I initially expected. She came up with every excuse she could, but I think she was more worried about putting us out and Shorty being forced to eat hard kibble." He shook his head. "I can't say I blame her. We're strangers she just met, asking to trust us to keep her, her mother and dog safe during a storm. She did panic about not having a sleep bonnet? Not sure why?"

"Black women have to cover their hair at night. With her hairstyle and Maeve's short afro, you can see they take care of their hair. I'll have to see if Noah has products for them." Josie held Logan with a look. "Why did you have us set Naomi and Maeve up at your place instead of the main house?"

Because he found the doctor fascinating, he thought. Spending time with Naomi, seeing her with the animals, concern for the well-being of her loved ones and not batting a lash at jumping in to help impressed him more than he expected.

Logan couldn't find a reason to justify her staying with him, but the idea of her being elsewhere caused him pain.

"I just thought they would like to be away from the chaos of the main house. Besides, Naomi is fostering two of the dogs. Maybe she would feel more comfortable if they were in my quarantine room. Give her a chance to bond in a quieter environment."

Josie rubbed her lips together and gave him a knowing, amused look. "You keep telling yourself that. Go get out of those wet clothes and grab something to eat."

"Aren't you eating?"

"I nibbled while I was getting the meal ready. Fiona and Maeve helped a lot."

"Thank you. I'll be back as soon as possible." He approached Naomi and Maeve. "Excuse me, ladies. We should get out of these clothes and eat something."

Maeve patted Naomi's arm. "Go. I put some dry clothes on the bed. Shorty is bonding with the three dogs in the house. I'll head over after I make sure Josie doesn't need me for anything."

Logan placed his hand on the small of Naomi's back and guided her through the covered walkway to the backdoor of his home. He toed off his boots once they stepped into the utility room that opened into the kitchen and living area. Naomi did the same.

Shorty, Tulip, Rosebud and Bluebell ran to meet them, tails wagging. They followed their owners to the closed door next to the kitchen. Logan kept dog beds, blankets, and toys in the room. He washed everything after he cleared the sisters, who now had a free run of the house.

"This is the quarantine area. I occasionally have patients that need medication every couple of hours, or puppies in need of nursing. Going back and forth to the clinic at two in the morning can be hard." He held the door open for her to cross. "Feel free to use it if you want to bring your fosters over. There is a doggie door that leads to the yard. You can see it better during the day. It's covered and bumps against the outside area for the clinic and pack."

Naomi nodded, and Logan closed the door behind them.

"Help yourself to anything in the kitchen." He opened a smaller fridge next to the large one. "Once you freshen up, here is the container for the dog food. I should have had Mom print the ingredients."

"It's fine. I like that it's fresh." Naomi looked around. "I thought you stayed in the main house."

He shook his head. "I'm there a lot, but we all have our own houses. I love my family more than anything, but you just need your privacy."

Naomi chuckled. "I'm learning that. My mother is my best friend, and I'm happy to have her with me. It's just sometimes, I think we both need our own space. For now, having the house on the property of the clinic works, but I think in the next year, we'll look for something close but separate."

A flash of future Naomi walking through his front door after a hard day and greeting all the dogs popped into his mind. Maybe the two of them spending the weekend hanging out with Fiona or helping Maeve and Josie with whatever chores needed to be done. Confused about what caused the image, Logan mentally shook his head. He'd barely just made up with the good doctor. Raising Fiona and helping the animals was his priority. Nope, romantic ideas couldn't take root despite how nice Naomi looked in her jeans.

He pointed to the guest room across the hall. "There are fresh towels in the closet. You and Maeve are more than welcome to use the washer and dryer if you need it. Will thirty minutes be enough time for you to clean up so we can grab something to eat?"

"It should be."

"Let me know if you need anything. I'm at the end of the hall." He rested his hand on the knob. "Thank you for today. I'm sorry you ended up stranded."

Her smile was a shot to his bloodstream. "I'm glad to help. Thank you for opening your home. I've always wanted to see the sanctuary and now's the perfect time."

Logan grinned as his imagined timeline of seeing Naomi permanently in his home moved up by six months. "I can't wait to show you everything. See you shortly."

Naomi stepped into the room. The click of the door echoed in the quiet space. Logan shoved his hands in his wet pocket and headed to the main suite. His bedroom had become his sanctuary. After the divorce, he'd remodeled the space and painted the walls in a soft slate gray. A view of the mountains greeted him each morning from his California king bed. A stack of books rested on a round table next to his brown leather chair. He pulled a pair of jeans and tee shirt from the dresser outside of the bathroom.

As he cleaned up, his mind drifted to the dogs they'd just brought in. Unfortunately, they were too old to be part of Caden's therapy dog training. He would have to sit with them and get a feel for their personality. If they were even-tempered, he could introduce them to be part of the pack. Or if they couldn't handle the energy and noise of a lot of dogs, he'd see if his brothers or workers wanted them as pets. It was something he'd have to discuss with them tomorrow.

Logan heard sounds from the kitchen and he hurriedly finished getting dressed. Maybe Fiona was home from helping her grandmother. He strolled down the hallway, slipping his shirt on as he went. He found Maeve standing in the kitchen, talking to Shorty, Tulip, Rosebud, and Bluebell as she searched through the cabinets for something..

"Everything okay?"

"Oh. Sorry. I was going to feed Shorty, but I couldn't find a bowl."

Logan chuckled and went to a cabinet above the fridge, pulling out a plastic wrapped bowl. "We sterilize them in case I have a dog staying in the house." He placed it on the counter next to the sisters' bowls. "I showed Naomi the food earlier."

Maeve spooned servings into the ceramic dishes. "Naomi told me she apologized. I hope you don't think any less of her for being influenced by outside chatter."

Logan's gaze snapped to hers. "I would never think that. I put off stopping by to welcome you because I also assumed she was like Walter. That was wrong on my part. As I mentioned to her, I want us both to move forward and work together."

Maeve studied him for a moment. Logan wouldn't shrink back and held her gaze. A few long heartbeats later, the corner of the older woman's lips curved up. "You're a good man, Logan Beckett. My daughter sees that *now*. I also see the way you look at her. Be patient while she severs the tether between her brain and her heart."

Logan understood what the woman meant; Naomi and her relationship with Walter. Their conversation in the van had opened his eyes a little. Oak Mountain was a fresh start for Naomi after a hurtful experience and explained the hesitation to put herself out there, not knowing if the town's residents would accept her. He got that and dealt with it himself. He appreciated Maeve's advice, but right now he wasn't sure if he wanted to pursue anything romantic because his focus was caring for their new arrivals and getting to know Naomi.

The woman in question strolled into the kitchen dressed in a pair of black sweatpants and a Hawkins Ridge Farm hoodie. She held a pair of sneakers in one hand. A different colorful scarf held her updo in place.

"Thank you for bringing my shoes from the car," she said to her mother.

Maeve settled herself in a kitchen chair. "I'll sit with the dogs for a bit. Let me know if you need me."

Logan nodded and motioned towards the back door. "Ready to grab something to eat and get started?"

Naomi blew out a breath. "Ready when you are."

Chapter 13

Naomi groaned as she stood from the Beckett's table. Josie's chili was amazing, and she'd promised her the recipe. The meal was filling and gave her the substance to face the long night before them. She'd probably ate too much, but she hadn't eaten since one o'clock that afternoon. Naomi gripped the travel mug of coffee like a life preserve.

Most of the meal was quiet, with everyone in their own head. Naomi's thoughts were of the conversation she over-heard between her mother and Logan.

His passionate response took Naomi by surprise. She could see Logan's gratitude for her being there and the help she provided. For him to declare he'd wanted to work with her again warmed her heart. The Becketts weren't the enemy; she saw that now. To think how close she came to letting Walter take control of her emotional state had the delicious meal roll in her stomach. Determined, once she returned home, she would talk to him and if it meant the end of their friendship, she would continue with her life.

"You okay?" Josephine said from beside her. Everyone be-gan filling cups with their beverage of choice and headed to-wards the back door to return to the rescues.. Logan watched her as he filled his own travel mug with coffee.

Naomi nodded. "Yes. Just briefly thinking if I have time to make a batch of chili to take home with me." *No need to tell the full truth*, she thought. Later, when it was just the two of them, she would share her epiphany with her mother later.

"Sweetheart, I would be more than happy to send you home with a container," Josie offered before setting two cookies wrapped in a paper towel on top of her travel mug. "I'll make sure you also get an invitation when I make pulled pork and potato salad next week."

Naomi's mouth watered. "You'd be my best friend if you did."

Everyone chuckled, lightening the mood. Maeve and Thomas were already standing at the counter in the clinic when the rest of their group hurried through the glass door.

"The two females strays the shelter dropped off earlier have gone into labor," the elder Beckett said, drawing everyone's attention. "There don't appear to be any complications. Both left the cage and are close, but not next to one another on the blanket."

"Pregnant females?" Naomi's gaze bounced between Logan and Thomas. It was Logan that spoke.

"Someone dropped off two females at the shelter last night." He wrapped his arm around his daughter. "The shelter asked if we had space because they didn't. Austin called before I could examine them."

Naomi nodded. It seemed the sanctuary had their hands full. Thomas cleared his throat.

"It's going to be a long night. Caden and his guys have the horses. Noah and the gardeners will handle the goats and making sure the crops don't flood." Thomas's gaze landed on

Naomi. "Luckily, we have the Doc and her mother to make up for the lost hands. We're thankful they're here."

Naomi's cheeks warmed when everyone voiced their appreciation. "Whatever you need us to do."

"Maeve, if you and Fiona wouldn't mind helping with the kitten feedings and administering their medication?" Logan pressed a kiss to the top of his daughter's head. "Then maybe get some rest. We'll be up early."

"Unless you need me, I'll go with them?" Josephine asked.

Logan shook his head and turned his attention to Thomas. "Dad, if you can check on the soon to be mothers, Naomi and I can take care of feeding and sitting with the new arrivals. Is someone with the pack?"

Thomas nodded. "The new vet tech, Claire."

Logan blew out a breath. "I'll send her home in about an hour. Are you okay with everything?" he directed his question to Naomi.

She knew nothing about the family pack, but she thought the dividing of jobs worked and she really wanted to get with the new arrivals. "That works for me."

The smile he gave her warmed her insides. She tightened the grip on her coffee, hiding her jittery fingers. Everyone murmured in agreement and went to work.

Josie showed her to the small fridge in the area they kept the medication and the bowls before heading out with Maeve and Fiona. Naomi periodically sipped her coffee while she scooped measured cups of wet food into individual bowls. A deep voice startled her.

"I thought nothing other than Fiona or taking care of animals would put a smile on my son's face again," Thomas said, bottles of water in his hands. "Despite the stress of the situation, you've made him smile, Doc."

Naomi shook her head. "I think he's just glad to have the help. We're colleagues."

Thomas' snort drew her gaze to the mischief in his green eyes. "You both keep telling yourself that."

The older man whistled as he walked down the hall to the room housing the soon-to-be mothers. What had he meant by that? Had Logan talked to his father about what Maeve mentioned in his kitchen?

Her eyes found Logan as he walked out of a storage closet with a stack of old blankets. He offered a grin when they passed the food prep area to the plastic laundry baskets stacked in the corner. Out of politeness, she returned the gesture.

Naomi didn't want to read anything in to what her mother and Thomas said. They only apologized a couple of hours ago. The idea of entering a romantic relationship so quickly seemed like a hopeful thought, especially since she was uncertain about his intentions beyond being friendly coworkers.

But if Logan flashed a dimple and called her Darlin', then all bets were off.

Chapter 14

The cold, refreshing water soothed Logan's dry throat while he rested his head on the wall behind him. He had returned to the new arrivals still in the decompress room an hour ago and made himself comfortable on a set of stacked mats in the corner. He was at the end of his wick and needed a solid six hours of sleep. Eight would be ideal, but he wasn't betting on it.

For the past few hours, he and Naomi had sat with the dogs and performed basic exams. When he checked on the pack to make sure they were calm during the rain, Clair had fallen asleep with the dogs curled up around her and decided they were okay.

The door to the room opened, and Naomi tiptoed in, handing him a granola bar. He ignored how her borrowed outfit accented her voluptuous frame when she took a seat beside him.

He asked about the new mothers. "How are they?"

"The brown and white dog had a litter of four. The other one had three. I cleaned up after them and made sure the pups latched on." Naomi looked around the room. "This is a quiet space."

"We try to keep it that way." He checked his watch. "Mom and dad will be here in thirty minutes to relieve us. I hope Noah can help with the baths."

"Wow. You guys do everything."

Logan chuckled. "The goats and the goat milk products are all Noah. He and Jace, my youngest brother, are responsible for the expansion into different areas. They went to the University of Pittsburgh to learn how we could expand past the rescue, stables and farmers' market."

"Did you think it would get this big?"

"Not at all. When Mom wanted to focus on the cats, Owen was the only one we trusted to supervise the staff. It's why my parents asked him to come out of retirement. He and my parents went to college together, and did investments before us kids came along. Owen's good with the staff and helped streamline processes to make everything more cost effective, allowing us to pay the workers a higher than normal wage. Now, he's married to my other vet tech, Samuel."

"So you each had your own specialty. Were you expected to become a vet because you were the oldest?" Naomi mirrored Logan's pose and rested her back against the wall. An audible yawn escaped her full lips.

It had been a long day for all of them, and Logan didn't want Naomi to feel she had to stay up with him. "It's okay if you want to head to the house," Logan offered. "They'll be here any minute."

Naomi shook her head. "I'll be fine a little longer. Besides…" she nodded towards the dogs. "I want to make sure they get another meal first. Talking also keeps my mind off my aching feet."

"I hear that. I don't know what possessed me to wear boots." He glanced down at his well-worn work boots. "To answer your question, I don't think expected is the right word. Not because I'm the oldest. People knew either I or Caden would be a vet because we were always with Dad or Mom when they took care of the animals or went on calls. Of course, that was when we weren't causing havoc on the property."

"My family knew I wanted to do something with animals," Naomi shared. "I was five or six when I got a pet hamster. I would always wrap bandages around it or listen to his heartbeat with my play stethoscope."

Logan smiled, listening to her story. For a moment, her face lit up, losing any sign of weariness.

"There was a neighborhood stray cat I would take care of. I would sneak him a bit or two of my dinner each night and leave it on the front porch," Naomi continued. "I swear my mother knew because she added small cans of cat food to the groceries." She chuckled. "One day, the cat brought me a half of a mouse it caught to say thank you and I screamed my head off. Scared the poor thing, and he never came back."

Logan laughed along with her. "Mice aren't one of my favorites. I've seen the mousers we have in the crops and stables proudly trotting by with them. I swear my stomach lurches each time."

"Back in Oklahoma, I had to bribe one of my colleagues when a man brought in his pet mice for their yearly exams. He had, like ten, entered them in competitions and everything." Naomi shuddered. "He always had two of them on his shoulders."

"Nope." Logan frantically shook his head. "They probably nibbled on his ears or hair."

"He let them sleep in the bed with him."

His mouth dropped open. "You're kidding."

Naomi flashed a scout's honor sign. "Deadly serious. The worse thing, his girlfriend had rats."

"What type of people are they?" Logan shuddered as he forced down the bile in his throat. "I'm all for what happens in your home is your business, but the thought of rodents scampering around the house… I'm going to have nightmares."

"Yep. I can laugh now."

Talking was the break they needed after a long night, and the tension in his neck and shoulder loosened. He watched as she whispered words of encouragement to the cautious dogs. Another meal with a dose of vitamins would do them well.

He slowly rose to his feet and stretched the ache in his lower back. "I'm going to grab a bag and pick up these disposable pads. Do you want to get their food together?"

"If you're sure?"

Their eyes locked for a moment as he held out his hand, gently tugging her to her feet. Logan took in the small flecks of light brown in her darker irises. Little lines creased the corner of her eyes. She truly was a beautiful, intelligent woman.

A tiny whimper pierced the quiet moment, causing them to take a step back.

Naomi ran her hands down the front of her sweatshirt. "You said you wanted to put vitamins this time?"

Logan cleared his throat. "Yes. There's a bottle above the fridge."

Before they could go about their duties, the door slowly opened. Josie poked her head in, a smile brightened her face.

"Tom and I got this. Go get some rest. There are leftovers in the fridge if you two are hungry."

"We can do this first." Logan shouldn't have spoken for Naomi and held his hands in a surrender pose. "I'm sorry. That was inconsiderate. Did you want to turn in instead?"

Naomi's melodic laugh settled his racing heart. "It's fine. I agree, though. We got this if you need to take care of something else first."

"I can help with the food. Thomas is already looking in on the mothers."

The dogs followed Logan as he quickly replaced the pads and picked up the water dishes to freshen. Naomi and his mother returned with portioned meals and set the bowls in front of the dogs. Once they were positive the rescues would eat, they headed to the lobby and met Thomas strolling out of the new mothers' room.

"You need to get some sleep. Come back around ten," Thomas ordered, handing him a bag of coffee beans.

Logan checked the clock—two in the morning. That would give him enough time to rest up. He agreed and held the door open for Naomi. He guided her towards the house, ignoring how natural his hand felt on the small of her back.

A rhythmic tone invaded Naomi's peaceful dream of skiing down a mountain of fluffy snow. She'd never skied a day in her life, but she felt relaxed as the wind whooshed past her face. The sound continued clearing the last of her sleep away.

Pulling her phone off the nightstand, Naomi tapped the green button.

"Hello?"

"Oh my gosh, I am so sorry I woke you," Isabella's apologetic voice sounded on the other end.

Naomi moved the phone from her ear and glanced at the time. She'd set her alarm to ring in ten minutes. "I needed to get up. How are you?"

"I should ask you that. Long night I take it."

She swallowed a groan when she sat up. "That is an understatement. I went to bed a little before three."

Naomi relayed the events of the evening, registering it hadn't been a full twenty-four hours since they'd gotten the call from Austin. After she finished, Isabella tsked on the other end.

"Just horrible. I'm glad they had you there."

"Me too." Naomi realized Shorty wasn't with her and assumed her mother had him. "How are things in town?"

"The park and some of the valley area flooded. There's a downed tree across the Stark bridge. Rumor has it the county is making the town take care of it." Isabella's husband was a deputy and in the know. "Right now, the focus is on stopping the waters from coming further into town. They think the winds will ease by this evening, but the forecast doesn't have the rain slowing until the morning."

Naomi's scarf had slid off while she slept. Thanks to the natural hair oil her mother borrowed from Noah, her locs hadn't frizzed from being in the rain. She put the call on speaker and went about styling her hair.

"Any calls for the office?"

"None yet. Everyone understood why we canceled their appointments." Isabella let out a sharp whistle. "Sorry, my cat dive bombed the poor dog, and now they're chasing each other. How are the Becketts treating you and Maeve?"

Being around the family, their hospitality and their obvious love for each other, gave Naomi a fuzzy feeling. The Becketts were good, caring people. Seeing Logan interact with the new arrivals, his patience when a dog would growl out of fear, not hiding his affection for his daughter, showed his passion for his career and the unconditional love for Fiona. He is a man that any woman would be proud to have as her partner.

"Fine. They're warm and friendly. Shorty has taken three pugs under his wing." Naomi also thought taking care of Bluebell, Rosebud and Tulip helped his rain anxiety. "I'm going to bring my fosters to Logan's house today so I can bond with them away from the dogs that are staying."

"See, I told you not to listen to Walter."

"I know. We'll see how today goes, but I'm hoping to head home tomorrow."

"Until they clear that tree and some of the water recedes, I don't see it happening. I'll keep you posted on the progress here," Isabella said.

"Thank you. I need to run and get started on the day."

Naomi darted into the bathroom for her morning routine, thankful she had showered before turning in. The hypnotic aroma of coffee drifted under the door. Her eyes closed and inhaled the rich intoxicating smell, causing her stomach to growl. Did Logan have food in the house, or did he eat all of his meals at his parents? He definitely had coffee. So that would do for now.

Maeve had washed their clothes and left them on the chair in their room. Naomi slipped on a pair of jeans and a borrowed long-sleeved t-shirt. After making the bed, she stepped into the hallway and paused, listening to the father and daughter conversation in the kitchen. Memories of trying to talk her father into letting her go to the library by herself flashed in Naomi's mind.

"Why can't I drive the four-wheeler by myself?" Fiona whined.

"It's still raining. The ground is too soft, and there's standing water between here and the stables. What if you flip it on yourself with no one around?"

"Daddy, I'll be fine. I did it before."

She heard what sounded like the refrigerator closing before Logan spoke again. "It was sunny. You drove it to the gate where Noah could see you the entire time. Did you ask Caden to come get you?"

"He said he was busy, but maybe this afternoon."

"I don't understand why you need to go to the stables now. You can't take Cinnamon out and don't tell me it's to help feed the horses because I know you better."

Fiona's exaggerated sigh reached Naomi's ears. "I'm bored. What am I going to do today?"

"You can help us with the dogs. See if Noah needs help with orders. Scoop the litter boxes or maybe clean your room. Perhaps read the book for the report you said you wanted to do on Friday at that boy's house. There's an entire list of things you can do."

Fiona argued. "But it's spring break,"

"Break from school, not the chores at home," Logan countered

Shorty outed Naomi's hiding spot with a short bark. She came around the corner and offered a smile. "Good morning."

"Morning Naomi," Fiona said. "I hope you don't mind that I took him out back with the pugs."

"Not at all." She looked towards Logan. "Do I smell coffee?"

He flashed her a lopsided grin. "You do. Cups are above the coffeepot. There's sugar on the table and cream in the fridge. If you're hungry, I was going to make some eggs and sausage."

"What can I help you with?" Naomi asked, pulling a black mug from the cabinet. She savored the first bitter sip. "That's fantastic."

"I think I have everything covered." Logan began cracking eggs into a bowl. "Regarding the coffee, Owen mixes different beans and then gives everyone some for mornings like this when we aren't going to the main house to eat."

Naomi sat beside Fiona, who gushed over the dogs. "Do you eat all your meals there?"

It was Fiona that answered. "No. Mostly, Owen or Nana will fix breakfast sandwiches so I can eat on the way to school. On the weekends is when we'll eat most meals there, but Dad tries to cook about three times during the week."

Logan sheepishly nodded. "It's true. Cooking helps me unwind."

"That's nothing to be embarrassed about. I used to love to cook, but since Mom is with me now, she insists on doing it. Now, I mostly read to help me relax."

"I read a lot, too," Fiona offered before turning her attention to her father. "So what can I do?"

Logan exhaled before placing links into a hot skillet. "After giving the rescues baths, Caden and I are going to introduce the dogs to the pack after lunch. You can help with that, and we'll see if Caden can give you a ride back to the stables."

Fiona rose to her feet. "I can go with you and Uncle Caden? For real?"

"Yes, but you have to pitch in somewhere else first."

"Deal. I'll see if Pop Pop needs help." She turned to Naomi as she bent over and gave each dog some loving. "Oh, your mom is with my Nana this morning."

Naomi had planned on texting her mother to see where she was, but now she didn't need to. Fiona slid on a pink rain slicker and headed out of the house, sadly, closing the door in the dogs' faces. Shorty came up to her and wagged his little bottom. Now that they were starting earlier, Naomi would have to find time today to spend with him while easing her new rescues into the mix.

"I wondered if your offer to bring the foster dogs here still stands?" Naomi asked Logan, standing to top off her mug. She wondered if they would throw in a bag of coffee beans with the chili.

"Of course. I wanted to spend one-on-one time with the arrivals after we give the new mothers an exam. Why don't you take a few hours and let them get to know Shorty?" He pointed to the bread box. "Actually, would you mind making toast?"

After another sip, Naomi sat her cup on the counter and washed her hands. "I spoke with Isabella this morning." She told him everything her friend had said. The four slices of bread popped up when she finished.

"That explains why Jace hasn't texted." Logan scooped fluffy, cheesy eggs onto a plate, along with three sausage links. "I may need to check if the sandbags around the goat barn are holding. I think Izzy is right. It will take a couple of more days before you head home. Once they're sure the creek won't crest higher, they'll tackle the tree."

Naomi dropped two slices on each plate and followed Logan back to the table. Shorty and the pugs sat on their rears, giving them hopeful looks.

"I have organic chew sticks for the dogs so you can eat in peace," Logan offered as he opened a door to a pantry. Pulling out a sealed bag, he handed it to Naomi. "See?"

She read off the short list before pulling out four and handed the bag back to Logan. She passed each dog one. As a crew, Shorty in the lead, they curled up on a large dog bed near the couch and nibbled on their treats.

"I probably would have snuck a piece of sausage to him," Naomi confessed, turning her attention back to her plate.

"It would be hard not to. He's adorable."

Warmth coursed through her as she looked at her little man. The pugs were helping him cope with the temporary situation of being in a new place. She wondered if Logan would let her bring him back for a play date once they return home. She also thought it would be good for Shorty to see his new friends. Maybe a play date for the owners.

Chapter 15

High winds whipped the steady downpour against Logan's screened-in yard, creating a rhythmic beat on the roof. Naomi closed her eyes, dropping her head back on the glider, and took a deep inhale of dewy fresh air. Shorty, Bluebell, Rosebud, Tulip, and her two fosters hunkered down on the only dry patch of grass near the back door.

She and Logan had finished the in-depth exams of the new arrivals before sending them off for baths. Once Thomas and Claire gave the newborn pups a once over, the mothers began a vitamin enriched diet. Logan suggested moving them to the decompress room the next day, after disinfection from the new arrivals, to give them more space.

In the light of day, Naomi could see the outdoor space behind Logan's home and the sanctuary clinic. Set in a triangle pattern with close to two acres of grass in the middle, Logan's home, the clinic and 'doghouse' gave ample space for the pack to stretch their legs. A high chain-link fencing acted as a barrier between the clinic and doghouse with enough overhang to keep rain, snow, and the summer sun off the animals. It is a pattern Naomi would have done if she had a sanctuary. It was practical for checking on all his responsibilities without using the front door.

Shorty's excited bark had her open her eyes and smile at her mother.

"I was wondering where you were. You can get lost on this land." Maeve sat beside her on the wooden bench and exhaled.

"I was thinking the same thing. I looked for you before I brought the dogs over. Were you in the main house?"

Maeve shook her head and reached down to pet the furry welcoming committee. "Caden drove me and Josephine to the greenhouse. A window sprung a leak, so while he worked on patching that up, we had to pump the excess water."

Naomi's brows furrowed. "I thought they had employees for that."

"Most of the workers live in town. The ones on-site are for the animals." Maeve rested her hand on Naomi's leg. "Noah met us there with more clothes. "

Naomi made a mental note to thank Noah later. With the number of animals at the sanctuary, it made sense for the workers to be close. The Beckett family believed in hard work, but they couldn't do everything.

"Thank you for getting those."

Maeve dismissively waved her hands. "No need to thank me. How are things going here? Where's Logan?"

"He's introducing the new arrivals to the pack. I didn't know they had another five acres set aside just for the dogs to run and enjoy the fresh air. Even have a small man-made pond for them to swim."

"Josephine said the entire property is five hundred and fifty acres. She offered to take us out on the four wheeler to the stables. Did you eat?"

Naomi nodded. "Logan made something before we went to the clinic, and Fiona brought us sandwiches before I came here. There's a jar of trail mix on the counter if you want something."

Maeve crossed her legs. "Nope. I'm saving my appetite for dinner. Josie started a brisket this morning. She froze some of their fresh collards and pulled an apple cobbler from their deep freezer. This may be my happy place."

"Mine too." Naomi glanced down at the dogs, including Logan's pugs, and smiled. "Putting your love for the food aside, what do you think of the Becketts and here?" She swept her arm out. Maeve answered after a long sigh.

"I think I've seen more of the family and the operation than you in the twenty-four hours we've been here. This family cares about one another and the animals. The stories I heard while we worked in the greenhouse only confirm that fact."

Naomi came to the same conclusion. She witnessed Logan interacting with Claire and the three employees that help him with the pack. Also, his interaction with Fiona spoke of the love for his daughter. The Becketts have been nothing but respectful to her.

"What made you ask that question?" Maeve asked, drawing her attention. Naomi slouched lower on the bench.

"I'm not sure, but I could use your opinion. Walter has called or texted six times since we've been here. I put the phone on silent after I spoke with Izzy this morning. I have a plan to talk to him at the office, either before we open or after closing. He needs to know that his actions aren't okay. I still worry about his pulling a John and try to make things difficult for me here, but I can't move forward mentally if I don't."

Oklahoma and Oak Mountain were vastly different. She moved to the rural town after marrying John. Naomi didn't know anyone and trusted him to be her guide to the people and potential patients. She achieved success solely because of her dedication and the positive reputation she had developed in the community. It earned her the loyalty of repeat customers. Taking a stand and establishing that hard line of what was acceptable was the next step in reclaiming her mental well-being

The sudden heavy patter of rain pinged off the roof of the screened in yard, causing the dogs to stop their game of chase and settle next to Naomi and Maeve.

"I'm willing to end the friendship if I have to," Naomi finally added.

Maeve pressed her shoulder against her daughter. "You control the outside influences in your life. If it means the end of the friendship, so be it."

Peace washed over Naomi. She'd needed this alone time with her mother. Seeing the friendship develop between Maeve and Josephine, she didn't think escaping the Becketts once they return home was an option. Deep down, Naomi was okay with that. Needing to change the subject, she glanced down at the two terrier mix fosters.

"You know I'm going to end up keeping them."

Maeve chuckled. "I know."

"We may need a bigger place."

"I agree, but something we can talk about later. Now, tell me what's going on with you and Logan."

Naomi choked on an intake of air. Maeve rubbed her back while she regained control, a knowing grin plastered on her lips. She playfully pushed her mother away.

"Nothing is going on. He's a knowledgeable vet, loves his daughter and has been nothing but kind and respectful to me. We're colleagues and chances are, will supervise visitation dates if Shorty has anything to say about it."

The dog in question was the only male in the group and took it upon himself to give the other pooches licks. Curiosity, however, nudged Naomi to ask a question.

"Have you heard anything about his marriage?"

Maeve snickered. "The only thing I've heard is that he has full custody, and the girl has video chats with her mother about once a month."

Naomi hummed. If the information from Austin was correct, Walter knew Logan's ex-wife. How was the million-dollar question? Logan said on the way to meet Austin, they would talk about the family's history with Walter at another time. She wouldn't push him.

For now, they needed to focus on getting the dogs settled and forming a working relationship.

Peals of laughter brought a smile to Logan's face as he watched his daughter run around the enclosed area with the pack from the comfort of a bench. The new arrivals were keeping close to Logan. They'd set boundaries with the pack and, after the initial introduction, the sanctuary dogs had turned their interest to Fiona. It would take time for the arrivals to learn this was their new home and their days of living in cages were over.

"Here," Caden said, tapping Logan's shoulder with a sports drink bottle. He reached down and petted the new dogs. "How are you holding up?"

Logan stretched his legs in front of him. "I need some sleep. I meant to ask where you were this morning?"

Scout lay near the new rescues but respected their space. Caden took off his cap and rested it on his knee. "One of the goat handlers noticed a crack in a greenhouse panel and called mom. I took her and Maeve over to help fix it and get the excess water out. The last thing we need is more humidity in there and ruining the crops."

"Why didn't you say something? I would have gone with you."

Caden shrugged. "You were asleep. I'm surprised Fi didn't tell you."

"No, but it explains why she wanted to take the four-wheeler."

Caden chuckled. Logan loved his brother's laugh. When he returned home from the service, he'd lost his smile and humor.

"She knows how to work her father."

"And her uncles." Logan took a gulp of his drink. "Did you look at the property? Any damage? I feel like I've put everything on hold for the past twenty-four hours."

Logan always dropped everything when arrivals came. He understood how stressful going to a new place would be for the dog or cat. It was why he spent as much time as possible with them, letting them know they were safe.

"We'll have to put more sandbags around the trail this evening. I'll know more once I head up home. One tree near the stables is leaning, but it shouldn't hit the bunk house if it falls. We'll deal with it after this passes. The horses are doing well." Caden nodded towards the screen porch on the other side of the clearing. "When are you planning on moving Doc and her mother to one of the tiny homes or the main house?"

Logan noticed Naomi bring the dogs to the yard shortly after he let the pack out. Though he couldn't fully see what they were doing because of the screen. "Why? No harm in them staying with me and Fi. I'm not sure how her dog would do with the cats. Besides, the road should be clear in a day or two."

"I think you're looking at close to two or three more days." Caden rested his arms on his thighs. "I see why you're attracted to her."

"I'm not attracted to her." Logan's gaze drifted to the back of his home. "Yes, Naomi is an intelligent, beautiful woman. But there could never be anything between us."

"Why?" A pack dog dropped a ball at Caden's feet, which he picked up and tossed. "She is everything Kaylee isn't."

"That's true. I guess I'm a bit gun shy whenever Walter's in the picture. We talked on our way to meet Austin and I got a bit more of her back story and what led to the misunderstanding. Though he made his opinion known about us, it seems her ex-husband ruined her reputation and basically drove her out of Oklahoma." Logan rested his arms on his thighs and focused on the uptake in wind speed. "I don't think Maeve is a fan of his."

"Can't say I blame her. Like I said, don't lump her in with what happened with Kaylee. You deserve to be happy."

The corners of his mouth tugged up as two of the new arrivals eased their way into the fray of the pack. He and Caden moved to the edge of their seats in case they needed to jump in.

"Thanks for listening," Logan said. "I think I'll keep Naomi as a friend while they are staying with us. Once I get to know her better…we'll see."

Caden stood and slipped his wet cap on. Scout ambled over, nudging his thigh. "That's good to know. Come on, Squirt, if you're going to the stables."

The rain went from a steady pace to a heavy downpour. The cover protected the pack, but the pitter-patter against the roof made a few nervous. He gave his daughter a hug, then ushered the dogs inside.

Logan used Walter meddling in his marriage with Kaylee as an excuse not to pursue something with Naomi right now. It was weak and a lie. He was afraid of not having the time for a relationship and Naomi losing interest. Between running the business and raising Fiona, he didn't think Naomi, or any woman for that matter, would accept not always be first in his life. Logan grew up seeing his parents working together to grow Hawkins Ridge. Though his mother was his father's vet tech, she still had her own thing and built the cat sanctuary. For a while during his separation from Kaylee, he wondered if she had her own responsibility, if that would have satisfied her craving to return to the rodeo.

It was something Logan wouldn't rehash again; he'd done enough of that. Logan spared a glance out the large window of the pack's sleeping area and noticed Naomi and the dogs had gone inside. Naomi's independence was an attractive quality, along with her love of animals. Maybe once Logan got to know her better, he may change his mind.

CHAPTER 16

"It's good to see Shorty calm during the rain," Maeve commented from beside Naomi on the large leather sofa in Logan's living room.

Naomi lifted her gaze from the e-reader app on her phone and glance at all the dogs curled up on an oversized doggie bed.

"I never thought giving him a companion would help."

"He may sense the nervousness of the other dogs and wants to give them support when they are doing the same for him," Maeve observed. "Did you decide on names, or are you going to keep the ones they have?"

"I'm leaning towards Mika and Tam. Don't ask me why, they just look like they need fun names." Naomi spared another glance. "Do you think it's weird we've all relaxed so quickly here?"

Maeve, also reading on her phone, sat the device down and shrugged. "I don't know. Part of me says no. They've shown us nothing but respect and openness since we pulled up yesterday. I think it helps that they aren't tracking our every move."

Naomi nodded. "Granted, they've had other things to focus on since over half their workers are in town."

"True. I guess my point is, these are down to earth, hard-working people. Do I think they'd let some random stranger stay in their private home? No. However, I think—"

The words died on Maeve's tongue when the front door flew open and a drenched Logan stumbled in.

"Ladies, we have a situation." He yanked off his boots. "An old tree has uprooted a few yards into the tree line near the chicken coop and run."

Naomi shared a look with her mother before speaking. "Is there flooding?"

Logan met her eyes and exhaled a deep breath. "That's what we are trying to avoid."

"Caden is bringing the axes and shovels," Thomas yelled as he stormed through the open door. He nodded to the women in greeting. "He'll meet you at the tree. The four-wheelers are ready to go."

Naomi shot to her feet. "What can we do?"

Logan yanked his Henley off and used it to run over his damp hair. The soaked tee underneath clung to his thick, muscled torso. *Now isn't the time to drool.*

"I don't know if we—"

"Don't start," Naomi sat her hands on her hips. "You need extra help. Mom and I are here. What do you *need* for us to do?"

"Actually, Doc, if you could help me, and a few workers with sandbags, that would be great," Thomas offered. "Maeve, if you could help Josie and Fi at the house. There's a cat in labor and past feeding time for the two kittens in the incubator. I can have Claire come sit with the dogs here."

"She doesn't have boots," Logan argued, heading towards the back of the house as Naomi, Thomas, and the dogs gave chase.

"Noah, grab an extra pair of galoshes," Thomas spoke into a walkie talkie Naomi didn't see him have. "What size Doc?"

"Eight." She headed to her room to grab a hoodie and the poncho from the day before.

A tug on her elbow when she stepped into the room caused her to spin around. Logan mimicked her pose from earlier, with his hands on his hips.

"Naomi, I don't want you to get hurt. Perhaps you could check on the cat that's in labor in case there are complications."

"That's not happening. Josie is still a vet tech. If there is a problem, she'll know what to do. Mom is better at helping with the feedings. You need the hands. I don't understand what the problem is. Don't give me some sexist remark cause you won't like my response." She squared her shoulders. "I'm helping your father."

"I would never say something sexist. Most of the women in my life are far more capable than men I know."

His concern for her well-being touched a part of her heart she'd thought long since died. Naomi took a beat, rested a hand on his arm, softening her tone. "Thank you for being worried. It means a lot, but I'm not changing my mind. The time we waste having this useless discussion could be better spent getting ready to go out there."

"She has a point, son." Thomas rested his hand on Logan's shoulder. "Noah will be here in a minute for y'all to head over and meet Caden. The longer that tree is down, the more damage could happen. I get why you're concerned about her safety, but she volunteered to help and we need it."

Logan held Naomi's gaze for a beat longer before dropping his head in resignation. "Fine. You're right. Darlin', the ground is muddy and divots are forming. Please take care of yourself."

Naomi fought the urge to smile in triumph. Now wasn't the time. Instead, she gave a quick nod and hurried over to the closet to grab the poncho. Maeve shimmied past a retreating Logan.

"Three minutes, Doc." The smile Thomas flashed her was one of amusement. She offered the gesture in kind and set about getting ready.

"You know I'm not going to try to stop you," Maeve said as she reached for her slip on sneakers. "Just be careful."

Naomi slipped on the hoodie Logan gave her before grabbing another pair of socks. She gave her mother a hug before yanking the poncho off the chair. "I will be careful." She hurried out of the bedroom and into the living area just as Thomas was setting a pair of black rubber boots on the tile in the foyer. Logan jogged past dressed in hip waders and a bright slicker. He stopped briefly and met Naomi's gaze.

"Thank you for helping with the sandbags. I apologize if you think I didn't want you to go because you're a woman. I don't want anything to happen to you." He turned to his father. "We'll radio when we have to tree chopped up, and the trench dug."

Thomas clapped his son on his back. "I got her. You be careful and if you need more hands, let me know."

Naomi called out, causing Logan to glance over his shoulder, his hand on the knob. "You be careful too."

The smile he gave her warmed her soul and thawed the wall around her heart.

For the past two hours, Logan, his brothers, and three workers dug a muddy trench and took axes to the old tree. Their focus that evening was to clear the blockage and prevent additional flooding.. Once the rain stopped, they would go back with chainsaws and do a better job of breaking the tree down,

A low groan escaped Logan's mouth as he shifted to climb out of the UTV, reminding him he wasn't twenty anymore. His shoulder and back screamed in annoyance at the workout they were put through.

"You make me not want to get old," Noah teased from behind the wheel. His close cut fade, and rich, medium brown skin damp from the work in the rain.

"You're three and a half years younger than me and don't think I didn't see you hold your lower back out there." The corner of Logan's lips easily ticked up. "Do you think we're good?"

Noah nodded. "The trench is working and Thomas radioed the water had stopped flowing towards the coop. Speaking of which, is he waiting up for you?"

Logan's gaze shifted to the set of benches under the overhang of the main house. Thomas had his legs crossed, nursing a beer. Concerned reared its ugly head. Had something happened to Naomi? Fiona? Instead of answering Noah's question, Logan flipped the hood from his slicker up and climbed out, leaving the door open so Noah could hear.

"Everything okay?"

"Yep." Thomas leaned forward to peer into the vehicle. "Just taking a minute."

Noah put the UTV in reverse when he and his father offered a wave.

"Do you think we're okay until this storm passes?" Thomas asked before taking a sip. Logan stepped further under the overhang, raking his fingers through his hair.

"I think so. Caden mentioned something about a tree on the north side of the property, but he didn't seem overly concerned. I'll ride over tomorrow. I'll see if Fi wants to go so she can check on the horses."

"She's passed out on the couch now. Your mother said she did amazing tonight, focused on feeding the kittens and running the food out to workers that stopped by." Thomas patted the spot beside him. "Take a minute."

Logan hated as a kid when his father would do the same move because it meant he was getting a talking to. He still did as he was told and took a seat in his wet clothes.

"What did I do now?"

"Nothing. I just wanted to tell you how your lady friend did tonight."

He wanted to ask, but didn't want his father to read too much into it. "Lady friend sounds like we're dating."

"That's only a matter of time. Anyway, she impressed every-one. She hopped right into the relay line. Not once did she complain. Even asked questions if there were other areas that needed to be made secure. She's a keeper."

"We aren't dating, but any man with half a brain knows she's a keeper."

"Son, you two look at each other like pieces of chocolate cake, so don't tell me you don't find her attractive."

Logan didn't want to have this conversation, especially when a hot shower, ibuprofen, and a beer were calling his name. "Naomi's beauty isn't an issue."

"It can't be brains because she's smart as a whip and has a giving personality."

Logan sighed, settling in to spilling his guts. "A woman like Naomi deserves a man that can give her more time than I can right now. Don't get me wrong, I'm not saying she needs someone to take care of her. She doesn't. But I honestly don't know if I'm worthy of her."

"Ah." Thomas took a long pull of his beer before he spoke. "Why do you think you're not?"

He shrugged. How could he explain what he battled during his divorce? "Walter put in Kaylee's mind that she could do better than me, this family, heck, even her daughter. Then there's the old-timers that still can't see me as qualified to care for their farm animals. If it wasn't for their children running interference, I'm sure we'd probably lose business." Logan raked his wet, tangled hair, his voice barely a whisper. "Even though I know Kaylee wasn't the one for me, I don't know if I can go through that pain again, especially with Fiona."

Thomas held his son in place with a look. "Regarding the farms, I went through the same thing when your grandfather turned everything over to your mother and me. The same ones causing a fuss had to run interference between me and their parents. They'll see you're far more capable than you give yourself credit for. Second, how long was Kaylee on this land and help with emergencies? If you would have told her to stay behind, she wouldn't have given it a second thought. If Naomi wanted to do Walt's bidding, she wouldn't have gone toe to toe with you earlier."

A ghost of a smile appeared on Logan's lips. Naomi's feistiness was one of Logan's favorite things about her. His father was right. His ex-wife would not have gone out in the rain to help with the rescues, stay up all night with them, let alone lift and toss dozens of sandbags. He still wasn't sure about Naomi and now wasn't the time to think about anything other than getting dry.

He stood and stretched his lower back. "I will admit Naomi sparks and interest, but she's only been here for less than forty-eight hours. She doesn't even know why Walter dislikes us. Until she learns the truth, I can't entertain anything more than colleagues."

Thomas followed his son and rose to his feet. He clapped him on the shoulder, splashing them with water. "Don't let the past stop you from finding happiness. Now, your mother sent some chicken and dumplings over with Naomi. Go eat and get some rest. We'll touch base at breakfast."

Logan nodded, flipping the hood up on the slicker. He could have stuck to the covered walkway, but darting across the open space would be faster. He watched his father climb the back steps to the main house before jogging to his home.

Light shone in the front windows. He shrugged off his coat and waders on the porch before stepping into the foyer. The sight before him took his breath away. Naomi stood in front of the stove. Her hair wrapped in a towel. She wore the sweatshirt and joggers he let her borrow. Though she swam in the top, the pants hugged her curves and bunched up at the ankles. He'd never seen a more beautiful image. The dogs, including Naomi's, ran to greet him.

"Hey. I'm heating some of the food your mother sent. Do you want some?"

He snapped out of the trance, closing the door behind him. "You don't need to do that, but thank you. Let me just take a quick shower."

"Would you mind if I had a beer?" Naomi asked over her shoulder. Logan swallowed a groan, beginning to accept the inevitable. He wanted to pursue something more than colleagues with Naomi.

"Of course. If you wait fifteen minutes, I'll have one with you."

"I can do that. I'll have this ready to go."

Logan flashed a smile and padded down the hall. Naomi Hendrix sparked something deep in him, and he was tired of denying it.

Chapter 17

Naomi's pulse waited until she heard the click of Logan's bedroom door before going into overdrive. What was she thinking? She'd just stepped into the kitchen and sat the saucepan on the stove when Logan came home. Seeing the man soaked to the bone put her plans of a quick bite before climbing into bed on the back burner.

Every part of her body hurt, but that didn't stop her from scurrying to the guest bedroom to pull off the towel and quickly tie her hair up in a scarf. Naomi refused to be one of those women who put on make-up so a man wouldn't see her natural face. Of course, she wasn't interested in Logan that way.

Getting a fresh start was Naomi's focus. Being more involved with the community, having the town see her as one of their own, drove her to be the vet the town needed. Helping Thomas and the workers satisfied that forgotten sense of purpose etched in her DNA. She wanted to be that person a neighbor could call if they had a problem. Naomi missed that part of her. Being at Hawkins Ridge, helping the Becketts sustain their hard work, was the first step in being the old pre-John Naomi.

But she'd be stupid to deny the butterflies when she thought about a relationship with Logan.

Taking a deep breath, she exhaled slowly, settled herself, and headed back to the kitchen. A flicker of the kitchen light startled her. Did Logan have candles or a lantern? She mentally chided herself. The family had pre-made sandbags and the ability to produce a size eight pair of goloshes on demand. Naomi felt confident a lantern, at the least candles, was within reach.

She was pulling the bowls from the cabinet when Logan padded in. Naomi tried to stop herself, but she did a quick glance at his sock covered feet. She smiled, not seeing any protruding bunions. The woodsy scent she associated with him apparently came from his soap.

"That smells good," he commented from beside her. "Is Maeve still at the house?"

Naomi shook her head. "She's asleep, but woke up long enough when I came home to make sure I took some ibuprofen before my shower."

"I took a couple myself. I don't think I'd be able to move in the morning if I didn't." Grabbing a ladle from the drawer, he balanced the bowls to the simmering pot. "Why don't you sit and I'll bring these to the table?"

"I don't mind."

"I insist."

Naomi didn't want to argue over something so trivial and gave a smile, taking the seat facing the stove. "Did you get everything taken care of? You don't think there will be additional flooding?"

Logan spooned servings into the bowl while he spoke. "We're good for now. Once the rain stops, we'll go back out there with chainsaws and break it down so we can use it for firewood this winter. The trench will need to be filled in once the ground dries some." He sat the bowls on the table. "Do you want a glass for your beer?"

"The bottle is fine. I'll take a glass of water in the bedroom with me if that's okay." She didn't want to assume it was okay to have drinks in the room. He waved off her concern.

"That's fine. Dig in."

Naomi took a tentative taste and swallowed a groan. Perfectly seasoned broth brought out the flavor of the tender pieces of chicken while the dumplings were fluffy, not soggy.

Naomi confessed, "I'm going to be spoiled by the food here."

Warmth shone in his eyes. "This is my grandmother's recipe. She used to make it once a week in the winter when we were kids. It's one of my favorite comfort foods."

"I can see why. Mine is probably my mother's macaroni and cheese. She doesn't make it that often, but I can look forward to it during the holidays."

"I hope I can try it one day."

The two ate for a minute in compatible silence, the spoons clinking against the bowl was the only noise. Naomi couldn't remember the last time she ate a meal with a man. At least not one who conjured romantic thoughts. Logan carried himself with a confident air who openly cared about those close to him. Qualities she looked for in a partner—sadly ones she thought John possessed.

Logan's deep voice pulled Naomi from her thoughts. "Are you adjusting to Oak Mountain?"

"Mmmm." Naomi followed her bite with a sip of beer. "We are. Mom has already found her group of ladies to have coffee with once a week at the diner. Though I've only been out with Izzy a few times, people have been welcoming."

"That's the advantage of close-knit towns. It took me going to a big school for college, and coming home once a month to appreciate that. I needed that small-town reality."

Naomi wiped her mouth, nodding in agreement. "I think that's why I chose a smaller school. Not being a real social person, I knew I could get lost at a large school. Not direction wise, but my values. I didn't want that." It was another reason she chose not to practice in a large city.

"I get that. My first semester, something similar happened to me and I started to lose my way and forget who I was. My family helped me see the error of my ways." The smirk on his face told Naomi there was a story there, but she didn't want to ask.

"Did you meet Fiona's mother at college?"

A scowl crossed Logan's face for a beat before he schooled his expression. He rolled his shoulders and grasped the beer bottle by the neck. "No. I knew her from high school. Kaylee loved horses, and that was what drew me to her as friends. We didn't become an item until the summer before I started veterinary school, despite my family and Walter's misgivings. In hindsight, we should have listened, but she became pregnant. I wanted to do the right thing, so we got married."

Naomi's brows furrowed. "Why would Walter have anything to do with your relationship?"

"Seriously? He's Kaylee's godfather."

Of all the reasons Naomi could think of, that was not on the list. It became clearer why Walter disliked the Beckets, especially Logan. It didn't explain harboring such disdain for so long. Not once in the years they've been friends did Walter mention having a goddaughter. Questions tumbled in her mind, but knew Logan couldn't answer them. Naomi took a long pull of her beer and added the piece of information to the growing list of why Walter wasn't the man she thought he was.

Logan fought a grin as Naomi's mouth dropped. He wasn't sure if she never asked Walter why he held such animosity or if he purposely kept it from her to control the narrative—the same as he did with Kaylee. Logan told his ex-wife about the history between Thomas and her godfather. Kaylee didn't believe him until she heard the truth from Walter during their divorce. She still took his side and burned any hope of a reconciliation.

Naomi had an inquisitive mind. He witnessed her asking questions about how the rescue ran, the diet for the horses and goats, and how they decided which animals to put up for adoption. However, Logan couldn't focus on that or if it was relevant.

His curiosity got the better of him. "You never asked?"

Naomi leaned back in her chair, crossing her arms. "I asked shortly after moving here because he was so adamant about staying away from you and your family. He just said it was nothing to worry about and he had my best interest in mind. I was so busy trying to adjust to the move and building the business, I didn't think about asking again. This whole feud, if you will, just seems more than you dating his goddaughter."

There was that brilliance Logan associated with Naomi. There was more to share, but it was late, and they were both tired. "His hatred for my father goes back to before I was born. It is a story I promised I would share, and I will. Not tonight, though. I am enjoying getting to know each other. I'd like to end the day on a positive note if that's okay?" Naomi's flirty smile wrapped around his heart.

"I think we can manage that. Before we go to happier subjects, I thought you should know that Walter introduced me to my ex-husband. He knew my former in-laws." Naomi shuddered and lifted her bottle. "He tried to talk me into staying with John, my ex. I knew that wasn't an option."

"Is that why you moved to get away from him?"

"More or less. My ex ruined my reputation, both profession-ally and personally. Female vets were not that common in the rural part of Oklahoma I lived, let alone a black one. As hard as it was for me to establish myself there, it took less time to strip the little trust the farmers had for me."

That explained her reaction during their first meeting. He wondered why she immediately brought up her race when she dressed him down.

"People in Oak Mountain respect you," Logan said. "I've heard from more than one person how kind and gentle you are with your patients. I've seen firsthand how you are with the animals. Harold Smith doesn't let just anyone take care of his dog and for him to come to you means a lot."

"I think that may have been a reason to see my mother," Naomi teased before sobering. "Truthfully, I didn't know what to expect when I moved here, but it wasn't for the town to feel like home as quickly as it has. I know I don't regret moving here."

Logan lifted his drink and pointed it towards her. "Here's to new beginnings."

Naomi clinked her bottle before downing the rest of her beer. They held each other's gaze for a beat too long before Naomi looked away.

"I should probably turn in." She stacked the dishes, but Logan grabbed them first.

"I got clean up. We're getting together for breakfast in the morning around eight."

Naomi covered a yawn, a sheepish tilt of her head. "That sounds good. Thank you again for everything."

"You're welcome. Night."

Naomi waved. Shorty, Mika, and Tam woke up from their spot on one of the dog beds and scurried after her. Rosebud, Tulip, and Bluebell looked between their four-legged friends and Logan, deciding to stay with their master. He expected the dogs to sleep with him, since Fiona was at the main house.

He quickly rinsed the bowls and loaded the dishwasher. He smiled, thinking back on the short time he spent with Naomi. She was easy to talk to, sharp, had a dry sense of humor and held an open mind to things around her. Clearing some of the air about his relationship with Walter helped their connection. There was still more to discuss later when they had more time.

After a quick check of the doors, he motioned for the dogs to follow. Maybe after breakfast, he could find time to spend with the enchanting vet.

CHAPTER 18

Intermittent rays of sunshine cut through the remaining clouds, heating Naomi's face as she stepped outside. Until that day, Logan's home, the clinic, and the main house were the only places she'd seen. Shorty, Mika, and Tam tugged on their leads, eagerly taking in the unfamiliar smells in front of Logan's home.

The rain stopped about two hours ago. Large puddles and sections of standing water decorated the gravel paths and grassy areas. In the distance, people scurried near the gate, pushing wheelbarrows of things Naomi couldn't make out.

But Josephine made good on her promise. Earlier, she drove her and Maeve around the property. The Beckett homestead took Naomi's breath away. Stables on the other end of the property housed thirty horses, ten of which were owned by Logan's family. They built homes for each brother, including Noah, close to their business responsibilities. Josephine finished the tour in the garden section. The small crop survived the wind and rain with minimal flooding. The closeness of the clan warmed Naomi's heart, increasing the desire to be a permanent part of the family.

Meaning she needed to leave that day or the next.

Being at Hawkins Ridge felt too much like home. Maeve spent her free time at the main house with Josephine, while Fiona played with the dogs so Naomi could check on the new mothers. The situation gave her a sense of rightness. Except for the breakfast Logan fixed and the meal they shared the night before, Naomi had eaten her meals with some iteration of the Beckett family. The conversations were easy, and the love was palpable. Naomi couldn't let herself enjoy it too much. She had a life off the property. Wishing to be part of this environment was not good for her heart.

Naomi greeted the workers with a smile, who stopped and gave her dogs the attention they wanted. She groaned when her phone rang, displaying Walter's name on the screen. Naomi avoided his calls, opting to text, saying she was busy and would call when she had a moment. Determination to confront Walter churned in her blood, but not over the phone. After bidding the workers a good day, she pressed the answer button.

"Hello Walter."

"Naomi, dear. I was worried. I hope you're not still upset about my conversation with Austin Harris."

She rolled her eyes and took a seat on a boulder near a tree. "I was, but I talked with him and agreed to take in two of the smaller dogs."

"Oh." Walter's pause made Naomi smile. "Will you try to find a home for them?"

"I doubt it. I'm already attached to the two cuties. They need a lot of love and stability. I don't think uprooting them in a couple of months would be beneficial."

"Probably not. Just as long as you have enough room for three dogs."

Naomi and Maeve discussed moving to a larger place, or perhaps finding their own separate homes. Their current house worked for them now while they settled into routines. Eventually, they needed their own space and Naomi a home office. But none of that was Walter's business.

"I'm sure there is enough space. Was there something you needed? I need to check on my mother." It wasn't a lie.

She wanted to see if Maeve had heard anything about access to town. It was also time to check on the new puppies and give the mothers their medication if Logan hadn't already.

"Right. Yes, I drove past the clinic and saw you were closed because of the weather. There wasn't an answer when I knocked at the house."

Ah! Walter wanted to know where she was. She could tell him, but his negativity would ruin her appetite for the roast beef Josie promised for dinner.

"Mom and I became stranded when visiting friends. We'll be heading home once they clear the tree and let traffic back into town."

"Oh. Well, be safe and we really should plan for lunch soon." Walter cleared his throat just as a group of workers walked by in animated chatter. "Where are you?"

Naomi still didn't offer information. "I'll call once I'm settled back home and let you know about lunch. Have a wonderful day."

She ended the call and slipped the phone in the hoodie pocket. Shorty stood on his hind legs, resting his head on her lap while Mika and Tam held curious gazes. In a short time, the terriers began picking up cues from Shorty, sensing the change in Naomi's mood. The last thing she wanted was to cause anxiety and pasted on a genuine smile.

"Ready to finish our walk, guys?" Naomi said to her pack of three and led them down the gravel road that took them close to the larger dog run for the pack.

Claire and another worker stood near the tall wooden fence, rinsing shallow buckets used for the pack's outside water. They confirmed Maeve was in the house helping Josephine clean the cat nursery and the dogs had received their medication. Because she didn't know how Mika and Tam would do around cats, she wrapped up their walk and headed towards Logan's.

Normally, she would look forward to some downtime and catching up on work. However, without her laptop, trying to even catch up on emails on her phone would be difficult. For the first time she could remember, she didn't feel like reading.

She led the dogs into the empty house. Logan and Fiona took the pugs with them first thing to spend the day at the stables. After removing her shoes and wiping muddy paws, she led them to the kitchen for fresh water and a small treat of boiled chicken. Looking out the window over the sink, she took in the bustle as she portioned out the food, adding a couple of drops of vitamins for the terriers.

Naomi leaned against the counter and pushed her conversation with Walter from her mind. She wouldn't let his passive aggressive words and action take another minute of her peace of mind. Oak Mountain was a fresh start and she wouldn't allow him to ruin it for her. She moved her gaze to the living room area and enjoyed the moment of alone time.

Logan's home was spacious and warm. She could see him lounging on the couch, flipping through the TV and chatting with Fiona about her day. When the image of her and all six dogs walking in from outside appeared in her mind, Naomi quickly shook her head.

Being at Hawkins Ridge made Naomi want something with Logan she wasn't sure she could have. If he wanted something more than friends, he had ample time to make his interest known. Yes, she could have said something. She was a modern woman, after all. However, men like Logan usually kept short, full-figured women in the friend zone. No matter how many times he tossed "darlin'" around.

Naomi picked up the empty bowls, then went about washing them. No, thinking about anything past a working relationship with Logan and the Becketts was useless. It was time to go home before it became even harder to say goodbye.

Logan adjusted his earplugs before tossing the last of the fallen branches in the chipper. He and a stable worker tackled the leaning tree Caden noticed a few days ago near the stable. Though the condition of the wood wasn't ideal for firewood, they could repurpose it for chips the goats could play on.

He and Fiona were at the stables by seven that morning to check on the horses and introduce the pugs to them. Scout served as support, gently nudging Tulip, Bluebell and Rosebud towards the gates. After breakfast with Caden, Logan examined each horse before letting them out into the paddock to stretch their legs.

His mind drifted back to his mother driving Naomi and Maeve around the property. Fiona took it upon herself to introduce their guests to the horses. The smile that lit up Naomi's face wrapped around Logan like a warm blanket. A feeling he could get used to.

For the first few years after the divorce, his priority was giving Fiona a sense of normalcy. With the help of his family, Fiona discovered who she was and gave her the self-confidence she needed as a pre-teen. Would dating mess up the progress Fiona had made?

Logan chuckled as he turned off the machine and shoved his work gloves into his back pocket. Naomi thought he was a jerk a few days ago. Why would he assume she went from apologizing to a sudden interest in him? Maybe having her leave would be the best thing for him.

The chirp of his phone stopped him in his tracks. He read the text from Jace saying the creek receded, and crews will start on the tree blocking access to town later that afternoon. It meant this would be his last night with Naomi in his home.

Logan could admit he enjoyed having Naomi on the property. Listening to her coo at the dogs made his heart tingle. His soul wept, knowing come morning, she and Maeve would leave.

Twirling his goggles by the strap, the aroma of sawdust and horse hit Logan as he strolled into the stables. He spotted Scout and the pugs sitting outside of two stalls. A short bark alerted Caden and Fiona of his presence as he made his way to them.

"Jace just texted," he said, reaching down to pet the pugs who had gathered around his legs. "Everything should be up and running first thing. They are tackling the tree this evening."

Fiona paused her brushing. "Does that mean Naomi and Ms. Maeve are leaving?"

"I'm afraid so. Naomi closed her business while she was here and I'm sure they miss their own beds."

"What about her dogs? The pugs really like them." Fiona spared a glance at the pups in question.

"I'm sure Naomi would be open to play dates," Caden piped in. Logan glared at his brother.

"That's a great idea!" Fiona went back to her chores. "Naomi is really nice and I think Nana is happy to have another older woman to be friends with."

Logan noticed Maeve's friendship with his parents and was sure they would keep in touch. It was time to change the subject before Caden said something else.

"Why don't we give her a few days to get the terriers used to their new home and then we'll see about having the dogs get together?" The downcast expression tugged at his heart. Fiona used the pugs as an excuse, but he could see her bonding with Naomi. He meant about giving the dogs a few days, but he would mention to Naomi later about bringing Shorty, Mika and Tam to visit. "I was thinking the storm kept you from having much of a spring break. Why don't we go into town tomorrow and get you those pink boots you wanted?"

"Really?!" Fiona threw her arms around his waist. "Thank you, Daddy."

Caden grinned, shaking his head as he slipped a couple of sugar cubes to the horse he was brushing. Logan had no shame in using material means as long as his baby was happy.

"You're welcome." Logan took a step back and leaned against a post. "I'm heading back to the clinic, then checking on the pack. You staying?"

She nodded. Loose strands of black hair escaped her two ponytails. "I have two more horses to brush, then uncle Caden said we can go four-wheeling."

"Like you said, she's had a horrible spring break," Caden teased, causing Logan to roll his eyes.

"Fine. Be back in time to wash up and have dinner with everyone. I'll take the pugs with me." He snagged the three-dog leash from a peg and clipped it to their collars. He turned his attention to his brother. "Can you spend time with the new mothers tomorrow? I want to separate them unless you think it's best they stay together."

Caden nodded, running his palms down his jeans. "Noah mentioned something before the rain about seeing if one of the new arrivals could work with the other livestock dogs. If not, we should start checking around to other shelters." Finding the right dog took time that Logan wasn't sure he had, but Noah wouldn't have asked if it wasn't necessary.

"There may be one. Let's talk about it after we finish the storm clean up." He kissed Fiona's crown. "Be good for your uncle. Call if you need me."

He waved and led Rosebud, Tulip, and Bluebell to his truck. Not knowing the terrain after the storm or how the dogs would do in the four-wheeler, Logan opted to drive his truck. He smirked as the trio stood on their hind legs to look out the window. Three black noses taking in the smells of their new home.

"I hope you guys like it here," Logan said. "Maybe Naomi will bring Shorty to play. Would you like that?"

They glanced at him over their shoulders before turning their heads back to the scenery. He guided the truck, careful of the dips in the road, and pulled up beside his house. Naomi's car sat off a few yards away. He wondered if Izzy told her the news yet about the road.

Maybe Naomi would like to have a date while the dogs played. Logan shoved the thought from his head and climbed out of the car, bringing the dogs with him. Until they had the talk about the history of Walter and his family, pursuing her was something he couldn't entertain.

After each dog marked their spots, they hurried to the front door, hopping in place. *"Shorty and the terriers must be inside,"* Logan thought as he turned the knob and came up short.

Naomi lounged on the couch with his favorite plaid throw over her legs, watching a show he couldn't identify. A scarf held her wild hair into a pile on top. A shy smile graced her lips.

"Claire said everything was under control and told me to rest. I hope you don't mind I made myself at home."

"Of course not. Let me clean up and I'll join you."

"I'd like that."

Logan unclipped the leash from the collars, a cue to start a mad case of zoomies with Shorty, Mika and Tam around the living room. Naomi's light laughter at the dogs' antics burrowed deeper into his heart. Logan left them to their enjoyment and headed down the hallway, pulling off his shirt as he went.

Maybe now would be a good time to have that talk.

CHAPTER 19

When Logan strolled through the door, Naomi lost all interest in the paranormal detective show. Muddy smudges marred the royal blue fitted henley shirt that clung to his broad shoulders and thick torso. Did he know there was a dirt clump in his hair?

Guilt washed over her for laying on his couch and she scrambled to a seated position. Hawkins Ridge buzzed with activity. The desire to help drove her to ask if anyone needed help. They assured her they had everything under control, even her mother and Josie told her dinner was taken care of. Naomi hated feeling restless and called Izzy before flipping through the channels. She learned plans were in place to clear the road later that evening and she'd be able to go home in the morning. Sadness sprung from nowhere at the thought.

In the short time with Logan and his family, Naomi saw the welcoming people the town cared for. She and Logan got past their dust up and became comfortable around one another. Yes, they still needed to talk about the history of the so call feud, but Naomi didn't care. She liked the Becketts, especially Logan and Fiona. Short of learning something horrific, nothing would change that.

Time away from her practice and home gave Naomi time to think. Though both were hers on paper, they still had a tinge of Walter to them. A coat of paint and bringing the business up to ADA compliance wouldn't change that. Maybe in a couple of years, she could build something that showed her personality, maybe add boarding or offer puppy training.

Growing up, Naomi had a dream of doing something like Hawkins Ridge, minus the crops. She only kept plants alive because of Maeve. After she married John, her dream took a backseat to help him build his business. Now that she was starting over, could this be the time for her to do something more with animals? Could she add dating to the mix?

A sloppy tongue pulled Naomi out of her thoughts. Shorty hairy tail whipped in a frenzy. "Do you guys want a treat?" she cooed and headed towards the kitchen. Laughter bubbled up as all six dogs yapped and jumped excitedly. She would miss the pugs, but she'd get to see them when she needed to bring her mother to visit Josephine.

Though Shorty, Mika and Tam had pieces of the boiled chicken earlier, she didn't mind spoiling them and giving them a little while she treated the pugs. Warmth wrapped around her as she watched the four-legged cuties. Shorty snapped his head toward the hallway and abandoned his chicken.

Running his fingers through his damp hair, Logan strolled into the kitchen. The sight of the man, dressed in a T-shirt and yet another pair of worn-out jeans, left her breathless.

"What are they eating?" he asked, making his way to the refrigerator and pulling out the pitcher of iced tea.

"Josie sent over boiled chicken for the dogs. I hope you don't mind? I gave them about three pieces each." Nervously, Naomi chewed on her bottom lip, praying she didn't cross a boundary. Logan shook his head.

"That's fine. I'll feed them before we leave for dinner." He poured a glass. Naomi declined the offer for her own. "Are you done watching TV?"

She picked up the small plates, setting them in the sink. "I wasn't really watching anything. You can look at whatever." She wanted to smack herself. It was his house. Of course, he could look at whatever he wanted.

"Unless I watch a movie with Fiona or football and baseball with my brothers, I don't watch TV that often." He leaned against the counter and crossed his arms, the glass dangling from his fingertips. "I'm not sure if you heard, but they are working on the tree this evening. You should be able to head home in the morning."

Naomi nodded. "I talked to Izzy, and she told me. I'm sure my mother will insist on having breakfast first."

Logan chuckled. "She's smart."

Naomi quickly washed the plates and set them on the drying rack. For the first time since their trip in the van, an uncomfortable silence filled the air. Logan watched the dogs attempt to drink from two water bowls at the same time. He glanced over his shoulder when she turned off the water.

"Actually, I was sort of hoping we could talk." He placed his glass on the counter before running his fingers through his thick hair. "I promised you some background on our relationship with Walter. You're owed both sides after the last few days."

She took a deep breath to settle her nerves. "I'd like that. You and your family have been so welcoming and kind to my mother and I."

"You're surprised?"

"I was, but only because we are, were, strangers." Naomi shrugged. "It took me by surprise."

"Fair enough," he said with a nod. "I hope seeing the real Beckett family has given you something to think about."

Logan gestured towards the living room, giving her the opportunity to take the lead. Naomi focused on her breathing as she made her way to the closest end of the couch near the oversize dog bed, where their fur babies contorted to cuddle together.

Logan spoke once they settled in their seats. "Has Walter given you any backstory to his dislike of my family?"

Naomi shook her head. "All he's done is share his personal perspective."

Rolling his eyes, Logan chuckled. "I'm not surprised. Full disclosure. When I started looking for a tech, I approached Izzy about coming to work for me, but she wanted to focus on motherhood."

Naomi smiled. "Is that part of the reason Walter has it out for you?"

"If only it was that simple." Logan scratched at his day-old stubble. "Walter blames my father for taking the job as the vet here."

Of all the things Naomi expected him to say, that wasn't one of them. Why Walter thought he would take a position away from the son-in-law of the owner's daughter her questioning his sanity. Naomi sat back and girded herself up for the tale.

"This is besides being your ex-wife's godfather." Naomi tucked her legs under her thighs and sat up straighter. "Why don't you start from the beginning because I thought your father had a private practice before? Didn't your parents meet at college?"

"Yes, they met at college, but Dad never had a private practice. You know this land belonged to my mother's family, right?" Naomi nodded, and he continued. "Back then, they focused on chickens and training horses. Walter's father used to be the stable manager."

"Seriously? He never mentioned that. He also never mentioned knowing your ex-wife, so..." Naomi shrugged. Logan took that as a sign to go on.

"When the previous staff doctor announced his retirement, Walter's father mentioned his son had recently graduated from veterinary school and was preparing to take the certification exam." Logan took a sip of his tea before proceeding.

"In the meantime, Mom brought Dad home for my grandfather to meet after they became serious. Once he learned Dad was going to graduate with a degree in biology that spring and starting vet school in the summer, he talked the on-staff doctor to stick around and hired additional help."

"Did your mother ask him to hold the job for your dad?"

Logan shook his head. "According to my mother, no. Grandpa liked Dad, and he knew marriage was in their future. He thought having him as the farm's vet would give them a solid start. Even though Dad was more of a city boy than rural."

Shorty attempted to jump onto the couch with Naomi. Her gaze asked a silent permission if it was okay. Logan nodded and helped the wiener dog, then the two terriers. Not wanting to be left out, Tulip, Rosebud and Bluebell whined to join their friends. They all took spots near Naomi's feet. A warm smile softened her face as she watched them figure out how they would curl up.

The steel band around Logan's heart snapped. Naomi was someone he thoroughly enjoyed being with. Every time he considered dating someone, having a love for animals, particularly dogs, was a must-have quality in any woman he found intriguing. Fiona's mother liked horses but didn't see the need for the pack or sharing a home with them. It's what led to him building the dog house.

Speaking of Fiona's mother, Logan needed to finish the story about Walter. First, he had to ask.

"You aren't giving them up for adoption, are you?"

The shy smile she flashed gut punched him. "No. I'll have to ease them into being the mascots for the practice like Shorty, but I knew once I saw them, I wasn't going to let them go."

"They have an adaptable personality and surprising low key for terriers. I think as long as they're with Shorty, they'll be okay."

Naomi spared another glance at the dogs before returning her attention to him. "So, your grandfather told Walter's father the job wasn't available?"

"Not exactly. According to Grandpa, Walter failed the board exams twice before passing."

"Seriously?" Naomi looked at her delicate hands. "He never mentioned it to me."

Logan remained silent. What could he possibly say? He kept going. "Eventually, Walter's father became upset and quit, then tried to bad mouth us to the owners of the horses."

"Like father, like son," Naomi said, no mirth in the statement.

"Basically. So, when Walter opened his practice, he wanted to break in with the ranches in the county, but they were loyal to my grandfather and then to my father." Logan took a healthy gulp of tea before continuing.

"Jump to high school when Haylee would hang out with us. Oak Mountain was smaller and everyone knew everyone. We didn't care who her godfather was. Her parents were friendly enough and didn't have a problem with us being friends. It was senior year that her folks died in a horrible accident and she stayed with Walter and his wife."

Naomi leaned forward, engrossed in the story. "You said you started dating before you went to veterinary school."

He nodded. "I was twenty-three. Walter wanted her to end it. My parents thought it was just a summer fling until it lasted through my first year. Kaylee was with an amateur rodeo circuit by then. It was what she wanted to do. When I graduated, she signed with a touring rodeo company. We tried to do a long-distance relationship because Caden was on his first tour and Jace and Noah were away at school."

"I can't imagine you had much choice," Naomi added. "I take it that didn't work out."

Logan ran his fingers through his hair, mentally making a note to get a haircut. "We were close to ending it when Kaylee became pregnant. I asked her to marry me and then we'd talk about her going back to the rodeo after the baby. I secretly hoped she would try to live our lifestyle."

The corner of Naomi's lips ticked up. "You mean home-body, farm work, and take care of the animals?" Logan couldn't resist chuckling.

"Exactly. Kaylee didn't understand my dream of expanding the sanctuary. She wanted me to put it on hold saying we could start that after she retired and Fi was an adult. After she signed with a company based out of Texas, we tried for about eighteen months traveling with her. It just wasn't working, and we got a divorce. A year later, she signed full custody over when she met another man on the circuit who didn't want children. Fiona and her mother still have video chats, but Kaylee doesn't want Fiona to be part of her new life. Walter thought I paid off Kaylee, saying a child should be with her mother." Logan snorted. "Since he has been trying to badmouth me. No one in town listens to him."

It was why his lies worked on Naomi. She was new. Oak Mountain had generations that knew the truth. No matter how hard Walter tried to ruin the reputation of his family, their actions contradicted everything the other man said.

Naomi placed her hand on his arm, pulling him out of his thoughts. "Thank you for sharing." He returned the gesture, clasping her hand.

"I didn't tell you any of that to turn you against Walter. I know you're close and you care deeply for him." Logan honestly wasn't trying to put a wedge between them.

Naomi shook her head. "I know. As I said before, he never offered a reason. I never asked more than once." Naomi shrugged. "I was so focused on trying to rebuild my life, it wasn't important to me. Now—"

The door flew open, interrupting Naomi and startling humans and dogs. Fiona's wind-blown cheeks, wild hair and blinding smile put him at ease. All the dogs scampered over to say hi.

"Nana said dinner will be ready in five minutes. Uncle Caden wants to talk to you before we eat." Fiona squatted and gave the dogs the loving they wanted. "Hi Naomi."

"Hi baby." She folded the throw and stood to her full height. "I'll feed the dogs if you need to talk to Caden and meet y'all at the house shortly."

"I can help," Fiona offered, motioning for the dogs to follow.

"Make sure you wash up," Logan said, placing a kiss on her cheek as she walked past. He turned to Naomi. "You sure you don't mind?"

"Not at all."

Logan held her brown gaze for a moment. A wave of calm washed over him and took up residence in his veins. He fought the urge to press his lips to hers, let her know his interest. A chorus of barks broke the spell. He gave her hand a squeeze instead.

"Thank you."

He watched Naomi head towards the kitchen and the smile on Fiona's face as she handed her Shorty's bowl. Logan thanked his mother for helping her through things he would never understand, but he wished his daughter had a younger adult to talk to. However, getting married solely to provide a mother figure for his daughter would have negative consequences. He longed for the love that his parents shared. He was uncertain if Naomi was the one, but she was the first woman since his divorce who made him think beyond his daughter and the rescue.

Maybe it was time to stop denying his feelings.

Chapter 20

Naomi closed her eyes and inhaled deeply as the sounds of nocturnal insects and animals drifted in through the small opening in the window. Casting a brief glance at the pair of dog beds by the doorway, she offered to take care of the pugs while Fiona stayed overnight at the main house to look after the kittens. Logan planned to spend the night with the pack so he could observe the newly rescued animals. She didn't stop the contented smile that graced her lips.

Her last dinner with the Beckett clan sat comfortably in her tummy. Perfect rare roast beef, savory almond green beans, and buttery rolls went well with the apple cobbler. Naomi tried not to think too hard on possibly not seeing any of the family again unless it was around town or if she drove her mother to visit.

The door to the en-suite bathroom opened, drawing Naomi's attention. Maeve secured her hair scarf as she made her way to the bed. They had spent little time together since the night of the tree emergency. Usually, her mother was asleep by the time Naomi came in from the last check on the animals. She was thankful for the empty house so she could talk to her mother about the conversation with Logan.

"What are you doing?" Maeve tilted her head toward the phone in Naomi's hands before climbing under the covers. As much as she loved Maeve, it had been over thirty years since they shared a bed.

"Glancing at a few emails, Izzy flagged. I have a lot to catch up on when we get home."

"Remember to add grocery shopping to that list since we didn't go before the storm. I'm sure things in the fridge have gone bad." Maeve squirted a dollop of lotion into her palm and rubbed it in. "Of course it helps that Josie is sending us home with a nice care package."

Naomi smiled. The matriarch of the family started putting together a tote with coffee, more preserves, and homemade jerky while Caden dished out their desserts.

"From what I've seen so far of the tote, we can wait a day or two to shop." Naomi set her phone on the nightstand and twisted slightly to face her mother. "Actually, I'm glad we have the place to ourselves. I wanted to tell you about my conversation with Logan and didn't think it would wait until we were on our way home."

"Okay. I need to talk to you, too, but yours sounds more like gossip, so go first." The twinkle in Maeve's eyes had Naomi laughing.

"We finally had that talk about the history with Walter, including being the godfather of his ex-wife."

Naomi filled her in on their conversation, including the one she had with Walter earlier, leaving nothing out. Maeve's eyes were wide by the time she finished.

"That is soap opera drama," her mother teased, then grew serious. "Josephine told me some of what happened with her father, but we were never alone long enough for the complete story."

"Why didn't you tell me?" Naomi didn't hide the hurt. Maeve rested her hand on her daughter's.

"She told me yesterday, and like I said, it was nowhere near as much information, but the stories are similar. Josie said nothing about the ex. Maybe she felt that was Logan's story to tell."

"Perhaps." Naomi nibbled her bottom lip. "Why do you think he never told me about his connection to the Becketts?"

Maeve shrugged. "Embarrassment about the exam is the only thing I can think of. I don't have an answer about the ex, especially since he probably still talks with her."

Naomi thought the same thing. She'd been in Oak Mountain long enough for him to mention something. She could see why Logan may be a thorn in his side, but it made little sense to hold a grudge for decades over a decision that Josephine's father made.

"Why do you think Logan brought this up now? Are you going to ask Walter?"

Naomi considered her mother's questions for a moment. "After I apologized for my actions, he said he would tell me his side. Why he did it now, I don't know. Regarding Walter, it just confirms my decision to step back and set firm boundaries or just flat out end the friendship. To now know he's capable of holding hate in his heart longer than I've been alive makes me question if I really know who he is."

The idea of him trying to ruin her standing among the citizens of Oak Mountain sent chills up her spine. The town was feeling like home. Naomi didn't think she had it in her to start over again. She clearly couldn't put her mother through relocating again. It was something she'd have to think about later, but it wouldn't stop her from what she needed to do with Walter.

Eager to change the subject, she focused her attention on Maeve. "You said you wanted to talk to me about something."

Maeve studied her daughter for a moment before she spoke. "Josephine offered me a part-time job."

Naomi's jaw dropped. "Really? Doing what?"

"Helping with the cats, ordering supplies, phones, just day-to-day activities." Maeve squeezed her daughter's hand. "I love helping you around the clinic, but that is your world. I want to do something for myself."

Naomi didn't know what to say. Her mother picked up her life to follow Naomi to Oak Mountain. She would miss her around the practice, but if working at Hawkins Ridge would make her happy, she wouldn't stand in her way. Maybe they'd let Maeve bring the dogs so they could play with the pugs.

"I think you'd be perfect for the position. Though something tells me there will be more laughing than working."

An enormous grin brightened Maeve's face. "Thomas said the same thing."

"Then it must be true." Naomi gave her a side hug. "I'm happy for you. Maybe once or twice you could bring the dogs with you. They're forming a bond."

"I can see that." Maeve glanced over the side of the bed to look at the sleeping fur balls. "I'm positive it won't be a problem. You sure you're okay with this?"

"Positive. I love you."

"Love you too, honey."

Naomi turned off the lamp, sparking to life the solar night light near the door. Time at the rescue had been an eye opening experience. The rescue exceeded everything she imagined. The Becketts weren't the evil family Walter led her to believe, and discovering the reasons for his lies made her question him as a person. His heart was not as open and caring as Naomi originally thought, and she wondered if there was an ulterior motive why he sold her the practice. Could he secretly be wishing she'd fail, hence all the questions about the business?

Then there was Logan. The man made her crave something she didn't know she wanted. At least not so soon after arriving in town. It felt pointless to hope for something more with Logan. They were leaving in the morning, and she didn't know if he held any romantic interest.

Naomi snuggled deeper into the covers and closed her eyes. Maybe once she returned home and focus her energy on getting back into her normal routine, the crush she had on Logan would pass.

At least, she hoped.

Logan slipped two fingers between his lips and let the shrill whistle echo in the night. "Okay. Bedtime!"

Thirty-two thundering dogs barreled into the house. After dinner, treats, and outdoor time, Logan was ready to curl up and call it a day. Once the last two seniors made their way in, he locked the door and made sure water was available. A minute later, a quick tap on the door preceded the click of the lock he just engaged.

Logan swallowed his sigh and followed the pack into the other room. Thomas devoted his attention to every dog, his laughter filled with pure happiness.

"Are you coming for a sleepover?" Logan teased as he lowered himself onto the firm couch.

"Tempting, but I prefer to cuddle with your mother." Thomas pulled a chair from the corner and sat across from his son. "I see you're sleeping here?"

"Yeah. I wanted to make sure everyone was adjusting. Also, I'm looking at how I can connect my house to the back."

"Why? I thought you said the pugs wouldn't do well with the pack."

Logan scratched behind a mixed breed who climbed on the couch. "I don't think they would do well with the more energetic larger members, but seeing them with Naomi's dogs, maybe. The last thing I want is for them to retreat into just themselves. I also want to walk through the back door of the den and into here."

Thomas looked at the ceiling. "We can sketch something together and talk to the builder when they're done extending the goat pen."

Logan nodded with a critical eye on his father. "So, why are you really here?"

"Do I need a reason to spend time with my favorite son?"

He snorted. "We're all your favorites."

"Fine. What's going on with you and the lovely doctor?"

"I should have let you finish beating around the bush." Logan ran his fingers through his hair.

How could he even answer that question when he didn't know himself? He spoke the truth when he said why he was staying with the pack, but the real reason was he was avoiding Naomi. The woman wormed her way into his heart and he didn't know what to do. Actually, he wanted to ask her to stay longer so they could get to know each other better. But Naomi had a life before meeting him. The happiness of sharing dinner with her and his family scared him, so he escaped to the one place he could think.

Using Walter as an excuse not to pursue something with Naomi no longer held merit. Pure fear drove him to hide like a shy teenager when the popular girl says hi. He could see spending the rest of his life with Naomi. He knew it was fast, but she was the exact opposite of Kaylee. She held nothing back, showing love to the animals. Fiona and his family adored her. More importantly, Naomi understood making your own path in life. She wanted the town to see her for the brilliant veterinarian she was, and he wanted them to see someone other than Little Logan Beckett.

Could that be something they worked on together? Giving each other the support to accomplish the same goal? Was she even interested in him that way?

Logan blinked out of his thoughts and met his father's scrutinizing gaze. "Nothing is going on between me and Naomi. We talked earlier about the history with Walter. A lot of things she didn't know. I think it opened her eyes even more to the man he is."

"Is that why you two kept glancing at each other during dinner?"

"We didn't."

"You most certainly did." The creases in Thomas's wrinkles deepen with his grin. "Back and forth when the other wasn't looking. Thought I was looking at two teenagers afraid to say hi to one another."

Logan crossed his arms. "I've never been afraid to talk to a woman."

"Maybe not, but there is something about this one that's different. She's taken away your Beckett swagger."

The two men laughed so hard that it made a few dogs excited enough to dance. Once they gained control of themselves, Logan continued the conversation.

"I will admit there is an interest in Naomi. I told Caden I didn't think I could go through another relationship where Walter had an influence on my partner. Now that I've gotten to know her, I don't think that would be an issue, but I don't know if I have time to give a relationship."

"I can't blame you on the Walter front. Kaylee was weak." Thomas stretched out his long legs and crossed them at the ankle. "Regarding time, I think you're grasping for a reason not to take a chance on falling in love again."

Logan bristled at the assessment. "I am open to falling in love again, but after Fiona is off to college." Thomas cocked a brow.

"Why are you lying to yourself?" His father held up a hand to silence Logan's coming protest. "Son, everyone, including you, knew Kaylee wasn't the one. You loved her, yes, but she wasn't the one to spend the rest of your life with. Either way, the pain she put you and Fiona through has made you a bit gun shy and that's okay. Most people would be. But your heart is too big and Naomi is too fine of a woman for you not to see if there's something there."

Logan buried his fingers into the wrinkles of a bulldog, blowing out a breath. Could the fear of being hurt again be the reason he made other excuses? He didn't want Fiona to experience that pain again, so it was easy to lock the idea of romance away. His daughter was older now and asked about him dating again. Did that give him the go ahead? Still, he didn't know if Naomi saw him that way or even wanted a relationship now.

Of course, he won't know unless he asked. Logan studied his father for a moment, curious about the sudden interest in his love life.

"Why are you telling me this?"

Thomas stood and rested his hands on his waist. "Because a couple of workers have asked about the good doctor. What's that saying: 'you snooze you lose'? Make your interest known, son, before your opportunity has passed you by. Fiona likes her and said to her grandmother, she wished you'd date someone like her. Also, Maeve took a job working with your mother and Owen."

He shook his head to make sure he heard correctly. "When? Doing what?"

"Earlier today. Helping them with day-to-day activities. I think this was just a way for your mother and Maeve to hang out. Once Owen is back, that's just going to be more laughing than working."

He agreed with his father about why they hired Maeve. His parents and Owen told their sons, over the holidays they were ready to fully turn everything over to them and travel. It was the reason he hired Claire, because Sam would go with them. It was something he would need to talk to his brothers about once Jace was home and rested.

"They're leaving after breakfast," Thomas commented as he walked to the door. "That gives you about twelve hours to get your swagger back."

Logan shook his head, a smile on his face. He said good night and headed towards the full-size bed. The information his father gave him played back in his mind.

Naomi had him wanting something he didn't think would be an option until Fiona was off to college. The workers weren't stupid. Naomi was a natural beauty, intelligent, with an unwavering love for animals. Any man knew she was a catch.

Was he willing to take a chance with another woman associated with Walter? The image of Naomi on the couch surrounded by the dogs flashed in his mind.

Yes. Yes, he was, because no one ever called him stupid.

Chapter 21

Naomi's gaze focused on the swaying trees while bleats from the goats, the bustles of workers, and playful barks of dogs played in the background. They were sounds she was getting used to.

And ones she would miss.

With a sigh, she tossed the shopping bag of clothes onto the floor of the backseat of the car and slammed the door. The warmth and love of the Beckett homestead wrapped around her like a grandmotherly hug. Her lips curled into a smile as thoughts of breakfast filled her mind.

Thomas and Josie went all out for her last meal with the family. Cheesy hash brown casserole, buttery biscuits, bacon, fresh squeezed orange juice, and the best coffee she had in a long time. Jace came in long enough to make a plate before heading home to sleep for the rest of the day. Even Noah joined the family before heading back out to feed the goats. It was a meal fueled with love and tugged at Naomi's heart strings.

She liked the clan. A lot. Everyone welcomed her with open arms and didn't care if she had a lot more curves than was socially acceptable or that her mentor tried to sway her opinion of them. No, the Becketts, and their workers, showed by their actions, Oak Mountain would be her forever home no matter the outcome with Walter. At least her mother will get a daily dose in two weeks when she starts work for the family.

Then there was Logan.

During breakfast, he opted to take the seat beside her. The familiar smell of his woody fragrance, combined with the tantalizing aroma of the food, caused her to let down her emotional defenses. As the overflowing platters made their way around the table, he scooped portions onto her plate before dishing out his own serving. Naomi didn't know what to make of the kind gesture, but she tried not to read too much into it. That was the last thing she wanted was to get her hopes up.

The past days gave Naomi an opportunity to see the life she wanted for herself. A close-knit family surrounded by animals and possibly children. John said he wanted kids down the road, even open to adoption. Naomi agreed because she wanted to establish herself with the farmers and focus on building their trust. Being around Fiona stirred that desire of a little one she could share her love of animals with and someone Maeve would spoil rotten. But Logan shown no romantic interest towards her. It was for the best she was leaving, so her mind could concentrate on being part of the community and not a silly crush.

Shorty, Mika, and Tam's joyful yips echoed in the air, bringing her out of her thoughts. A soft laugh bubbled forth as she watched them play with the pugs in the grassy area near the car.

"Their tiny legs are so cute when they run," Fiona remarked, approaching from the side of the house and stopping next to her.

"Isn't it adorable?" Naomi glanced at the young girl who stood about an inch shorter than her five one height. "Are you excited about getting your new boots?" Fiona's face beamed as she nodded.

"I have the perfect hoodie to go with them. I'm sure Dad will try to talk me into getting a color that goes with everything, but he doesn't understand." Fiona crossed her arms, determination in her blue eyes. "Pink goes with everything."

Naomi disagreed with the girl's statement, but said nothing. Although Fiona had a lot of pastel colored tops in her wardrobe, maybe pink boots *would* go with everything.

"I'm sure he'll let you get whatever you want." Logan would give his baby girl the world if she asked.

"Maybe." Fiona reached into her jean pocket and pulled out a small pouch with the logo of the farm printed on it. "I made this for you."

"Oh, sweetie…" Naomi spoke around the lump in her throat.

Fiona held a special place in her heart. She was a ball of excitement when she helped in the clinic and eagerly volunteered to take care of Shorty if Naomi was busy. With a gentle tug on the strings, she effortlessly opened it up and retrieved a wide strip of brown leather with Naomi's name burnished on one side.

"It's beautiful," she whispered. "Can you put it on for me?"

Fiona beamed and eagerly snapped it around Naomi's wrist. When she was done, Naomi pulled her in for a hug.

"You really like it?" Fiona asked before taking a step back.

"I do. I'll only take it off when I perform surgery on the animals and showers." Naomi ran her hand lightly over the girl's hair. "Thank you. It means a lot that you made it for me."

"Uncle Caden helped. He creates a lot of stuff we sell at the stand we set up for the Farmer's Market."

Naomi would have to stop past their booth when it opens next month. The two watched Mika and Tam slow down before sitting on their rumps. They were older than Shorty, Rosebud, Bluebell and Tulip, and tired quicker. Seeing their playmates stop, the others followed suit and rested.

"Will you bring them back to play?" Fiona asked as she shoved her hands into her jeans.

Naomi nodded. "My mother is going to bring them on the days she works."

"But I'll be at school. I won't see them." Observing the pout on the young girl's innocent face, Naomi instinctively put her arm around her shoulder to offer comfort.

"I'll talk to your father about bringing them sometimes on the weekend."

"He says the dogs are welcome anytime." They looked over their shoulders, hearing Logan's deep voice.

"Yea!" Fiona cheered, pumping her slender fist in the air, causing Naomi and Logan to chuckle.

"Sweetheart, why don't you take the dogs inside to get some water before they head out?"

"Okay." Fiona turned to the tiny pack. "Come on, let's get you something to drink."

Fiona's infectious giggles filled the air as all six pups were on her heels, tripping over each other. For a moment, the thought of coming home to Fiona worked its way into Naomi's heart and took root. *Yep, it was time to go.*

"I see she gave you the bracelet," Logan commented, glancing down at her wrist. She nodded and held her arm closer for him to see.

"It's beautiful. I've always loved leather bands and bracelets." She ran her fingers over the buttery soft material. "I didn't know Caden created leather pieces."

"He took up the hobby when he returned home. It helped channel his emotions. That and the animals."

Naomi liked the quiet brother. "I'll have to check out his pieces when the market opens." Naomi glanced back at the main house, willing her mother to exit. "I feel like a parent waiting for their child to finish saying goodbye to their friends."

Logan chuckled. "When I came out, your mother was with the kittens, saying her farewells."

"It'd be rude to honk the horn, right?"

"I've learned from personal experience, the horn has no effect whatsoever." Logan motioned towards the bench for them to sit. "I'm glad we have a moment, actually."

Naomi ran her damp hands down her jeans. What could Logan want to talk about? She stripped the bed and put fresh linen on before she went to breakfast and started a wash with the items they used. Did he want the Hawkins Ridge shirts back? When his thigh pressed against hers, all questions stuttered to a halt. Naomi fought the urge to lean into him and instead cleared her throat, meeting his gaze.

"What did you want to talk about?"

Logan sighed. "I tried to deny my feelings the entire time you were here."

Naomi's blood boiled. Was their kindness an elaborate joke? What about her mother's job? Is that why her mother was still in the main house, because they were laughing at her? Naomi's heart and trust couldn't handle anymore betrayal.

"Feelings? I thought we'd move past everything. Was being nice just an act?"

He frantically shook his head and latched on to her wrist when she tried to stand. "That's not what I meant."

"Then what did you mean?"

"I like you, Naomi. I don't mean as a colleague. As a woman."

"Oh."

Her pulse raced. Again, she'd jumped to an assumption and wished for a hole in the ground to swallow her up. Then his words sunk in. Could he be saying what she thinks he's saying? Did he really see her as a woman he could be interested in? Logan was an attractive, compassionate man and someone she could see herself dating. Was she *really* ready to take that step?

Logan raked his fingers through his hair. "I'm messing this up."

"No, you're not." Naomi rested her hand on his arm to stop his motion. "I was being super sensitive for no reason. I'm sorry. What did you want to say?"

With a soft smile, he admitted, "I've been drawn to you since the first time I laid eyes on you. Even when you tore into me, I just wanted to kiss the anger out of you."

Naomi thanked her skin tone for hiding the heat rushing to her cheeks. "I thought you were attractive, too. When you stood in the doorway, you had the whole sunny, back light thing going on. You know the one where the hero makes a dramatic entrance and the bad guys tremble in fear just from the sight of his silhouette."

He raised an eyebrow and flashed the charming dimple she was getting used to. "That was one of the nicest compliments anyone's ever given to me."

Naomi licked her lips, twisting the hem of her shirt. "So, now what?"

"I'd like to take you to dinner next week. I know you have to get the dogs settled and catch up on work."

Speaking of the dogs, it didn't take this long to give them water and her mother should have been out by now. Did they know Logan wanted to talk to her? Her suspicions grew, but kept them to herself.

"I think dinner next week would be nice."

"Great. I'll call you so we can make plans." Logan stood and held out his hand. She ignored the zing when their fingers laced or how right it felt when he pulled her into his arms. "I'm going to miss having you here."

Oh, she was a goner.

Naomi took a step back for fear of swooning, but let him rest his hand on her shoulders. "I'm going to miss you, too. Thank you for sharing this with me and my mother."

Logan gave a grateful nod. "You're welcome here anytime. Maybe next time, we can go horseback riding."

She couldn't remember the last time she went riding. "That sounds great."

As if on cue, dogs spilled out of Logan's screen door, followed by Fiona looking at her phone. "Dad? Can I spend the night at Megan's? Her mother will be there."

Before Logan could answer, the back door to the main house opened to Maeve and Josephine, laughing like loons. Thomas brought up the rear with a small box in his arms.

"Yes, you can spend the night," Logan answered. "I'll drop you after we finish shopping." Fiona's fingers flew across the screen, bringing a grin to Naomi's lips.

"I should get going before your parents have us stay for lunch."

"They already offered," Maeve said, stopping beside her daughter. "I told them it's a tempting offer, but we need to head home to see if there's any damage."

"I was serious when I said to let us know," Thomas commented, sliding the box into the car. "We can send one of the guys over and there's plenty of room here if you need a place to stay."

The possibility of damage hadn't crossed Naomi's mind. Walter would have mentioned if there were noticeable flooding, and the sale papers said he had the roof replaced five years ago.

"Thank you for the offer and for opening your home. We'll let you know if there's a problem." Naomi held out her hand.

Josephine took her outstretched hand to pull her in for a hug. "Don't be a stranger. You're always welcomed."

Thomas followed suit with a fatherly embrace, echoing the same invitation. Naomi ushered the dogs into the car before wrapping her arms around Fiona. "Your father has my number. Send me a picture of the boots."

"I will." She turned to her father. "I'm going to pack."

Logan shook his head at his daughter's retreating figure before setting his gaze on Naomi. "I'll call you later. Be safe going back."

The touch of his lips to her forehead startled her, but she welcomed the move. Naomi rested her hand on his flat stomach for balance and swallowed a sigh. It was definitely time to leave. She took a step back and tilted her head.

"I'll text you when I get home."

Naomi nodded before climbing behind the wheel. After a last wave, she pulled off. Her mind drifted in a million places as she maneuvered out of the rescue.

"So, Logan asked you out?" Maeve said once they were off the property and on the mountain road. It proved the delay in her mother leaving was to give him time.

"He did. I see you and the Becketts made sure of that." Naomi gave her mother a quick stink eye and returned her gaze to the road.

Though the creek receded, it still swelled with fast moving water. Naomi slowed for an officer directing traffic during a stretch where crews shoveled mud and cleared branches and debris. Hawkins Ridge experienced its share of destruction, but seeing the damage the town endured sobered Naomi, thankful the Becketts gave them a place of refuge.

Once they cleared the roadwork, Maeve continued their conversation, keeping her eyes out the passenger window. "Logan asked for a few minutes so he could talk to you. Did you say yes?"

The hug and quick peck should have served as a response. She had a feeling Maeve wanted verbal confirmation so she and Josie could gossip later. "I did."

"He's a good man that comes from a wonderful family. I think our time there proved that Walter is wrong about them."

Naomi sighed. "I know, you don't have to speak their praises."

Maeve rested her hand on Naomi's thigh. "You're responsible for your own happiness. If you want to see where things go with Logan, that needs to be your decision. Don't let Walter or anyone else put doubts in your head."

Naomi sighed as they crossed the town limits and the more residential area. "I like Logan and admire what the Becketts are doing up there. The plan to talk to Walter is still a top priority in the coming days. I'm still wrapping my head around his dislike, based on an imagine slight before Logan was even born." The car splashed through standing water before Naomi finished. "For the rest of the weekend, I'm only focused on getting Mika and Tam settled and catching up on paperwork."

Maeve squeezed her wrist, before commenting on the state of some yards they passed. Naomi welcomed the change in subject. It kept her mind off Logan, the possibility of a relationship, and her inevitable conversation with Walter. For now, she just wanted to wash her hair, cuddle up with the dogs, and sleep alone in her own bed. Anything else could wait until the morning.

CHAPTER 22

Logan's belly laugh echoed in the back room as the pugs attacked the dust broom he was using on the hardwood floor. He turned it into a game and raced out of the room, down the hallway and back, dragging the perceived enemy behind him. The joyful barks solidified his choice to adopt them as pets.

"Okay, y'all. Enough playing for now. Let's get you something to eat before your uncles get here."

Logan shoved the broom in the utility room and bent over to give each dog a scratch behind their ears. It seemed everyone on the property was taking advantage of the break in weather. Stable hands and garden workers planned a gathering around the fire pit on the west side of the land. Logan gave Claire the night off to spend with her cousin and his wife in town. His parents decided on a date night of dinner and a movie. With Fiona at a sleepover and Naomi and Maeve back home, Logan invited his brothers over to hang out.

The pugs did their bouncy food dance when he pulled their bowls from the drying mat. A pang of longing washed over him, seeing the bowls Shorty, Mika and Tam used while they were there. Logan meant when he said he would miss Naomi.

In a few short days, they'd developed a routine, and it brought him comfort.

When he initially offered for Naomi and Maeve to say on the property, he didn't expect to fall for the voluptuous woman with a love for animals that marvel his. As he sat the bowls on the floor, he smiled, thinking of her text earlier, letting him know she was home. When he dropped off Fiona after shopping, it took willpower he didn't know he possessed not to stop by her house. They agreed to talk the next day because she had paperwork to do and to double check the clinic to make sure there wasn't water damage.

Mentally shaking his head to clear the image of Naomi in his home, Logan pulled the frozen pasta sauce he had thawed in the fridge and set it on the counter. He had raided the main house for food for him and his brothers. Opting for spaghetti, garlic bread and the apple crumble from the night before.

He placed the sauce in a pot on low to melt the remaining ice crystals and simmer. The front door swung open at the exact moment the pugs finished their meal. Scout trotted into the room, closely followed by Caden who was carrying two six packs. Once they had a satisfying sniff, the dogs eagerly began a spirited game of chase.

Caden pulled off his boots before crossing the open space to place the beer in the fridge. "I saw Jace and Noah headed this way."

Jace and Noah built their houses near each other, between the goats and the farm.

"I'm surprised they aren't hitting the bars."

Caden bent at the waist to give the pugs some loving. "I think they're finally acting their age. Truthfully, Jace is still hoping he can sweet talk Claire into giving him a chance."

"Claire isn't a casual woman. She's also my employee who I want to take over for Sam when he and Owen decide to call it a day and travel with the folks." Logan had a warm spot for the bookish vet tech and didn't want to lose her once Jace became bored with her. "Besides, she's not his type."

"She's a single woman in a town of fifteen thousand. She also ignores him. Claire is a challenge," Caden argued.

Logan snagged a wooden spoon from the drawer and stirred the sauce. "I'll talk to him."

"Talk to who?" Noah's deep voice had Logan and Cade turning around. Both men made quick work of their shoes.

"Jace."

"Me?" His youngest brother's crooked grin was quick. "I haven't been home in days. What could I possibly have done?"

"Claire. Stop harassing her. I don't want to lose her because you can't keep your hormones in check."

Jace snorted as he passed his older brothers with two more six-packs while Noah brought up the rear, carrying a container of his herb-infused goat cheese and a box of crackers.

"Yeah, that's not gonna happen." Jace handed each brother a beer before putting the rest in the fridge.

Caden nodded his thanks. "Why?"

In response, Noah smirked. "Claire is his one," which immediately grabbed Logan and Caden's attention. "Or so he thinks she is. He moaned and whined last weekend when he was helping me box orders."

"Are you serious?" The last time Logan heard his brother confess seriousness about a woman was his sophomore year of college.

Jace nodded in response, scratching his close-cut beard. "Her laugh is the most beautiful sound I've ever heard. She's smart—"

"Since your usual conquests don't know what a book is, I can imagine that would be a plus," Noah interrupted, earning a playful shove from his best friend. Jace continued.

"Whatever. I just know that Claire is amazing, and I just want to wrap her up and bring her hot chocolate."

Logan, Caden, and Noah shared a look before bellowing in laughter.

"I hate all of you," Jace's announcement was void of heat. His gaze went to Logan. "I don't know why you're laughing. Rumor has it you finally had the nerve to ask the doc out."

He expected Naomi would come up in conversation at some point that evening. Logan would rather handle it now to free up their attention for the poker game and to talk about the homestead plans. Returning his attention to the stove, he set the oven to preheat.

"I finally got past using Walter as an excuse."

Noah pulled a stockpot from the cabinet and filled it with water. "Do you expect it to be a problem if things progress between you two?"

Logan shrugged. "I doubt it. We had a chat the other night, and I explained the history. She was shocked and I think a little hurt he hadn't been forthcoming with why he hated even though she asked." He left out the conversation they shared and the one with Thomas.

"I may have insight into what's happening with that friendship." Caden leaned against the counter, dangling his beer bottle between two fingers. "Walter has been the passive aggressive jerk he always is. His speaking on her behalf with Austin was the final straw, and she plans on putting him in his place now that the storm is over."

Logan didn't know when they became gossiping hens, but he appreciated it now. He saw Walter's manipulation first hand with Kaylee and the damage to his marriage. It also confirmed his father's point that Naomi wasn't Kaylee, and he didn't need to compare the two. However, Logan wondered where his brother got the information.

"Did Mom tell you this?"

Caden shook his head. "Maeve. The day we worked in the greenhouse. Mom asked what brought them here; Maeve shared."

"Why didn't you say something sooner?" Noah asked, as he dumped the crackers onto a small saucer.

"I figured he," Caden pointed his bottle towards Logan, "would never ask her out because of Walter."

Logan turned the burner on under the water filled stockpot. He faced his brothers and blew out a breath. "I found Naomi attractive the day I met her and probably would have asked her to have coffee if we didn't have that dust up. Y'all know I haven't wanted a relationship because of Fi and trying to get everything straight to take over for Dad. But not knowing at the time what was up with Walter, I used it as an excuse." Logan took a pull from his beer, then continued.

"Once we cleared the air and getting to know her these past few days, I knew she was someone I could see myself spending time with later down the line. Maybe once she became more settled. Then I talked with Dad yesterday and he said some workers were sniffing around. Jealousy I didn't know I had reared its ugly head."

"But did that make you want to wrap her up in a wool blanket and bring her cocoa?" Caden teased, earning a growl from Jace. Logan smiled.

"I'm not sure about the blanket, but she brings out my protective instincts." Especially knowing what her ex-husband did to her reputation. Naomi is a brilliant vet. The farmers who listened to her ex saw how well she handled their animals and shouldn't have given in to an obvious smear campaign.

Caden sat on the floor near the table and pulled Rosebud into his lap. "Well, I like Doc. She didn't have a problem jumping in and helping take care of the animals, nor hesitate about going out in the rain to help when we needed it. More importantly, Fi likes her." He held Logan's gaze with the last part.

Noah agreed. "Fi had nothing but nice things to say when she came to help feed the goats."

"She's also getting a reputation in town," Jace added. "Several guys at the station have taken their pets to her and have said she is nothing like Walter."

They didn't need to sell Logan on Naomi's appeal. He's seen her skills and gentleness first hand with the rescues, not to mention her instant love for the terriers.

"Like I said, I woke up and realized I would be an idiot if I didn't ask her out." Logan turned back to the stove to stir the sauce, needing to take the attention off of him. "Regarding Claire, give her some space. She's been in Oak Mountain for two months. According to Sam, she's trying to get herself settled and not looking for anything now. Maybe try being a friend first."

"That's the same thing Mom said." Jace rolled up the sleeves of his shirt. "I'll step back a little, but if I hear or see anyone sniffing around her, all bets are off."

Logan knew Jace's backing off would last a week unless they kept him busy. He'd have to talk to his father and brothers to come up with projects. Speaking of which…

"I'm thinking about connecting the dog house to here or build an addition. Caden also mentioned expanding the therapy dog training and the need for a new livestock dog. There may be a fit we can try out next week. Otherwise, I'll make some calls to some shelters."

Noah spoke from his spot at the table, "With the folks turning over the reins, we need to talk about where we see the future of the homestead. I know Josie hired Maeve to help, but Dad is already putting together a job description of his duties and seeing if there's someone on staff he trusts enough to train."

When Logan's parents asked Owen to help with Hawkins Ridge, they let him build the position of manager to what worked for him, knowing Josie would be there to help. Owen and Noah were family and part owners with had equal say to the future of the business. Knowing they might have to find someone outside of the family concerned Logan, but he already begun thinking about the same thing.

For a moment, the thought of sharing the future of Hawkins Ridge with Naomi crossed his mind. They still had to go on their first date.

"Okay, enough touchy feeling nonsense," Caden pulled himself to stand. "We can talk about that on Monday. I'm ready to eat and play poker."

Trash talking began, causing Logan to smile. Business and fantasy thoughts of Naomi could wait. It was time to beat his brothers.

The desire to toss her phone across the room overwhelmed Naomi. After three deep breaths, she gently placed it on her desk and buried her head in her hands. Maeve sat a hot cup of red rooibos tea in front of her before joining Shorty, Mika and Tam on the worn leather couch in her office.

"No one can come out and look at the damage until Tuesday, but the adjuster will be here Monday afternoon." Naomi wrapped her fingers around the warm cup. "What are we going to do?"

The overwhelming smell of mildew as soon as they opened the front door dashed Naomi's hopes of coming home and getting the terriers settled. The soppy wet carpet, clearly the culprit. She and Maeve located a hole in the roof over the hallway. The exact day of the damage is unclear, but it happened early in the storm, allowing the water to seep beyond the hallway into the bedrooms and causing a few tiles in the kitchen to buckle.

They spent over an hour laying towels and blankets. After a call to Izzy to see who rented a wet-vac, the emergency crew showed up to soak up what they could. A few minutes later, Isabella and her brother arrived and covered the roof with a tarp as a temporary fix. It might take days, if not weeks, for her home to be suitable for living. They sought refuge at the clinic and made efforts to air out the house as much as possible.

"The fire chief said we could sleep there tonight, but we needed to find other accommodations." Maeve sighed. "A hotel isn't cost effective."

Naomi would never have her dogs sleep in a house with mildew spores in the air. She shook her head. "Not with three dogs. It was nice of Isabella to offer to set us up, but with two young kids, four animals in a three-bedroom house…"

"That would be way too chaotic," Maeve finished the thought. "I see you haven't called Walter."

Naomi took a long sip of tea, letting the natural sweetness coat her tongue. Walter and his wife had room and would welcome them with open arms. A night was one thing, an extended stay wouldn't be wise. She was still struggling with the information she learned from Logan and now questions about the condition of her house. Mentally, it wouldn't be healthy for Naomi, Maeve, and the dogs to subject themselves to that toxic environment.

"I know I need to talk to him," Naomi finally replied. "But in my current state, I can't guarantee that I wouldn't threaten him with body harm. Besides, I don't want or need him in my business."

They were silent for a moment before Maeve spoke. "Why don't you call the Becketts?"

The thought had crossed Naomi's mind more than once. When she texted Logan to say she was home, she mentioned nothing about the damage. Why, she couldn't answer. The last thing she wanted was for them to think they were taking advantage of them.

"I don't want to share a house with Logan and Fiona, and I don't know how Mika and Tam would do around the cats if we stayed in the main house. Besides, Logan just asked me out a few hours ago, and I don't want to put pressure on something that hasn't even started."

"And, no offense, I don't want to share a bed with you again unless I have to," Maeve teased.

Naomi smirked. "I thought the same thing, but wanted to spare your feelings." The two shared a laugh before getting serious. Maeve lifted her own mug.

"I don't think we would stay at the house. They have those tiny homes throughout the property for visitors and employees. Claire lives in one and I'm sure if we talked to Josie, it wouldn't be a problem." Maeve glanced at the dogs. "It would be better for them as well."

Naomi decided on the way home that Maeve would take the car and dogs when she started with the Becketts. Her fur babies loved running around the property and would be better than taking Maeve to work and leaving in the middle of the day to pick her up.

While she may have been overthinking, she didn't want Logan to think she was manipulating him. Logan was the first man since her husband she'd even considered going on a date with. He was handsome, so very handsome, but also passionate about the animals and the rescue. His love for Fiona and his family was clear and made him a catch in any woman's book.

"Do you think they would let us rent out one of the houses? I don't want them to assume they'd let us stay there out of the goodness of their hearts."

Maeve chuckled. "We've just met them, but something tells me they won't take a penny from us."

Naomi didn't think so either. She spared a glance at the dogs, who were sleeping peacefully. The frantic commotion earlier ticked up Mika and Tam's anxiety, but now, with the calm restored, they can finally relax. She held out her hand with a heavy sigh.

"Give me your phone. We all know Josie is the law on that property and I only have Logan's number. I'm don't want to go tonight. It's late and we need to pack up the house."

Maeve unlocked the device and handed it to her. "It's just waiting for you to press call."

"You knew they were our only choice."

The smirk on her mother's face gave it away. "I did. I also told her what was happening and promised not to tell anyone until we knew the full extent of the damage."

Naomi exhaled. "I'm serious about offering to pay rent."

"I know you are, dear."

She shook her head and pressed the call button.

Chapter 23

Logan slipped his feet into a pair of work boots. Despite having a busy day ahead, he couldn't start without a strong cup of coffee. Scout, followed by Rosebud, Tulip, and Bluebell, pushed past him and sat patiently for the door to open. Caden lived on the other side of the property near the stable, and after a few beers, neither wanted him driving the ATV home, so he spent the night.

Spending time with his brothers was what Logan needed. Each of them had responsibilities and expectations to uphold for Hawkins Ridge to succeed and periodically, they needed a break to just relax and be brothers. Logan stored the pennies used for the ante in a jar at his place and has been using them for almost a decade. For them, it was never about winning despite the trash talk, but about reconnecting.

"What time are you moving the mothers and their pups over?" Caden asked, slipping his hat over his mussed hair.

"In about two hours. Fi wants to help, so I'm picking her up after breakfast."

"Okay. I'll bring the pugs back when you're done."

Logan opened the door, and the dogs bolted for the front lawn. "You're not eating with everyone?"

Caden shook his head. "I'll be at dinner. I have two owners coming in an hour to take their horses for a ride and need to get cleaned up." Both men turned their heads when the dogs ran to the side of the house. "What's got their attention?"

They followed and noticed the house set aside for visiting family door wide open. Logan met his brother's gaze. "Did we miss something?"

"I didn't think Uncle Frank was coming until May."

They hurried across the gravel road just as their father stepped out carrying a wooden rocker, setting it on the small porch. Josie followed with the other.

"Morning boys," Thomas said in greeting. "How was poker?"

"Good," Logan answered. He moved his hands between the chairs. "What's going on here?"

Josie grabbed a cushion from a basket on the porch, speaking as she tied it to the seat. "Maeve and Naomi will be with us for a spell. Storm did some damage to their home."

"Seemed there was rot in a spot on the roof," Thomas added. "The chief wanted to stop them from staying last night, but Isabella stepped in."

"It helps that the fire chief is her father," Caden pointed out. "So mildew?"

Josie nodded. "They tried to use fans and the vac, but the damage had been done. Izzy's brother put a tarp to cover the hole, but he noticed potential issues in other areas. With the forecast for rain late next week, Naomi is worried about more leaks."

Logan's brain caught up with the development that he would have Naomi back on the property with him and only a few feet away.

"She mentioned nothing to me when she texted yesterday. Why doesn't she stay with me?" Logan swallowed the hurt.

Josie chuckled. "A few days is one thing. You're looking at them being displaced for weeks. Besides, both of them said sharing a queen-sized bed for that long would be torture."

Logan could see that. The designated family house had two bedrooms and an open living area with a kitchen and would give them enough privacy.

"You know Naomi offered to pay rent," Thomas snorted. "We compromised and told her she could help with the dogs on the weekend. She's a keeper."

Logan shook his head at the wink his father shot him. "Why wasn't the roof inspected before the sale? She's only own the home for what, six months? A professional inspector would have caught that and had Walter pay to fix it before she took ownership."

"Maeve said Naomi is pulling all the paperwork to look over today. They need to be out before the chief comes back and red tag the place." Josie rested her hand on her hips. "Poor thing can't get anyone out there until Tuesday to look at the damage. The adjuster is coming tomorrow, but she has a day full of clients."

Thomas wrapped his arm around Josie. "I'm laying a heavier tarp over the hole once we're done here. Your mother plans to make breakfast sandwiches for them."

Logan refused to let his father be the hero for his woman. He knew it was possessive and had a feeling Naomi would bristle if she found out, but he couldn't help how he felt.

"If you can pick up Fi, I'll go help Naomi and Maeve and take care of the tarp. I'll see if Jace or Noah can help." Logan pulled his phone from his jean pocket. "I don't understand why she didn't tell me, but I'll take that up with her."

Thomas rested his hand on Logan's shoulder. "She's a proud, independent woman, son. If you go there acting all alpha, you will push her away before you even had a chance. Let her tell you what she needs."

Logan rolled his neck to ease the tension coursing through his body. Multiple feelings fought for dominance over his emotions. Hurt because Naomi called his parents instead of him for help. Anger because roofs don't instantly spring a hole no matter how wet of a winter they had. Though he didn't have proof, something told him Walter knew the roof wasn't up to code. Happiness that Naomi would be back and he and Fi could see her daily.

Logan gave a tight nod and jotted off a text to Jace before sending one to Fiona. By the time he was done, his parents were closing the door. Caden gave a low whistle, signaling the dogs it was time to go. He turned his attention to Logan.

"I have to run, but it's interesting she's not staying with Walter. I agree with Dad. Let it go about her not telling you. She's going to need you when he pull the same guilt trip he used with Kaylee. Naomi is smart. I'm willing to bet washing every dog on the property that she suspects Walter knew about the roof and didn't tell her." The dogs heeled at Caden's feet. "Let me know when you get back."

He watched his brother lead the dogs to the ATV. No way Logan would take that bet, he suspected the same. Naomi wouldn't ask to stay unless she not had a choice. Mika and Tam would not have done well with Izzy's houseful of energetic animals. Walter and his wife didn't have pets and plenty of room, a perfect option. But he suspected she didn't reach out because Naomi had an inkling of the truth. Walter screwed her over. The million dollar question was, did he do it willingly?

"What time did you tell them you'd be there?" Logan asked as they walked towards the main house.

"In about forty-five minutes. I already have the ladder and tarp in the work truck." Thomas tossed him the keys. "I'll swing by after picking up Fi to see if you're still there. We told them they could bring a few things."

Logan assumed they meant more than clothes. How much would they have to throw away or salvage after this?

"Come get some coffee and eat before you head out," Josie fussed. "I'll see if a worker can help me finish taking over the dog beds and food staples in case they want to spend the evening in."

If the carpet was wet, it would make sense that the dog beds got ruined. Jace's dirt bike stirred up dust on the road before parking on the side of the main house and met them at the back door. They gave him a brief rundown as they stepped into the warm kitchen. The intoxicating fragrance of slow roasted chicken filled the air.

His younger brother voiced the same concern he had about the timing. Something didn't sit right with Logan, but he pushed it to the back of his mind. The important thing is that

Naomi would be close. He smiled as a rush of peace washed over him.

"Can you add putting a pause on cable to the list?" Naomi called out to her mother in the other room. She tossed a handful of clothes from her dresser into a large plastic tote. "I should be able to ask the post office to just deliver the mail to the clinic, right?"

"This list is getting longer by the minute." Maeve poked her head into the room. "You need to take a break."

"I can't. Thomas will be here soon, and I want to have things ready to go."

"You also work a few yards from the house. Anything we forget, we can get tomorrow." Maeve stepped over a suitcase and rested her hand on Naomi's shoulder. "You need to step outside and breathe."

"I just have one more drawer to empty, then I'll meet you outside. I promise."

Maeve held her daughter's gaze for a moment before nodding and leaving the room. Her mother was right. Though they wore surgical masks, staying inside for extended periods wasn't good for either of them. She had kept the dogs out of the house since they discovered the leak. Their little lungs couldn't handle the mildew spores. It was why they slept at the clinic last night.

Or attempted to sleep.

Naomi's mind couldn't shut down enough to rest. She wasn't an expert in home building and architecture, but she also wasn't stupid. If Walter replaced the roof five years prior, nothing short of a lightning strike or sabotage would make a hole that size. The picture Izzy's brother took proved nature did not cause it.

The question that ran on a loop in her mind was, why? Why didn't Walter tell her? Why did he sell her the house, knowing the roof wasn't up to code? The one that she couldn't shake: why did he purposely hurt her? Nothing short of God testifying Walter's innocence would have her believe he didn't know. Concern over the condition of the clinic's building also ran through her mind and another item to add to her growing list of things to do.

First, she needed to get as much packed as she could before leaving her home for the next several weeks.

Naomi made quick work of tossing the clothes into another case and zipping it up. Despite having all the windows and doors open, the musky smell still permeated the air. It was why they were taking all their clothing. The thought of replacing an entire wardrobe made her itchy.

Minutes later, she stepped onto the front porch, removed her mask, and took a long, deep breath. Crisp, cool air cleared her sinus passage and momentarily settled her racing mind. Seated on a kitchen chair they had moved earlier, her mother drank from a bottled water and offered Naomi one. She gladly accepted and dropped into the seat next to her.

She took a long pull, watching Mika and Tam tilt their muzzles to the sky before laying down in the early morning sun. "Thanks for bringing the dogs out front. They're doing better with this than I thought."

"Having Shorty and knowing they're safe helps." Maeve linked her fingers with Naomi, giving them a gentle squeeze. "You don't have to do everything today."

"I know that here." Naomi rested her hand on her chest before tapping her temple. "This is the part that's struggling to get the message."

"You get that from your father."

Naomi gave a warm smile. "He always had four or five contingent plans, it seemed, for every scenario."

Love coated Maeve's laugh. "He even had a back-up plan for our wedding day just in case something happened to the church or the pastor."

"I can see that." Naomi took another sip of water. When she spoke, her tone was serious. "I have questions about the roof that I'm afraid to get the answers for. It's not just a leak. It's a hole."

Maeve exhaled, sparing a quick glance at the house. "I'm sure we have the same questions, but we can't answer them now. For today, we have to be thankful we have friends that have opened up a home for us."

"Even though Thomas and Josie won't let us pay."

"Friends wouldn't charge or expect anything in return. Besides, they offer the homes for employees new to the area or in a hardship. I'm an employee." Maeve patted her thigh. "I'm sure your young man will be happy to have you back on the property."

"Logan? I wouldn't classify him as my young man. I haven't even talked to him since I sent him the text." The sound of an approaching vehicle drew their attention. Seeing Maeve's devilish grin made Naomi's stomach come alive with fluttering butterflies.

"Oh, I think he knows."

Naomi squinted as the truck moved closer. Recognition had her jaw drop. "What did you do?" she hissed at her mother, her hand adjusting the scarf holding her wild hair in place.

"Nothing. Thomas told Logan what happened, then Logan volunteered to rescue you." Maeve waved as she rose to her feet. "I told you to tell him yesterday."

"And I told you why I didn't."

"And look how that turned out." Maeve stepped off the porch. "He cares about you."

Naomi stopped beside her mother. "We haven't even had a date."

"Yet, according to Josie, he didn't hesitate to tell his father he would take care of things. Don't be difficult and accept the help."

"Why are you assuming I'll be difficult?"

Maeve pinned her with a look. "Remember the first time you met Logan?"

Before Naomi could come back with a retort, the men climbed out of the truck. Shorty, Mika, and Tam abandoned their spot on the grass to greet Logan. He dropped to a crouch and gave them the attention they wanted.

"You better be careful. A woman might get jealous if you keep greeting the dogs before saying hi to her," Naomi teased, stopping a few feet away.

"Believe me, darlin', if you ran to me the way they did, I'd definitely show you the proper greeting first." Logan rose to his full height and closed the distance in two long strides. "Instead, you stood there, looking beautiful as always, knowing I'd prefer to greet you first."

Naomi's cheeks burned. "Good save."

"Brother, never talk about me being sappy again," Jace commented from the side of Maeve. "Morning, Doc."

Naomi nodded a greeting just as Logan wrapped his arms around her waist and tugged her to him. She returned the embrace, and for just a moment, everything felt right. She didn't want to admit how happy she was he came to help. The last thing she wanted was to be viewed as weak. Naomi never wanted to be the damsel in distress. Even during her marriage, she rarely asked John for help.

Yes, she still had to work on her pride. The last thing she wanted was to appear as ungrateful. But knowing she wasn't alone gave her the strength she didn't know she needed.

Logan spoke after pressing a kiss to the crown of her head.

"How are you two holding up?"

"As best as expected," Naomi focused on the pups. "The dogs are a little confused about what's going on. Shorty didn't understand why we were sleeping at the clinic."

"Slept is a relative term," Maeve mumbled. "Thankfully, we found an old air mattress."

Jace rested his hands on his hips as he looked through the screen door. "I'm glad neither of you tried to sleep here. I can smell the mildew from here,"

Logan nodded in agreement. "That makes two of us. The important thing is that you're okay. Mom sent breakfast sandwiches and a thermos of coffee for you. Why don't you two sit and eat? Jace and I will secure the tarp on the roof. Then we'll get you packed up." Naomi fought the urge to pout when he let go of her hand.

"How big is the house? What about furniture?" Maeve accepted the insulated lunch bag from Jace and passed the coffee to Naomi.

"The place comes furnished, but if there are any items you'd like to keep, we can remove them," Logan explained, while holding a large piece of tarp on the side of the truck. "First eat, then you can decide on what you want to take. We want you both to feel at home."

"Thank you." Maeve settled on the porch. "Will our king-size beds fit?"

He nodded. "Both rooms have them already, but if you're bringing yours, we can have them moved by the time we get there."

Naomi's eyes widened. "Don't you dare ask your mother and Thomas to do that?"

Logan chuckled, shaking his head. "I would never. They'll ask a couple of workers."

Relief washed over Naomi. She'd never forgive herself if his parents hurt themselves by moving heavy furniture. She twisted the lid of the thermos and inhaled the rich, nutty aroma. "Oh, my gosh. This coffee is one of the best advantages of staying on the property."

"Hey!" The twinkle in Logan's eyes softened his offense.

"Sorry. Seeing Fiona and having room for the dogs run are at the top too." Naomi joked, patting Logan on the arm. "I'm kidding."

"Sure." He wrapped his arm around her shoulder, tucking her to his side. "It just means I need to step up my charm."

Maeve and Jace laughed, lightening the mood. Naomi's shoulders felt lighter as the stress of the situation eased. She didn't realize how drawn she was to Logan. Naomi could admit she missed him, but didn't realize the extent until that moment with him standing beside her.

It meant a lot. Logan didn't arrive with an attitude for not calling him or go on a tirade about Walter and the house. Perhaps he recognized how fragile the situation was. It just put another check in the pro column about why she wanted to give their relationship a chance.

For now, she was thankful the Becketts opened up their home and gave them a place that would allow them to still have a sense of privacy.

"We should get started," Jace called from the side of the house. "I'll text the chief to see when he's coming back out."

Another reminder they needed to hurry if they had to dismantle their beds.

"I'll grab some cups," Naomi offered and smiled as the dogs followed Logan to the bed of the truck.

The mildew smell had lessened, but she noticed more of the kitchen floor had buckled. Remodeling had been on her list a few years down the road when she was in a better place financially. The universe had other plans.

She snagged two cups and thought of the situation. Naomi told herself, staying on the Beckett's property would be different this time. She wouldn't be in Logan's home. It would keep the fantasy of turning his home into theirs at bay.

Picturing a future with Logan was easy. His kind heart warmed the souls of those around him. His relationship with Fiona was one of his best qualities. But it was something she couldn't entertain at the moment. They still needed to go on their first date.

Her gaze drifted to the hallway ceiling and the peak of electric blue plastic fabric showing. No, her priority was to get her and Maeve settled in their temporary home. Then address a roof that should not have a hole in it six months after purchasing.

Naomi had questions for Walter, and she would get them answered.

Chapter 24

Logan set the tool chest and tarp on the grass at the foot of the ladder. Jace was already on the roof.

"You stay here," he told the dogs who followed him wherever he went. "Make sure your mom eats." They sat on their haunches and looked lovingly at him.

If only he could get Naomi to look at him that way.

She seemed open toward his touches, and he counted that as a win. The urge to tuck her and Maeve in the truck and let him and Jace handle everything rode Logan hard. Not because they were women. Because he could see the exhaustion on their faces and in the slump of their shoulders. They had their lives completely uprooted twice. They may have argued about accepting help, but each time, the women held their heads high. He smirked, picturing Naomi's determination to pay rent, but when Josie Beckett said no, nothing would change her mind.

Speaking of which, he sent a quick text to his mother regarding the beds and to keep the workers close for additional furniture. They had a storage unit behind the greenhouse where they kept furniture for the workers to use in their homes in case they needed it. Once he received acknowledgement, he called up to Jace and tossed the tarp. Logan draped the fabric carrier for the tools over his shoulder and deftly climbed the ladder. The roof of the single-story house had a slight incline, but was mostly flat. Jace stood with his hands on his hips, shaking his head.

"This is a mess."

Logan set the bag beside him and carefully walked to his brother. He saw the hole and surrounding rotting wood planks.

"Why is this here? The rest of the roof uses shingles. How did they make it through the winter without losing a portion of the roof?" Logan squatted and ran his fingers along the deteriorating material. "This didn't come from the storm."

"Nope. There's no way a qualified inspector would have signed off on this."

Logan didn't think so, either. He leaned closer to his brother's ear. "Do you think Walter knew?" Jace answered with a shrug.

"I don't know. If it was just old shingles, I'd could give him the benefit of the doubt. This is untreated pieces of lumber hammered in this section and another one on the other side of the chimney."

"Meaning it was a quick fix for a previous leak." Logan pulled his ball cap off and ran his fingers through his hair. "Do you know what he used this place for? He and his wife have been on the other side of town for over a decade."

"Walter isn't on my list of concerns. It's easy to find out, though." Jace pulled out his phone when it dinged. "Chief is going to be here in an hour to put an 'unsuitable for habitation' sign."

"Then we better get moving."

Logan unfurled the heavy plastic material. After double checking the nail gun, he and Jace went to work. They laid the material, removing the thinner tarp Isabella placed the day before. As Logan nailed, Jace spoke.

"You have feelings for Doc? I haven't seen you affectionate with a woman since Kaylee."

Logan also hadn't dated since her. He blew out a breath and crawled to the next section. "I wasn't expecting it, but yeah. Like I said last night. I thought she was attractive the first time I met her. Seeing her with the animals, interacting with the workers, showed me her heart. That's when I knew I wanted more."

"Are you up for another relationship with someone close to Walter?"

"I don't think she's as close as we thought." Logan gave a rundown of his conversations with Caden and Naomi while they worked. "The fact she didn't reach out to him for help when this happened speaks to their relationship. He's not manipulating her like Kaylee." That fact helped Logan know Walter wouldn't be a factor in his relationship with Naomi.

Jace pulled the next section of fabric taut so Logan could secure it. When they moved to the plank near the chimney, Jace continued the conversation.

"Mom and Dad wouldn't have offered the family house if they didn't like them. One of the smaller, one-bedroom ones, sure."

Logan thought the same thing. "I know. I think it's half their friendship with Maeve and the other half is Naomi. Her volunteering to help with the rescue and work the sandbag line gained Dad's respect. Not complaining impressed him."

If Logan was truthful, it impressed him as well. Despite his concern about her safety, it meant a lot that she wanted to help his family.

The sound of tires on the packed gravel drew their attention. Logan stiffened when he recognized Walter's signature vehicle. It was a newer model than when he was married to Kaylee, but it fed into his pompous attitude. Seeing the pearl white Suburban had Logan's blood boiling. Barking had him setting the nail gun down and wiping his hands on his jeans.

"Can you text Dad? Tell him to just head home with Fi."

Jace pulled out his phone. "As the smartest brother when it comes to women, I would advise to let her handle this."

Logan snorted and walked to the ladder. "You aren't the smartest, and that's my intention. I just want to be close in case she needs me."

"Okay. I'll finish this and be down."

He wouldn't need Jace if things went sideways. However, Logan would step in if the other man threatened Naomi or Maeve. Not that he would ever hit Walter, he hadn't in the past, but sending his father straight home avoided the possibility of fists flying.

Mika and Tam met him at the last rung and pressed themselves against him. They picked up the increased tension, either from Shorty or Naomi. He rested his hands on their necks to comfort them.

Logan sent a silent prayer that Naomi wouldn't cower to Walter. He had feelings for Naomi and wanted to see where their relationship would go. Logan didn't need someone from the outside ruining it before it got started.

Naomi growled as she placed her suitcase into the back of her Subaru. She was not in the mood to deal with Walter. His surprise visit couldn't have come at a worse time.

Thirty minutes ago, she'd received a call from the fire chief that he would be there soon to tag the property. Once they removed the bedding, she and Maeve worked on moving boxes and belongings to the front yard. She planned on asking Logan and Jace to help with the dismantling. Dealing with a potential confrontation between Logan and Walter would cut into the small window they had.

The sound of heavy footsteps spilled from the house. Naomi had a hunch that it was Logan who came in through the back door. Although she was grateful for his help, she knew she had to handle this situation by herself.

"He's standing by the door, just in case," Maeve commented as she stepped onto the porch. Shorty took the sentinel position in front of her. It steeled her confidence with the knowledge she had support, but they trusted her to take care of everything.

Walter pulled in next to Logan's truck and killed the engine. He stepped out a moment later, slipping his white Stetson on to cover his thinning hair. His smile seemed weary.

"Mornin' Naomi, Maeve. Is everything okay?" He went to hug her, but she took a step back. She didn't miss the scowl that ghosted his lips.

"I wasn't expecting you this morning. You need to call first, even if you're in the neighborhood."

The older man cleared his throat. "I just wanted to check on you. We haven't talked for a couple of days. Since the storm was over, I was curious if you were still with friends."

Naomi crossed her arms. "You still should have called. As you can see, now is not a good time."

Walter took in the suitcases by the car. "Going on a vacation? I'm surprised you're able to go away with the business and all. You're just now getting a standing with the town. People will talk if they can't get a hold of you for their pets."

Naomi fought the urge to roll her eyes. Isabella had rescheduled all of her appointments. Of course, that was none of his business. "My patients have nothing to worry about. Because a hole in the roof caused major water damage, we need to move temporarily. I don't know how, since the roof passed inspection at closing." She held his gaze and didn't miss the tick in his jaw.

"It passed. My guy has been doing real estate inspections for over thirty years. You should have called. I have plenty of room. I hope you aren't wasting money on a hotel," Walter took a step closer to Logan's truck. "Do you have workers here now?"

The vehicle gave no sign it belonged to Hawkins Ridge. Walter didn't hide his curiosity by glancing through the driver's side window. It may be petty, but Naomi looked forward to seeing his face when she told him who was there.

"Logan and Jace are here to put a tarp on the roof. We'll be staying with the Becketts while I deal with this." She had no intention of giving him information about the adjustor and contractor. "They took us in when we became stranded during the storm and made us feel at home. Josie eagerly offered us shelter once she found out about the damage to our home."

Walter took a step forward, but Naomi held her ground. He had close to a foot on her, but she wouldn't cower at any man. Though something told her Logan would be by her side if she needed him.

"I told you to stay away from them. They are horrible, arrogant people. You think they're letting you stay there out of the goodness of their hearts?" Walter snorted. "Please, they will expect you to bow down to them. Tell you how grateful you should be."

"Now you just wait right there…" Maeve yelled from the porch, but Naomi held her hand up to stop her mother. It was time she put Walter in his place.

"I understand you may have hard feelings toward them because your goddaughter's marriage didn't work out." Shock registered on his face for a moment before going back to his patent scowl. Naomi pressed on.

"Yes. They told me about Kaylee. I am surprised you never told me the reason behind your hatred of them, one that has consumed you for decades. You attempted to poison me with that foulness because you knew I would think it was stupid once I found out."

"Logan tricked my goddaughter into giving up custody for Fiona."

Naomi again held up her hand. Not for Maeve, but for the man she knew would burst through the screen door at that moment if she let him. She ran her fingers over the bracelet Fiona made her and squared her shoulders.

"What happened between Logan and his ex-wife is between them, not you. I'm sure you helped her get a qualified lawyer who explained what it meant by giving Logan full custody. I observed him with Fiona, and all I see is unconditional love. Every Beckett loves and protects her. She is a good kid. Sadly, you'll never know because of pettiness."

An unhealthy tinge of red colored Walter's cheeks and highlighted the hatred burning in his eyes. "You know nothing. They've already turned you against me."

Naomi shook her head. "No, *you* did that. I never gave you permission to speak for me to anyone. But you took it upon yourself to do it with Austin. Why? Because he was working with the Becketts. You also sold me a house with a rotting roof."

"I said I knew nothing about that."

"And I think you did. I can't prove it at the moment, but you can believe I will find out the truth. When I was at the lowest in my life, I ignored your passive aggressive comments because I didn't see them for what they were. Now I do." Naomi scooped up Shorty when he pressed against her leg. She used his comfort to continue.

"I'm thankful to you for giving me a new start here, but I don't think we can continue as friends. Now, if you'll excuse me, I have to finish packing before the fire chief arrives and tag my home as uninhabitable."

"Ungrateful is what you are. I took you under my wing when you were preparing for the boards because no one thought a black woman from rural Oklahoma would succeed as a vet. I listened to your whining when John left you for a skinner, a more public friendly woman. Then, I sold you my business for a song, gave you a new lease on life and this is the thanks I get." He took a menacing step forward, Shorty let out a low growl. "Where would you be without me?"

The squeak of the screen door hinges had her stand taller. The days of letting a man control her were over.

"I would still be a black woman that graduated at the top of her class, passed the boards in two states on her first try, and, according to my patients, a better vet than you. Now again, I am asking nicely to get off my property."

Walter spared a glance at Logan before dragging his gaze to the side of the house. Something told her Jace had showed up for the party.

"You've earned an enemy today. Good luck keeping patients." He walked backwards towards his truck. "Don't come crying to me when that family kicks you to the curb."

"I can guarantee you that won't be happening," Logan said, coming up beside her, wrapping his arm around her shoulders.

Walter climbed back into his truck and peeled out of the driveway. Naomi waited until he pulled into traffic to release the breath she was holding. Logan pulled her into a full hug and rested his chin on the top of her head.

It meant the world he let her handle the situation and stood beside her as a partner. The conversation with Walter was days in the making. The house solidified the end to what she thought was a friendship, no she didn't know what it had been. A pity acquaintance? It didn't matter. Starting over meant getting rid of every harmful part of her past. That meant ending everything with Walter.

Shorty, still squished between them, licked Logan's throat. He chuckled and took a step back.

"Are you okay? Don't listen to anything he said. He is a hateful man."

She took in the woodsy aftershave before tilting her head back. "I see that now. He became angrier since I've been in Oak Mountain. I always made excuses for him. Now, I see that was a mistake. I'm thankful he sold me the business. I wouldn't have met you or your family."

The flirty smile he gave her wrapped around her heart. "That is the best thing he's done since I've known him."

He pressed his lips to her forehead before taking a step back. "Let's get you packed up and get you settle back home. We'll deal with everything later, together."

Home.

Together.

Naomi didn't want to get her hopes up on a future with Logan. But he was making it hard.

Chapter 25

Naomi's temporary home had a slight chill in the main room. The log cabin, her description, brought a smile to her face. With her furry companions right behind her, she took in the space as she made her way to the refrigerator.

The open-concept living space had stainless steel appliances in the kitchen and a movable island with a butcher-block design. A corner fireplace complimented the rich dark furniture, light wood and the twelve-pane front window. There were three doorways leading to the bedrooms, with the bathroom positioned in between. At the edge of the kitchen, someone arranged the borrowed dog beds next to her room's entrance. It felt cozy, welcoming, and just right.

"Let's get you guys something to eat," Naomi said in her best cooing voice.

She set about distributing their food, while her mind playback the events from the day. Walter's hateful glare and demeaning comments were on a constant loop. Though she appeared strong, he knew his words hit at her insecurity.

Naomi confided the derogatory words of classmates and her ex-husband to him. Throwing them back to her solidified the end of any relationship they had. She still didn't know what his end game was. Why mentor her if he felt that way? Did he consider her an easy mark to unload his business? Did he not know of the prior damage to the roof? The last question troubled her the most.

Jace outlined the essential elements of building a roof. While most of the structure seemed in good shape, the area with the hole lacked a leak barrier, had old decking, and used thin planks unsuitable for roofing. Either Walter hired an inspector that took his money or both knew and submitted a false inspection report. Naomi was more inclined towards the latter. She would need to deal with it after the inspector's visit the following day.

She placed the bowls on the doggy mat and prepared a chicken sandwich using the tender meat Josie sent over. Maeve shared dinner with the family, giving Naomi the alone time necessary to process her thoughts and restore a positive mindset. Despite her immense gratitude for the Beckett family and their generosity, the excessive energy of their family meals would not have helped.

"Let's get y'all some fresh air and I can have my dinner," she said to the dogs while they licked their chops.

She slipped a hoodie over her t-shirt, wrapped a throw around her before grabbing her plate. The dogs eagerly bounded down the stairs, staking their claim on the nearby bushes. Naomi shook her head and settled in the rocker.

She lost herself in the view of the setting sun through the trees. The red and gold contrast against the dark silhouette of the mature oaks. Though it was the third week of spring, the crisp mountain air caused goosebumps to sprout.

Shorty took off on a trot, tail high in the air and wagging. A moment later, Thomas strolled up the stone path. Even in the waning light, she saw a smile on his face.

"Evening Tom."

"Doc. Beautiful evening. I wanted to let you know your mother started watching one of those Hallmark movies with Josie."

Naomi chuckled. "Was that your cue to leave?"

"I consider myself a romantic, but there's only so much a man can take." He let Mika and Tam sniff his hands before giving them a gentle scratch behind the ears. "I didn't mean to disturb your dinner."

"Not at all. I could use a little company." Although Naomi didn't want to come across as rude by turning the older man down, his fatherly presence, filled with warmth and compassion, was something she could benefit from.

"I was hoping you'd say that." He stepped onto the small porch and lowered himself into the remaining rocker. He relaxed and set his cowboy hat gently on his knee. She could see Logan in thirty years and fought the urge to smile. The patriarch plucked at invisible lint on his jeans. "Are you settled in?"

When they arrived earlier, Tom was helping Caden with the horses. Naomi nodded. "We are. I wanted to thank you for opening up the home to people you've only known for a short time. I'm appreciative."

Tom shook his head. "Has nothing to do with how long we've known you and Maeve. Both of you wrapped your way around our hearts on that day we rescued these beauties," he leaned his head towards Mika and Tam. Naomi felt the same.

"I forgot my manners. Do you want something to drink? Snack?"

"I think I've eaten enough today." He patted his slightly pudgy stomach. "You go on and eat. I have some things to say and if you're chewing, you won't get all sappy on me."

Naomi bit her lip to keep from laughing. She picked up her sandwich, motioning with her head for him to start. Thomas crossed his legs and focused on the tree line.

"Logan said he told you about our history with Walter. To this day, I never understood how someone can hold so much hatred towards a family because of a missed job opportunity almost forty years ago. I think it has more to do with Josie refusing to go out with him in high school, but I can't prove it." Thomas shook his head before shifting his gaze towards the dogs who curled up next to his feet before continuing.

"Since then, he's persistently worked to try to ruin our reputation in town, among the regional horse training community, and other rescue organizations. Except for having a part in Logan's marriage ending, no one pays him no mind. I say that because Logan told us what he said about turning your patients against you. Don't let it get to you, Doc."

Naomi exhaled, setting her sandwich back on the plate. The savory meat took on a bitter taste. "I didn't think my ex-husband could kill my business. The farmers that gave me a chance quickly found vets in other counties willing to drive fifty miles for business. The sad part is my ex said he would have left my business alone if I had just agreed to split the monthly earnings of my profits with him."

"Sounds like a real prize."

"More like booby prize." She didn't hide the sarcastic tone. "His new wife convinced him he was entitled. The judge thought otherwise."

She wrapped her fingers around her sandwich and motioned with her head for Thomas to continue.

"Well, I stand by my statement; don't worry about Walter and your business. You've developed a solid reputation, whereas Walter continues to ruin his. The pull he has is only in his mind. You know, he planned on shutting down the practice before he sold it to you because he hardly had patients."

Naomi stopped mid chew. She swallowed before she choked on her words. "He told me the practice was getting to be too much for him and wanted to spend more time with his wife. Izzy said people took their pets to the city or the next town over. I thought she was kidding."

Thomas shook his head. "Blamed us, of course. Saying Logan was seeing town pets on the side. Which brings me back to my point. Walter lacks the power to support his words. According to what I hear, the town adores you. I've seen for myself, you're good with the animals. Don't let him take your confidence away."

"He was my sounding board for close to ten years." Naomi pushed her plate towards Thomas for him to grab a chip. "He hit every insecurity I had because he knew them. Especially about your family kicking me to the curb."

"You're worried about Logan doing that?" Thomas gave her a side glance. Naomi shrugged in response and studied her glass. He continued. "I get it Doc. I do. Your experience tells you it can and will happen. Walter fed that doubt. In my younger days, I would meet him behind the barn for a chat."

Naomi couldn't stop the giggle that came forth. It returned the smile to Thomas's face. He plucked a chip from the plate and spoke around the bite.

"My family is loyal to a fault. Betrayal is the only thing that would have us turn our backs on anyone. I've seen your heart. You know firsthand the pain it causes." He leaned conspiratory closer to Naomi. "Josie has already started a list of eligible widows and divorcees for Maeve, so we can double-date." Thomas tapped his chin. "Maybe that's why she offered her the job. She and Owen need help, but it's a subtle way to introduce her to these men."

After her father died, Maeve had shared coffee with a few gentlemen back in Oklahoma, but Naomi wasn't sure her mother was looking for another marriage. If having a companion would make her mother happy, she was all in.

Thomas barreled on. "I can't predict where your relationship with Logan will go, but I know my son. He promised not to date until Fi went to college, unless he met a special woman who caught his attention. He hasn't until you. My son loves hard. Every one of my boys, including Noah, desires the love their parents have. If there's a chance to have that, they will fight to keep it."

Naomi took Thomas's words in and set them aside to process later. Examining her feelings for Logan couldn't be done with his father. There were other things she needed to process first. She pulled a piece of chicken from her sandwich and handed a small bite to each dog. Since Thomas was there, she had one last question before going inside.

"Let me get your opinion. Do you think Walter knew about the damage to the roof? Also, do you know what he was using the house for?" A low whistle escaped his lips.

"I'll answer the easy question first. He used it as a rental property until about eighteen months before you moved in. People here for seasonal workers or the construction crew when they built the new exits to the highway. People that didn't have ties to the town."

Thomas scratched his chin, then met her eyes. "Regarding the roof. I don't see how he could *not* have. That home sat unoccupied through two rough winters and last spring was exceptionally wet. Jace knows roofing. What he saw would never have passed any legitimate inspector and if the coding office found out, there would be a fine."

She rested her arms on her knees. "That's what I thought."

"Since we brought up the subject. Jace took pictures of the flooring and the hole from the inside. Doc, that hole caused about half of that damage. I think you have some foundation issues."

The sandwich flipped in her stomach. Until two weeks ago, she trusted Walter. Thought he had her best interest in mind. It seems she didn't truly know the man at all. She had a decision to make after she met with the adjuster the next day. One she wasn't looking forward to.

"Thank you," she said. "I need to hear what the insurance person says tomorrow before I can fully process anything."

Thomas stood and slipped his hat on. "Please don't interpret what I'm about to say as a question about your abilities. Just hear me out. I think you should have either myself or Logan with you when the adjuster comes out, especially if you have

Maeve meeting him. I've encountered adjusters who try to sound knowledgeable by spouting nonsense when they see a woman. You need someone in your corner with this because my gut tells me you're going to have a battle on your hands with the insurance company and Walter."

Sadly, she knew he was right, and it had her blood boiling.

"I'll ask Logan." She flashed a calm smile. "I'm afraid you'll take people behind the house and *talk* to them if you go."

Thomas's deep belly laugh drew the attention of a worker walking by. The man tossed up a wave and moved on. Thomas gently rested a hand on her shoulder, care twinkled in his eyes.

"You're not alone in this, Doc. I can promise we won't run roughshod over you. You're a smart, independent woman. You'll let us know what you need help with, and we'll do what we can."

Warmth flood her veins. It was the difference between him and Walter. Thomas asked, whereas Walter took control without talking to her. What did they say about hindsight?

"Thank you again. I'll text Logan before going over charts for tomorrow."

Thomas gave a quick nod and strolled down the stairs. Naomi gathered her dishes, giving the dogs a quick whistle as she went inside.

Her brain told her to be cautious about trusting the Becketts. She trusted Walter and look at where she was. However, her gut and heart told her it was different. She sat the plate in the sink and reached for the empty dog bowls to wash.

Naomi had a fight on her hands with the damage of the house. She still considered herself new to Oak Mountain. She didn't think she would win unless she had the help of the family, who didn't hesitate to offer her shelter.

Chapter 26

"Grab your lunch bag and breakfast sandwich from the table. Meet at the truck in five minutes!" Logan called out to Fiona as the screen door closed.

With the sun barely cresting the trees, he jogged to the clinic a few yards away. It would take a few days for them to settle back into the school routine after a break. Logan had a busy day ahead, which included supporting Naomi during her meeting with the adjustor.

When he got the text the night before, his brain bounced between shock and elation. She spoke about her chat with Thomas, and although it could have upset him, it warmed his heart she trusted his father enough to talk to. The fact she picked him instead of his father was a bonus.

After Naomi and Maeve settled in, Logan looked forward to spending some quality time together. When she asked to be alone, he swallowed the hurt. He understood her need to reflect on the day's events; her encounter with Walter, and being in another unfamiliar home. Yet, deep down, he wished she would open up about her emotions with him. It was a lot to ask.

Logan was the designated problem solver among his brothers. But Naomi wasn't his brothers, or even a worker. She was the woman he hoped to form a relationship with. He admired her independence and had no intention of taking it away. What matters is that she asked him to stand by her side today, and he agreed without hesitation.

He had to get Fiona to school first and pushed the door open, smiling at seeing Claire behind the desk.

"Good morning. Are you feeling better? If not, it's okay to take the day off."

The woman pushed her glasses up and nodded. "I am, thank you. My cousin brought enough cold medicine, juice and soup on Saturday afternoon. I didn't have a choice but to feel better."

"Well, don't overdo it."

He punched in the code to the storage area, which held the medication. Logan loaded his special case with the syringes he filled the day before. He stopped briefly at the counter.

"I won't be back until three thirty. Naomi and Maeve are staying with us for a bit."

"I thought I saw her car pulling off when I was leaving." Claire adjusted the compression glove covering the burn on the back of her hand. "I really like her."

He agreed, adding a wink, "that makes two of us. I know you're checking on the goats today, but would you have time to call some of the foster homes we work with? Jace and my mother are going out this morning to catch a stray cat and her kittens he saw yesterday."

"I can foster. I used to do it back home all the time."

"Seriously? That would be great. Grab whatever blankets you need from here, and Dad can bring over the extra large crate for them to start in." He checked his watch, scowling. "I need to run or Fiona's going to be late. Call if you need me, and thanks again."

Claire offered a wave as he darted from the building. A quick glance at his house showed his bag was missing from the porch and the front door was closed.

"Sorry." Logan pressed the fob to unlock the doors. Fiona leaned against the passenger door, typing on her phone. Her backpack hung from one shoulder. "Clarie's going to foster the cat Jace and Nana are tracking."

"Why can't we do it?"

Logan held off on answering until they were settled inside. "We have two mother dogs now. Bringing a stray cat with her own kittens into the house would not end well."

"We could keep her in my room?"

They both waved to Noah in the goat pasture before he answered. "What about Rosebud, Tulip and Bluebell? That's their sleeping domain. It works with the mothers because they have their own space in a closed room. This is a feral cat, even Nana doesn't want it in the cat sanctuary. For now, sweetheart, it's going to be a few weeks before we can bring in new animals to the house."

"Fine."

As Logan maneuvered the mountain road, they fell into a comfortable silence. A mist settled over the creek. It was the perfect weather to go fishing and wondered if it was something Naomi enjoyed. It was just the tip of the iceberg of what he wanted to know about the beautiful doctor. Once today was over, he would start planning for their official date.

"Do you think Naomi will have dinner with everyone tonight?" Fiona's eyes never leaving her phone.

Logan hoped. "I'm not sure. I'll ask when I see her in a few hours."

His daughter's gaze glanced out the window when they crossed the town limits. "I like her and Ms. Maeve."

"That makes two of us. Though this time differs from last week when they stayed with us. Naomi and Maeve will need privacy for some meals. Just like when we eat by ourselves because we want chili dogs."

A smile graced Fiona's lips. "We should totally do a dog and movie night this weekend."

Though it would be something he'd want to share with Naomi, it was too soon and Fiona opened up more when they had a father/daughter night. "That sounds fun."

"Oh, Uncle Jace said you and Naomi are dating."

Logan wanted to kick himself after he punched Jace. He planned on mentioning something to Fiona when they had more time to talk and wished his brother hadn't forced his hand. Her school rose in the distance as they crested the hill. "We haven't been on a date yet, so I don't think we can say dating."

"But you *like her,* like her?"

Logan chuckled, falling in place of the drop-off queue. "Yes, I like her, like her. Are you okay with that?"

They hadn't talked about him dating anyone. If she wasn't okay with it, he'd have to talk to Naomi about waiting. Fiona spoke as they waved to the principal.

"I like Naomi. She'd be good for you because she likes animals as much as you." Fiona had the door open when she continued. "She would also give me a beautiful baby sister or brother. Bye Dad!"

She scurried out of the truck before Logan's brain could plan a response. A child? Logan hadn't thought about having another child. Maybe a stepchild, but not one of his own. Did Naomi even want children? Could she?

A honk from behind pulled him from the almost panic and he tossed a hand in the air in apology. He shook his head and continued along the road to take him to the more rural area and the many farms.

It was crazy to think about something life-changing before his date with Naomi. There was still much to learn about each other. He wanted to know more about her marriage. Childhood. Did she enjoy snowball fights? He needed answers to these questions before he could envision a future with the attractive doctor.

"There will be lawyers champing at the bit to help you," Isabella commented as they slipped the harness on to the black Newfoundland, his tail wagging at full speed.

"I'm not sure I will need a lawyer. At least not yet," Naomi replied.

"Trust me. You're going to need one. I should have listened to my folks and not taken the job when Walter was here."

"Then you wouldn't have worked for me." Naomi flashed a cheeky grin before guiding the fluffy dog out of the exam room.

"I'm just saying, someone other than you needs to be held accountable," Isabella said, hurrying behind Naomi.

"Agreed, but I can't think about that until after the inspector."

They pushed their way through the low swinging door and greeted the owner, who was in deep conversation with Maeve. Ophelia Norris was an imposing figure with dark skin, a short gray afro and a shapely muscular build. She owned the butcher shop with her husband and was friendly with her mother. The woman scowled at Naomi, causing her to take a step back.

"Girly, don't you dare let that snake get away with what he did. Since the day he said our prime rib was stringy twenty years ago, I ain't have nothing to do with him." Ms. Ophelia turned her gaze to Isabella. "You've had our prime rib. Have you ever complained once?"

Her friend shook her head. "Every piece of meat has been great."

Naomi nodded in agreement. Ophelia's organic beef and chicken were worth the money over the local grocer. Their acknowledgement gave the older woman fuel to push forward.

"I banned him and his wife from getting anything from us. The man tried to ruin our reputation, said we wouldn't give him his money back. He had the nerve to say we injected hormones into our cows. My husband's family has raised beef for two generations. Everything they've fed those cows has been natural and organic. Nobody believed him, of course. Just cause his wife doesn't know how to cook prime rib, don't take it out on us." Ophelia turned her attention to Maeve. "Don't let that man try to get back in your daughter's good graces."

Naomi spoke up, taking control. "I won't let that happen, Mrs. Norris."

"And don't worry none about him talking ill will about you." Ophelia took the dog's leash. "In less than a year, you developed an excellent reputation in town. Everyone was a little worried when you first started not going to lie to you. But you proved you're a better vet and person than that old snake."

Naomi's heart swelled. "Thank you for saying that."

Ophelia patted her shoulder. "You got the town behind you. Once word spreads about your problems and who caused it, we'll help you make it right."

Unable to speak around the lump in her throat, Naomi nodded. The sound of the bell caused everyone to look towards the door. Naomi's mouth went dry when Logan casually walked in. His navy flannel shirt and well-fitted jeans caught her attention, but it was the roses he held that left her speechless.

"Ladies." The dog bumped against his thigh. He gave the dog a scratch. "Bruno."

Ophelia's gaze darted between him and Naomi before the corner of her lips upturned. "Lord, today, so the rumors are true." She addressed the rest of her statement to Izzy. "Your father came in to get some bacon and ground beef for the station and said these two were dating."

"I didn't even know." Her assistant crossed her arms. "We chatted the entire time during the storm and spent all morning together. Why didn't you say anything?"

"Because it's new," Logan spoke, pink colored his cheeks. He closed the distance and wrapped his arm around Naomi.

"When your father came to place the notice on the door, he saw us holding hands."

"And he did nothing to remove it," Maeve piped in before winking at Ophelia. "Logan stood beside my baby, but let her handle Walter yesterday. That's a secure man."

Naomi's cheeks heated and needed to end the conversation. The adjuster was due any minute.

"Bruno's fine Ms. Norris. I'll see him again in six months."

The knowing smirk on the older woman's face made everyone chuckle. "I'm going. You call me later, Maeve, so we can make plans for lunch. Logan, you tell Owen his order will be ready tomorrow." Ophelia tossed up a finger wave as she let Bruno pull her from the building. Naomi glanced up at Logan, shaking her head.

"Our business is going to be all over town by the end of the week."

He chuckled, handing her the multicolor bouquet of roses. "Please. Mrs. Ophelia is probably already on the phone with her sister. Our business will be all over town by tomorrow morning."

Naomi wasn't embarrassed about being in a relationship with Logan, but it would help if they went on an actual date first. She was familiar with how quickly gossip traveled, having grown up in a small town. Her heart swelled that Logan did nothing to deny his interest.

She pressed her nosed into the bouquet, inhaling deeply. "Thank you."

"Why don't I take those," Maeve said, coming from around the desk. "You need to get your paperwork ready before that adjuster gets here."

Izzy gave her a playful stink eye. "We can talk after lunch. In the meantime, let him see the name on the inspection papers. He'll back up what I said."

With an eye roll, Naomi reluctantly passed the flowers to her mother. "We can get a vase from the house for those. In the meantime, I think there's a container in the supply closet. Come on."

Logan followed to her office. He gave the space an appreciative once over before taking the papers from her. A scowl marred his handsome face a moment later.

"This can't be right. He let his license expire." He flipped through the folder. "Darlin', this is proving more and more that Walter knew the house wasn't up to code."

Naomi dropped hard in her desk chair, the weight of the situation overwhelming. "I know. I came out two weeks before the sale was final. Everything looked fine. I had my real estate agent back home handle the paperwork. How was she supposed to know this guy forged the expiration date of his license? I had so much going on I was just happy to have a new opportunity."

Logan squatted in front of her, taking her hands. "Darlin', you can't blame yourself. You trusted Walter. He was the one that betrayed you. None of this is your fault."

"Deep down, I know that, but it doesn't change the fact, I should have hired an independent inspector. Of course, I thought Walter had hired one. Not use an old fishing buddy. I don't even know if the insurance company will pay on the claim once they get a look at the roof and foundation. What will I do then?"

"Then that is a decision to be made once they check out the house. You and Maeve are welcome to stay as long as you want, so don't let that be a worry."

"But what if this doesn't work?" she motioned her hand between them. "I wouldn't expect you to let us stay there." He shook his head.

"I'm thinking we have a long future together. Yes, this is new, but I never felt a connection with a woman the way I have with you. Not even with Fiona's mother."

"Logan…" He put a finger to her lips.

"That's a discussion for later. Just know you and Maeve have a home at Hawkins Ridge. Today, is finding out what the insurance company has to say. I should let you know that if I think he is mansplaining or trying to roughshod you, I'm going to say something."

A smile overtook her lips. The man before her had wormed his way into her heart. Despite not knowing what the future held for them, she was thankful that Walter was wrong about the Becketts, especially Logan. She leaned forward and pressed a kiss to the tip of his nose.

"That's why I asked you. I want you here just in case."

A quick tap on the open door drew their attention. Maeve's approving grin had Naomi shaking her head.

"The adjuster is here and Isabella just left for lunch."

Logan groaned as he stood, causing Naomi to laugh. "Old knees?"

"Knees, back, whatever." He took her hand and brought it to his lips. "You got this Darlin'. Things will work out."

Naomi hoped so.

CHAPTER 27

Logan used the hem of his shirt to wipe the sweat beading on his forehead. A pack member dug a hole near the entrance to the run and had to be filled before someone twisted an ankle. The strenuous chore helped work out the anger coursing through his veins.

Running the meeting with the adjuster back through his mind, he slapped the new dirt with the flat side of the shovel. The problem was worse than Naomi imagined, and she faced a tough decision. Instead of seeking solitude, Naomi asked to talk to his family over dinner.

Izzy's assessment for legal action was correct. According to the adjuster, the home should not have passed inspection and Naomi was fortunate there wasn't more damage done. It left no doubt Walter's culpability in the matter. Logan needed to give his father a heads up prior to dinner. The sputter of an incoming ATV brought him out of his thoughts.

As the vehicle came to a stop, Shorty, Mika, and Tam swiftly jumped out and scurried over to him. He gave each dog the needed love as Thomas strolled up a moment later.

"You'd think they missed you more than Naomi." Thomas took a seat on an old tree stump. "What did you need to talk about? How'd things go today?"

"Not good." Logan watched the dogs start a spirited game of chase as he lowered himself onto the ground. "First, Ophelia was there when I got there. I'm sure people will know about us dating by the morning."

"You're not ashamed of your relationship, are you?" The disappointed look on his father's face had Logan shaking his head.

"You know I'm not. I just wanted to start with the good news first. She'll also have the meat order ready, so I need to schedule time to make dog food this week." Logan blew out a breath. "Did you know Dale Young signed off on the inspection papers?"

"What? How is that possible? His license expired." Thomas leaned forward, resting his forearms on his thighs. "That explains how the roof wasn't an issue. I wonder how much of a cut he received."

"That makes two of us." Logan was still mad about that piece of information. "You were right about the foundation. The land is sinking and caused the foundation to shift and crack. According to the inspector, this didn't just happen in the past year."

Thomas spewed the same curses Logan did after he left to pick up Fiona. They were still tame compared to the ones Naomi and Maeve uttered.

"What about the clinic?" Thomas asked.

"It's not in immediate danger, but she'll need to shore up that foundation in the next couple of years. The adjuster promised to contact her soon. Naomi gave him copies of the sale and inspection papers. He suggested talking to a lawyer." Logan raked his fingers through his hair and smiled at the dogs tracking a couple of squirrels. "Before we met with the guy, she was worried about how long they could stay, if things didn't work out between us."

"You planning on ending things with her?"

Logan chuckled. "Why are you thinking the worse?"

"I'm not. Just want to make sure you do nothing stupid."

"You don't have to worry about that. I know I have something special with Naomi. I'm not trying to mess it up before it even gets started."

Thomas grunted in approval. "Walter took advantage of her and he knows it. I don't understand how he could look her in the eye when he handed her the keys." Thomas scratched the scruff on his jaw. "You told her they could stay as long as they need to?" Logan nodded in agreement.

"Because he's a horrible person. It also explains why he looked nervous when he first pulled up and saw Naomi packing the car. Even more when she told him her suspicions." He plucked at a piece of grass. "I'm worried about her leaving. If the insurance company doesn't pay on the claim, or if the settlement it's not enough to fix the problem, what will she do?"

"I don't know, son. What I *know* is we need to support whatever decisions she makes and show her she's not alone. She's good for you and Fiona, and the town finally has a vet for their pets that they trust." Thomas stood and stretched his lower back. "Doc and Maeve became part of the family in a short amount of time. We, nor the people of Oak Mountain, are going to let Walter and his shadiness run her out of town. I sure as heck have no intention of losing out on the possibility of another grandchild."

Logan blinked rapidly, rising to his feet. "You were the one that told Fiona to bring up a baby to me."

Thomas whistled for the dogs and shrugged. "She reminded me and your mother you're still young enough to have a kid. Do you want a ride back to the house? It's about time for Naomi to come home."

Logan grabbed the shovel and fell into step with his father. It was time to divert the baby talk to this youngest brother. "You know Jace has the hots for Claire." Thomas cut his gaze to Logan.

"You're kidding? Uh. Maybe he's finally growing up. Once we get Naomi's problem situated, we'll help your brother tackle the uphill battle in front of him."

Logan helped the dogs into the back of the ATV before climbing into the front. The talk of babies wasn't something he wanted to focus on. Making sure Naomi didn't leave Oak Mountain and ultimately their relationship was at the top of his list.

After sparing one final sniff of the roses sitting on her dresser, Naomi clicked off the light. Shorty, Mika, and Tam, on her heels as she walked to the kitchen to grab her contribution to the meal — two six-packs. The Becketts weren't wine drinkers and Josie cooked better than anything Naomi could have bought from the bakery.

Considering what she wanted to discuss with the Becketts, it was the least she could offer.

The adjuster stated that her home wouldn't be habitable for the foreseeable future. The cost to bring it up to code was more than the home was worth. It didn't include the building for the practice, which would endure the same fate if she didn't take action. To say she was angry was an understatement.

Plain and simple, Walter took advantage of her. He lied to her face about his knowledge, and it hurt to her core. The reason was no longer important. Making it right was. If Walter thought she would just accept it, he was mistaken.

Then there was the Becketts. Naomi didn't want to consider where she and Maeve would be if Logan held their first meeting against her. Could it be why Walter tried to keep her from them? To limit her options when the inevitable damage to her home happened? He wanted her reliant on him, another assumption he made. Maeve raised her to be a survivor. She picked herself up after John, and she'd do it again. She wouldn't run away and had every intention of fighting.

After saying goodbye to her babies, she walked out the door, closing it behind her. By the time she reached the back door of the main house, Caden was climbing out of his ATV.

"Evening Doc." He took her package from her. "Did Dad tell you he brought the dogs up to the stable?"

Thomas hadn't told her. "How did Mika and Tam do? Shorty's been around horses before."

"Better than I thought. Mostly they stayed in the shade with Scout, terrorized the barn cat a little, and won over the workers." Caden held the back door open for her. "Overall, they were easy. I don't have a problem with them staying up there while you're at work."

Naomi's soft spot for the quiet brother grew. Initially, the plan was for Maeve to bring the dogs with her when she began working at the property. Knowing her mother and dogs were safe brought her comfort. They would be residents of Hawkins Ridge for the foreseeable future.

"Thank you, Caden. I'd like that. It will give my mother the chance to focus on her new job."

He flashed a quick smile as they stepped further into the house. Through the bustle of the kitchen, a figure of arms and legs barreled towards her.

"Naomi!" Fiona wrapped her arms around her, causing them to sway slightly. Laughing, she returned the loving gesture.

"Hey, sweetie." After kissing the pre-teen's forehead, Naomi took a step back. "How was your day at school?"

Fiona's patent eye roll had Caden snort as he walked by. The girl ignored him. "No one noticed my new boots except my friends and that's because I told them yesterday I was going to wear them today."

"What she means is none of the boys noticed her new boots," Logan pointed out as he stepped behind her.

"Whatever. I don't really care." Fiona pouted.

"I'm sure you don't." Logan nudged his daughter with his hip. "Can you help feed the cats so we can eat?"

Naomi smiled as she watched Fiona exit the kitchen with Caden in tow. Logan's fingers gently brushed down her arm before intertwining with hers. Her frayed nerves found solace in the warmth of the connection.

"How are you holding up?"

Naomi tilted her chin up and gave a soft smile. In a short amount of time, this man had become important to her. She wasn't ready to say the L word just yet, but she couldn't deny it would get there.

"I still have some thinking to do, but I want to talk to your parents and make sure it's okay for us to stay and to work out an arrangement." She put a finger to his mouth when he protested. "I know I don't have to, but I need to. Charity is not something I'm comfortable with."

"It's not charity. We care for you and Maeve."

"I get that and I feel comfortable in speaking for my mother when I say we care for your family too."

"Darlin', we want you here." Logan stepped into her personal space, causing her to tip back her head. "I want you here."

Before she spoke, Naomi squeezed Logan's hand. "I know. We like being here."

She studied his face for a moment. When Naomi moved to Oak Mountain, starting a relationship was low on her list. She wasn't expecting someone like Logan, but she was thankful she met him. It shouldn't be an option to trust the Becketts, given what she was going through. But she trusted her mother. She never like Walter or John. If Naomi listened to her mother, she could have avoided some problems she experienced. However, in hindsight, she would avoid repeating the same mistakes.

After pressing his lips to her forehead, Logan took a step back. "I still want to take you out on Friday."

"I'd like that."

"Okay, you two, enough lovey dovey. Let's move everything to the table." Thomas said from his spot near the industrial refrigerator.

Logan kept his fingers linked with hers as they moved further into the kitchen. Thomas passed out items for everyone to take something to the large table. He gave a wink to Naomi when he gave her the soup spoons. It was then she saw the stock pot of what looked like a thick, meaty stew. Her stomach growled in appreciation. Maeve, Josie, Fiona, and Caden strolled out of the cat sanctuary, deep in conversation. Josie broke off from the group and pulled Naomi into a hug.

"I didn't have time to see you yesterday when you arrived."

"Neither did I," Fiona yelled from the sink as she washed her hands. Josie ignored her grandchild and linked her arm with Naomi, pulling her away from the table.

"I know you have a lot going on, but know you will always have a place here. We'll respect your privacy, so don't feel you have to eat every meal with us." Josie leaned closer. "Now, I love these men with every fiber of my being, but they will drive you crazy. At least once a week, I'll disappear to the edge of the property with a book and a thermos of tea. You just say the word, and I'll show you where to go."

"It's no secret where you go," Thomas said, walking by. "We just let you think you're getting away with something because we know you need time for yourself."

"Please. You walk like a dinosaur. I heard you follow me thirty years ago when the boys got into that huge fight." Josie's eye roll was identical to Fiona's. "I just wanted to protect your ego and let you think you were getting away with sneaking up on me."

Naomi couldn't help but laugh. It made sense Josie would understand. Until Fiona, the matriarch of the family, spent decades being in a house with only men. Finding that moment of peace was something to be cherished. She glanced at Logan in conversation with Thomas. Both wore genuine smiles. Would he understand she needed a few minutes after work to decompress?

Caden carried the stock pot to the table and sat it on a colorful metal trivet between him and Thomas's place near the head of the table. Noah and Jace hurried in just as everyone was taking their seats. Naomi found herself between Logan and Fiona.

After a quick prayer of thanks, a conveyor line of soup bowls passed through hands while Thomas doled out servings. Everyone spoke of their day, including Jace and Josie's success at catching the stray and her kittens. After everyone settled with savory stew and buttery crusty bread, Thomas turned the conversation in Naomi's direction.

"What happened with the adjustor, Doc?"

Naomi shook her head at Logan's low growl and told them the story of the falsified inspection report, damage to the foundation, and predicting the land quality. By the time she finished, scowls graced all the faces. It surprised her when Noah spoke first. He and Caden were the quiet ones of the group.

"Walter took advantage of you. Knowing the house had little time before it crumbled." Noah looked around the table. "Do you know if he tried to sell the business or land before Naomi?"

Thomas and Josie shared a look. "There were rumors. He planned to fold the business and travel."

"That's when Izzy asked if I was looking for help," Logan added.

Josie piped in. "Then a month later, he said he found a buyer for the clinic and land. When he said it was one of his former students, the town wasn't happy." She turned her gaze to Naomi. "Sorry."

She shook her head, sitting her glass of sweet tea on the table. "No. Izzy told me the concerns of the town on my first day. For the record, I was never a student. He was an advisor for the school."

"The town loves Naomi," Jace said around a bite of bread. "A lot of the guys at the station now take their animals to her."

Naomi's cheeks warmed. She liked Oak Mountain and wanted to spend the rest of her life in the town. The residents exuded warmth and hospitality. She wouldn't let Walter take that from her.

"I love it here," Naomi started. "Oak Mountain is my second chance and I have no intention of running. I should hear from the insurance company by the end of the week. In the meantime, I would like to know if your offer to stay in the house still stands?" She directed the question to Thomas and Josie, both already nodding.

"Of course it does," Josie answered for both of them. "For as long as you like."

"Thank you." Naomi took a deep breath. "I insist on paying something for staying here. Rent or helping wherever you need me. I am grateful for your hospitality, but my parents raised me to pay my way."

Maeve turned her gaze to Josie. "My daughter's right. I know your argument is that I am an employee, but the houses are only for full-time workers and you charge fifty dollars a month which you take from their paychecks. We insist on paying double that since I'm part time."

"Also, I will help with the rescue or the farm on the weekends." Naomi pinned Thomas with a look. "That's not negotiable."

The patriarch of the Beckett clan studied Naomi for a moment before laughing. "I knew I liked you for a reason, Doc. I want to reject your offer and tell you we're doing it out of the goodness of our hearts, but something tells me I'd lose that argument."

Noah's deep voice drew everyone's attention. "I know I could use the help with the orders. I asked Fi to help, but having an extra pair of hands will help."

"Yes, I get to hang out with Naomi." Fiona's fist pump lighten the mood.

The table buzzed with plans for the coming weeks, and Naomi took it all in. No one brought up the obvious question, but she had talked to her mother on the way home that evening.

No matter what the insurance company's final decision would be, Naomi planned to sue Walter. His negligence and out right lie could destroy her. She vowed after her husband, she would never let another man take advantage of her.

It was time to become the strong woman her parents raised her to be.

Chapter 28

While shimmying her hips, Naomi carefully placed her favorite cup and matching saucer onto a tray. She lifted the container of chamomile tea with lemon and inhaled the fragrant aroma. A smile graced her lips as she spooned the loose leaves into the infusing basket and poured the boiling water over the tea and into the stainless-steel teapot. She pressed the lid in place and flicked off the light.

Three days had passed after her talk with the Beckett family. True to their word, they didn't push family meals on her. She had dinner with them the night before because Fiona asked. That evening, however, Josie invited Maeve to a book club and let Fiona tag along. Naomi saw it as an opportunity to have the place to herself and brought home a pizza with the desire to enjoy time with the dogs and a good book.

Shorty, Mika, and Tam were curled up on the large dog bed near the corner fireplace. Though it was early spring, Oak Mountain was experiencing a cold snap. It was a perfect night to snuggle on the couch and catch up on some reading. Naomi sat the tray on the table and added another log to the fireplace. The heads of all three dogs popped up a moment before there was a knock at the door. The irritation died in her throat when she peeked out the window and saw Logan standing on the welcome mat.

He and Jace left the day after the dinner to help a new rescue in a town called Point Harbor. Though he called and texted each day, it had been over forty-eight hours since she'd seen him.

She ran her hands down her outfit of yoga pants and a long thermal shirt and hurried to the door; dogs in tow. She flung the door open and greeted him with a smile.

"You're back."

He snaked an arm around her waist, pulling her closer. "I am. I missed your smile."

In his arms, she felt the same way. "I missed you too." She stood on tiptoes and pressed a kiss to his lips. Furry heads attempted to wedge their way in between, causing them both to smirk. "It seems I wasn't the only one."

The couple took a step back so Logan could greet the dogs. It was then she noticed he had something in his hand.

"What's in the bag?"

Logan flashed a devilish grin. "Dessert."

The magic word. "Okay, you three, give him some room."

Naomi lifted Shorty in her arms, knowing his sisters would step back. Logan crossed the threshold, closing the door behind him. She sat her fur baby down and grasped the offered bag so he could untie his work boots. She peered inside.

"Isaac, the person who contacted me about the rescue, his sister owns a bakery there. These red velvet cupcakes are the best I've ever had." He stood to his full height and took in the space. "How did you and Maeve transform this into a cozy space in a matter of days?"

Once Thomas and Josie agreed to the terms for them to stay there, Maeve wasted no time adding pictures and their personal knickknacks. With the weekend approaching, they planned to move their couch and recliner.

"Mom wanted to be comfortable. We both did. The only way we could do that was to add our own touches." Naomi padded to the kitchen. "I have pizza if you want some."

"No, thank you. I will take some water if you have it." He leaned against the counter and crossed his arms. "Caden shoved a sandwich down my throat when I stopped past the main house to get Fiona before coming here."

"Josie said it was okay for her to go to the book club." Naomi thought it was a great idea. The pre-teen was missing her father. He shook his head as he accepted the glass of cold water.

"It's fine. I wasn't supposed to be home until after midnight, so they weren't expecting us. My mother is always looking for a reason to show off her grandchild. Given that the book is for thirteen and up, I don't mind."

Naomi carefully pulled the pink box from the bag. The large cupcake was big enough for two and packaged to prevent it from sliding. It warmed her heart that he remembered red velvet was her favorite.

"Will you have some with me?"

"Of course." Logan closed the short distance between them, linking their fingers together. "I almost came to blows with Jace because he thought I bought it for us to eat on the way home."

That wasn't the romantic saying she expected and snorted. "I'm glad you're willing to fight your brother to save my gift. We can enjoy this on the couch. I'm having tea."

His gaze shifted to the dogs, who were waiting in anticipation for him. "I'll grab the napkins and maybe some beef chews for the dogs?".

"Go ahead." Naomi made herself comfortable on the couch with her back against the arm. "You're spoiling us all with treats."

"If I could spoil you all every day, I would."

Swoon.

Logan set a stack of napkins on the coffee table and gave each dog a treat before joining her on the couch. "Caden mentioned you had something to tell me about what's going on with Walter."

Naomi didn't want to spend the evening talking about Walter, but was glad his brother gave her a chance to tell him.

First, she wanted to taste the sugary goodness on her lap.

She slid the fork through the crumb dusted, pink tinted, cream cheese icing into the moist cake. Her eyes rolled back in her head as the bite dissolved in her mouth. Chocolaty perfection that wasn't too sweet. Naomi couldn't stop the moan even if she tried. She opened her eyes to see Logan with a wide grin.

"Sorry."

He handed her a napkin, shaking his head. "Don't apologize. That was the same reaction I had yesterday when I tasted one."

She handed the box to Logan to take a bite while she poured a cup of tea and caught him up to date. "I'm suing Walter. The insurance company said if I could prove I didn't have knowledge of the false inspection, I have a case. They will still adjust my policy and pay half of the claim because of the foundation. I had a phone consultation with Guy Brown."

Izzy wasted no time providing a name for a lawyer when Naomi shared her decision. She did her own research and spoke with Thomas and Josie before calling to make an appointment.

Logan responded after swallowing. "He's good. I played football with his son."

"You played football? I wondered why I pictured baseball."

Logan nudged the box to her before helping the dogs onto the couch, despite their ramp. "We all played. I think we just liked the idea of tackling each other. Did you play a sport?

An unladylike guffaw escape before Naomi could take a bite. "Coordination, especially in high school, was not my thing. I was too much of an introvert to be part of debate or student council. So I joined the science club."

It didn't surprise her that the Becketts brothers played sports. They had the looks and built to make any teenage girl heart go pitter patter. Naomi was positive she wouldn't have turned his head years ago.

"Science was my favorite subject," Logan drew her attention back to him. "I wanted to understand the components of things, what made chemicals react a certain way."

Naomi bobbed her head in agreement. "I was hooked the first time I saw an egg get sucked into a beaker. I think I was seven or eight."

"Mine was when we heard you could use cola to remove rust. Caden and I found this old gasket and poured almost a six-pack of coke over it." Logan chuckled. "Our grandfather was spitting nails because he had hidden the soda. He wasn't supposed to have it."

"Were you close to your grandfather?" She passed him their shared dessert after taking a bite. She pulled the throw off the back of the couch.

Setting the box on the coffee table, Logan rose to his feet. "We all were close to him in different ways. I always found my way to be near him when he went to check on animals. He taught Caden the secrets of training horses." He tossed another log onto the dwindling fire and return to the couch. "But Jace was his buddy. They both had a way with people. Neither one ever met a stranger. It's why he cared for Noah, too."

Naomi ignored the fuzzy feeling of watching Logan feed the fire because he noticed her get a chill. She couldn't remember John ever doing something that caring. During their first year of marriage, he showed kindness and affection, but he never took notice of her discomfort. In the short time they've known each other, Logan had. Something she hoped he continued.

Naomi nestled the cup near her body, warming her hands. "I never met my maternal grandparents. Being the only girl, my paternal grandfather spoiled me, but he was closer to my cousins because they were boys. He couldn't be rough and tumble with me. I was okay with that since I got all of my grandmother's attention."

"I can see that. You and Maeve are close. Did your grandmother like your mother?"

Naomi nodded as she swallowed a sip. "My grandmother said she liked my mother because she wasn't bougie. Her words." Her lips curved as she recalled a memory. "My father's brothers married women they could spoil and looked good on their arms. My mother was always with Granny in the kitchen helping clean greens or fish. They'd get sweaty working in the yard and had me with them when I was older. I think it also helped that my mom had a job. My aunts didn't work."

"That's where you get your work ethic from." Logan passed the last bite of cupcake to her. "Are we still on for dinner tomorrow night?"

Before she could answer, the front door open revealing Maeve, with a basket full of goodies and a wide smile. Logan hurried to help her while Naomi flung the throw off and scurried to her feet.

"Mom? What's all this?"

"Thank you. You're back early," Maeve said to Logan as she closed the door and hung her lightweight jacket on the coat rack. She greeted the dogs before answering her daughter. "They are a gift from Harold Smith."

Naomi and Logan stopped in their tracks and stared at each other before turning back to Maeve. It was Logan who spoke.

"You mean the same Harold Smith whose dog always gets in his prickly pear patch? The one that makes his own moonshine and owns the farm five miles down the road."

Maeve giggled—actually giggled—and took the basket from Logan and strolled towards the kitchen area. She put an extra little swing in her hips. Naomi and Logan were on her heels. "One and the same. Josie and I stopped by his place yesterday to drop off his order of eggs and cheese. He invited us to stay for a cup of coffee. Once he heard about the book club meeting and said he'd stop by. He gave it to me when it was over."

"Harold Smith has a good ten years on you," Naomi shook her head. "He's interested?"

Maeve shrugged. "He may be older, but he doesn't act it."

"That's the moonshine keeping him pickled," Logan joked. At least Naomi hoped he was joking. "So, are you going to spend some time with him?"

"I don't see why not." Maeve started unpacking the basket. Naomi snagged the jar of olives. "He's funny, enjoys old movies, and invited me on a horseback ride this weekend." Maeve placed the bottle of wine and summer sausage in the fridge. "Your parents sang his praises, but I think Josie's hoping I'll chose Frank."

Logan's eyes went wide and fumbled the box of crackers he was holding. "My uncle Frank?"

Naomi bit her cheek to stop the laughter, threatened to come out. Maeve nodded, setting the empty basket on the small kitchen table.

"He called about two days ago when I was helping with the cats. He is quite the charmer and has called during lunch ever since. Even said he may move his visit up." Maeve beamed at Logan. "Are you staying for tea?"

"I'm sure he wants to see Fiona," Naomi volunteered for him. She also wanted to grill her mother about the sudden onset of suitors.

Logan blinked, shaking his head. "She's right. I wanted to surprise her. You have a pleasant night, Maeve."

"You too, Hon." Maeve used a knife to cut the cellophane wrapper on a package of shortbread cookies.

He held his hand out to Naomi. "Walk me out?"

She grabbed the throw and wrapped it around her shoulders while he laced up his boots. The dogs followed them outside and sniffed for a spot. The star-filled sky played a perfect backdrop for the owls calling out a hoot. Logan tugged her closer and rubbed his hands up and down her arms.

"Dinner tomorrow?"

Naomi nodded. "I should be home by six."

"Great. See if you can find out who else is on my mother's list."

"Thomas said that it was most of the divorcees and widows."

Logan's head dropped back. "Oh, good grief. If you want, I'll try to rein my mother in."

Naomi made a dismissive gesture with her hand. "It's good for my mother to meet people."

"Okay. Just say the word." His fingers lightly grazed her cheek before tilting her chin up. "I had a nice evening."

"Me too."

He pressed his pillow soft lips to hers. Warmth coursed through her blood as she rose to her tiptoes. Naomi couldn't remember the last time a simple, chaste kiss left her breathless. Laughter in the distance ended the moment, but neither took a step back. The dogs darted onto the porch and pressed themselves against the couple. Logan rested his forehead against hers.

"I better get going. I'll text you in the morning."

Naomi nodded before giving him a quick peck and putting distance between them. "Tell Fiona I said good night."

Logan agreed and shoved his hands into his pocket. She watched him cross the gravel roadway towards his home and the main house. His silhouette was graceful under the spotlights that ran along the road. She was falling for Logan fast, and it didn't scare her.

She let out a deep breath and went back inside. Maeve was pouring boiling water into a cup. It was time to catch up with her mother.

"So tell me everything."

"Please don't eat anything with garlic or onions," Fiona pleaded from the middle of Logan's bed. She sat cross-legged with Rosebud in her lap. "Do you want me to run to the main house and get fresh mint leaves?"

Logan poked his head out of his walk-in closet. Concern marred his features. He hadn't planned on getting the fragrant vegetables. Deep down, he'd hoped there'd be a lot of kissing that night. The question was, how would his eleven-year-old daughter know about kissing?

"Why shouldn't I have garlic?"

"Duh, women don't want to kiss men with bad breath."

"How do you know this? Has someone tried to kiss you?" He'd hate to make a boy disappear.

"It's in all the books. Also, Nana pushes Pop-Pop away after he's had a large helping of garlic mashed potatoes."

Logan laughed as he stepped out of his closet. His daughter's frantic head shake stopped him in his tracks. "What?"

"Wear the blue shirt."

"Why?"

"Everyone wears white or plaid button down with jeans. It's so boring."

Logan rested his hands on his hips. "A white button down is a classic."

"Maybe next time, but this is your coming out date. You have to look your best."

He stared at his daughter with a slack jaw while he processed her words. "Coming out date?"

She nodded. "Everyone knows you two are an item. By the way, Brittney's mom is devastated. She was hoping you'd ask her out. Anyway, this is the first time you and Naomi are going to be out on the town. You're confirming the rumors. You need to look good doing it. If my friends see you in something like that, it will reflect badly on me."

"How? What?" Logan shook his head. "More importantly, if people know we're dating, as you claim, how is seeing me out in public a good or bad thing?"

Fiona's patent eye roll reminded Logan his girl was older than her years. "Everyone is going to talk and a lot of women will be upset that you're off the market. There are also single men who were hoping to ask Naomi out. That's what Jace, Noah, and Nana said anyway. My point is, you two have to look hot together so that everyone will know to back off and they don't have a chance."

His daughter left him speechless once again.

Logan spun and went back into this closet to put on his blue shirt. He couldn't understand how going to the steakhouse became a statement for the town, but he wanted to impress Naomi.

He had questions about the men interested in the beautiful doctor, but he wouldn't ask his daughter. It didn't surprise Logan that men found her attractive. He wanted to pummel

Walter when he tried to put doubt in her head about her appearance and why her ex-husband cheated on her.

It took a strong man to appreciate her. Naomi had a kind, strong-minded and a natural beauty. He'd met women, Fiona's mother included, that would expect a free place to stay. Naomi wanted to work for the house. She didn't have to, but he understood why she *wanted* to. Deep down, Logan was glad. He wanted her to see the hard work generations of his family did and become familiar with the different branches of Hawkins Ridge.

He wanted her to be part of its future.

Logan stepped back into the bedroom, carrying his black cowboy boots. Fiona looked up from her phone and gave an enthusiastic thumbs up.

"You clean up nice, Dad."

His cheeks warmed. "Thank you, sweetheart. What do you and Caden have planned?"

"We're going to do some wood burning. He wants a supply for when the booth opens."

"Hello?" Caden called from the front of the house. Scout trotted into Logan's room by the time Fiona and the pugs climbed off the bed. Shorty, Mika, and Tam were hot on his tail. Caden poked his head into the room a moment later.

"Naomi's still going to look better than you," his brother teased. He gave Fiona a side hug and rubbed the pugs' head. "Don't worry about hurrying home. We have a busy night planned."

Logan shoved his wallet and cell phone in his pocket and gave a quick once over as he crossed the mirror on the dresser.

"Thank you for dog sitting. We're just getting dinner. We both had long days and shouldn't be any later than ten."

The dogs led the way down the hall. Caden had sent his tools and a small stack of wood on the dining room table. His brother was talented and his artwork sold well at the farmer's market. He pulled the bouquet of wildflowers from the fridge before sitting on the couch and slipped his feet into the boots.

"Please don't give her too much sugar. She'll be up all night reading and not want to help Noah in the morning."

"Right. Celery and carrots for us." Caden finished with a mock salute.

"I'm going to regret this." He gave Fiona a hug, said good-bye to the dogs and offered a last wave before stepping outside.

Normally, he would walk the short distance to the other house, but he wanted to do the date image right. He climbed into his truck and made a U-turn, stopping in front of the stone pathway.

The evening was warmer than the night before, but there was still an early spring chill in the air. He flicked the car heater on low so the cab would be warm when she stepped in.

After grabbing the flowers, he strolled to the door that opened before he could knock. Maeve greeted him with a smile, wearing a thick cardigan and makeup.

"Evening Logan. You're looking nice." She spied flowers and nodded. "Good call on the flowers. Baby, Logan's here!"

"Thank you, Maeve. Are you heading out?"

Maeve stepped onto the porch. "I have a night of card playing with your parents and Harold. Don't wait up." She tossed a finger wave over her shoulder and hummed while heading towards the main house diagonal from them.

"I can't remember the last time she smiled that bright," Naomi said from behind, causing him to turn. Twice in a matter of minutes, Logan was at a loss for words.

"Wow." His gaze took in her shapely form. She wore a purple V-neck sweater, black jeans, a leather jacket, and black boots to add a few inches to her short stature. Naomi was an absolute sight to behold. "You look amazing."

"Thank you. You look handsome yourself."

He wanted to tell her Fiona dressed him but decided against it. "Thanks. These are for you."

She took the flowers and held them up to her nose. He noticed she did the same thing with the roses. "These are beautiful. Let me put them in water, then we can go."

When she turned her back to him, he noticed her hair was down. Her twisted locs hung midway down her back. Logan had only seen her hair pinned up and secured with a scarf.

"I like your hair." He stepped further into the room. "I've never seen it down."

Naomi pulled a vase from a bottom cabinet and sat it in the sink. "It gets in the way when I'm with patients and most cats try to play with it. You'll see it up more than you'll see it down."

"I like it both ways."

"Thank you."

Naomi filled the vase while removing the small tubes from the stem. A minute later, she turned the water off and grabbed her purse from the couch.

He held his hand for hers. "Ready?"

Naomi linked her fingers with his as they walked onto the porch. He was finally ready to start the next stage in his life.

Naomi ran her damp palms down her thighs as Logan put the truck into park. She didn't remember the last time her nerves got away from her.

The steakhouse was on one of the local farms on the other side of the creek. According to Maeve, between her run-in with Walter and her budding relationship with Logan, she was the talk of the town. There were a few negative things being said, but Naomi had to ignore them. Oak Mountain was her home. She was building friendships and wouldn't let a few whispers force her to leave.

"I've never been here," she commented. "How do they keep the special fragrant of cow from ruining people's appetite?"

Logan chuckled and motioned for her to wait. He jogged around the front of the truck to open the door. His truck was high off the ground and she needed help.

"There's a stretch of land that belongs to the state in the middle of the farm. So, even though it's two thousand acres, they keep the cattle and processing on the other side of the land."

"Why would they sell just a piece?" Naomi understood the farms in the county were family owned and passed down through generations.

Logan linked his fingers with hers and guided them to the front door. "Long story, but there is a section of the river that runs through the land. The state gave them a fair offer about eighty years ago to help conserve the waterway. The family was struggling and took it."

Naomi took a deep breath as he opened the door and motioned for her to enter. Garlic, rosemary, and grilled meat tickled her nose as she stepped in.

"Oh man, it smells great in here."

"I figured you'd like it." He guided her to the hostess station. "Evening Mary. How's everything going?"

The woman, Mary, offered a warm smile and came around the stand to give him a hug. "Logan Beckett, it's been too long. How's that little girl of yours?"

"Growing up too fast. What about your boys?"

"Please. I'm ready to ship them off to military school." The woman gave Naomi a side look.

"My apologies. Mary, this is Naomi Hendrix, the new vet in town."

"You're Naomi?"

Unsure what to say, she nodded and held out her hand. "Nice to meet you."

"It is a pleasure to meet you. My sister-in-law can't shut up about working for you."

"Izzy's husband is Mary's brother," Logan offered. "I would have mentioned something if I knew she was working tonight."

Mary grabbed two menus. "I switched with someone. Let me show you to your table."

Logan rested his hand on the middle of her back to guide her. Instrumental music became noticeable as they made their way down the short hallway. Naomi appreciated how the dark, rich wood gave a ski lodge feel. Exposed beams, heavy chairs and votive candles on each table gave an elegant look but casual feel.

Naomi recognized a few of the townspeople and gave a slight nod in greeting as they wove their way to their table near the large pane glass window. It gave a romantic view of the half moon highlighted with multitudes of stars. She removed her jacket and placed it on the back of the chair Logan was holding out for her.

Mary set the menus in front of them once they settled. "I'll take your drink order and have the server bring it over."

They each ordered a beer, along with glasses of water. Mary said her goodbyes after they promised to stop by the hostess desk on their way out. Naomi glanced over her menu at the few gazes pointed in their direction. She sat straighter in her seat and projected a confidence that her nerves didn't agree with.

"People are trying not to stare, but failing," she whispered, reading the appetizer page.

"They're noticing how beautiful you look."

She swallowed the snort threatened to escape. "Thank you for the compliment, but according to my mother, I'm the talk of the town. People seem to side with me with Walter. Also, I snagged one of the coveted Beckett bachelors and women are mourning."

It was Logan's turn to cough out his laugh just as the server came with their drinks. The young man couldn't be any older than twenty-two, but gave them a warm welcome. After placing their orders, Logan responded to her statement.

"Since we are going down the gossip trail, Fiona referred to this as our coming out date. This is to show the town we're an item."

"Are we? An item?" Naomi hated how unsure her voice sounded, but they'd only recently admitted their interest in one another. She wasn't a casual person and didn't suspect Logan was, at least not with Fiona in the picture.

He exhaled and glanced at the roll on his saucer. Naomi's heart rate ticked up. It was too early to bring the subject up. Logan spoke just as she opened her mouth to apologize.

"The term 'an item' isn't appropriate to describe us. The same with 'girlfriend' or boyfriend. I just feel that after the age of twenty-one, especially for divorced people, it seems childish." He emphasized the last word with a shrug.

"I think saying we're in a committed relationship is best," he continued. "I promised myself I wouldn't consider showing the side of my life that included Hawkins Ridge with anyone I wasn't serious with."

The server brought their appetizer of stuffed mushrooms with melted parmesan cheese. Naomi pondered his words while they placed a couple on their plates.

"You were stuck with me though because of the weather," she said. "You didn't have a choice but to show that side of you."

Logan flashed a smirk. "We had three empty houses, including the one you're in now when the storm started. There are guest bedrooms in the main house. Did you ever wonder why I wanted you in my home?"

"I thought it was the only place. I didn't know there were guest rooms." Naomi furrowed her brows. "Why would you do that?"

"Because I found you breathtaking from the moment you went toe to toe with me. I wanted to see if there was anything there, if there was depth beyond the looks. I made that mistake once, and I didn't want to do it again."

She popped a mushroom cap into her mouth while she worked through her emotions. The crispy bacon and spinach complemented the smoky parmesan flavor.

Naomi's feelings ranged between flattered and irritated. She settled in the middle on curious. "What if I only wanted to stay colleagues or friends?"

"Then I would have accepted that for a while before turning on the charm to make you change your mind." Logan gave a saucy wink, almost causing her to choke on her appetizer.

After ensuring she wouldn't go into a coughing fit, Naomi shared her feelings.

"I thought you were handsome when you walked in and felt the chemistry between us. I figured I wasn't your type or my mouth ruined even a working relationship, and thought no more about it." She held up her hand when he tried to speak. It was then the server came with the meals of rib eye steak, garlic mashed potatoes, and green beans. She wanted to finish her statement before digging in. Once the young man left, she continued.

"Spending time with you, seeing your family and how you ran the rescue, I hoped, if nothing else, we could be friends. It surprised me when you said you wanted more." She blew out a breath to organize her thoughts. "I guess what I'm trying to say is I want to build something with you, see where this goes."

He wrapped his hand around hers and gave it a little squeeze. "I'm glad we're on the same page. Now that we've had the hard conversation, my stomach is growling and we should dig into these steaks while they're hot."

Naomi giggled and took the knife to her piece of meat. Knowing she and Logan wanted the same thing from this relationship eased her mind. Now she could focus her worrying on to what she was going to do with her house, the land, and Walter.

Chapter 30

The rising sun filtered orange and pink rays through the leaves of the white oak trees. The branches created a thick canopy of the forest hugging the mountain road. Naomi didn't fight the smile that crept on her lips as she zipped towards the neighboring town of Riverdale. Spring was in full bloom, and she was in love.

A month had passed since her dinner with Logan, and their relationship had been going great. They'd taken to having dinner together when they didn't join the family. Naomi made sure that he had plenty of time with Fiona and his brothers. It gave her time to spend with Maeve and she formed a friendship with Claire. They were neighbors, after all.

Naomi didn't want to compare her relationship with Logan to the one she shared with John, but the sharp contrast made it hard not to. Logan made her feel cherished, protected, and valued. He encouraged her independence and sought her advice on two patients and even encouraged Harold to keep Naomi as Vader's vet. She learned from her past mistake and treasured her relationship with Logan.

Thanks to her lawyer, the insurance company agreed to a settlement on her house, provided she demolished the structure. There were also plans to serve Walter with lawsuit papers any day. She hadn't spoken to him since the day she moved. She'd seen his wife in town, but she only scowled. Naomi didn't care. His blase attitude about the condition of the house showed his true feelings for her.

Squirrels darted across the road in a game of chase. A soft giggle beside her had Naomi shifting her gaze. Fiona moved her arm in a wave against the current with the passenger window down. Naomi flashed back to doing the same move when she accompanied her father on one of his trucking runs during summer vacation.

It was Naomi's first time alone with Fiona. They've been together, but there was always some version of a Beckett buffer with them. Logan's overnight emergency derailed their plan to drive to the farmer's market opening as a family. A mare was giving birth for the first time and its anxiety worried the owner there might be complications. He promised to join them as soon as he could.

"Have you ever worked on a squirrel?" Fiona twisted in the seat to tuck a long leg under her.

"Not one like those, but I had the chance to examine a flying squirrel during my summer job at a zoo. He was snippy but cute." She smiled at the memory.

"We have them on the property, but they stay away from the barn because of the cats. I think they like teasing the dogs."

"Shorty barks like a loon when he sees them. He knows he can't catch them, but he likes to try."

Fiona nodded. "The pugs saw one the other day and tried to chase it. The squirrel was clear across the road and up a tree by the time they got their little legs working. Pop-Pop laughed so hard I thought he was going to choke."

"Your grandfather has a joyful laugh." It was one of many things she liked about Thomas.

The two fell into silence as the GPS barked directions. Fiona spoke when they were told to drive two miles.

"Are you going to get another house in town and move off the property?"

Naomi didn't know how to answer the question because she didn't know. She loved staying at Hawkins Ridge and been told frequently the house was theirs for as long as she needed it. Maeve decided if Naomi opted to leave, she would stay and move to a smaller house.

"I don't know. I'm happy at Hawkins Ridge. But the house isn't mine." Naomi doubted her grandparents would allow her to build one.

"If Dad were to ask you to marry him, would you stay?"

She and Logan hadn't talked about marriage. They hadn't said the L word yet. Naomi didn't want to give the young woman false hope, but she wanted to be honest.

"Your father and I are still getting to know each other. I care for him and we both want to build something that'll last. If he asks me to marry him, of course I would stay. I just don't know when that would be." Naomi spared a glance at her as she took the exit. "Does that make sense?"

"It does. But I just don't think you should rush into leaving."

Naomi laughed just as the signs for the municipal park came into view. "I promise I will be there through the summer."

"That works." Fiona pointed to the first entrance. "Turn there."

Naomi followed the girl's instructions and stopped to inform the attendant who they were with. They both wore

Hawkins Ridge shirts and directed where to go. A moment later, Naomi pulled beside Thomas' truck. She saw Maeve and Josie talking with Ophelia on a bench.

The three ladies on the bench waved as Naomi and Fiona approached.

"You had us worried," Maeve announced, passing off a cold water bottle.

Naomi leaned her head towards Fiona, who adjusted the back of her baseball cap. "Someone, I'm not mentioning any names, couldn't find the right hat to go with her boots.".

"I need to look my best when I represent the family." The pre-teen tilted her chin. "I'm going to see if three are any breakfast sandwiches left."

Fiona jogged towards her uncles. Naomi offered a soft smile before putting on her work face. "So where do I go?"

Josie guided her to a small set up next to the merchandise tent. Naomi surveyed the merchants' arrangement. Hawkins Ridge had a tent in the middle across from another farm. Noah mentioned the other vendor offered crops they didn't grow and were friendly with each other. A line of baked goods, sundries, and artwork filled out the remaining spaces.

"There are more vendors during the summer," Josie informed her as they made their way behind the table.

Twelve kittens frolicked in a portable playpen underneath the shade of an umbrella. Naomi performed the spay and neutering on the five-month-old babies two weeks ago. They wanted to give the new owners peace of mind that the kittens were healthy and taken care of.

"They're letting people in," Thomas bellowed as he walked towards their group. His gaze landed on Naomi and Maeve.

"Remember, all of us, blood or choice, are a family. No matter how today goes, we love each other and are proud of the work we do."

Everyone cheered in agreement before plastering a welcoming look on their faces.

For today, Naomi thought of herself as a Beckett.

Logan rolled his neck as he turned into the back lot for the farmer's market. Given the number of cars he could see in the front as he drove past, it was going to be a busy day. He was ninety minutes late. Once the maiden mare relaxed, she delivered without complications. Logan had enough time to head home, take a power nap, shower, and fill his travel mug with strong, dark coffee. He wanted to be there for his family, especially Naomi.

The talented vet was the bright spot in his life he didn't realize was missing. He thought Fiona, his work and family would be enough. He was wrong.

True to her word, every weekend since their dinner, Naomi had helped around the land. Between filling orders for Noah, working with the pack and taking on the training of some pups, she'd become an integral part of Hawkins Ridge. What Logan loved most is that she was independent and didn't hover. She didn't need to have him glued to her hip and didn't complain when he wanted to spend quality time with his brothers, unlike Fiona's mother.

Speaking of his daughter, her love for Naomi was obvious. When Naomi wasn't around, Fiona would ask when the next time she would be over. She worked with his daughter on whatever chore she did. The night before, Fiona asked if he thought about marrying her. Logan had for the past week. He could see her fitting in with his family. Heck, his parents already thought of her as a daughter-in-law. Not something she knew. He at least wanted to get them, saying I love you before talking about their future.

Logan climbed out of the truck. Keeping his fingers crossed, Ophelia had jerky and his family had a donut or three left. He noticed Jace broke away from a group of men and headed his way, falling in step next to him.

"How'd everything go?"

"Good. The mare had a girl. The mother took right to cleaning and nudging it." Logan slipped his cap on and nodded towards the men. "What was that about?"

"A potential partnership with a vet group here. They knew Naomi from some online message board. They bought a couple of bags of treats after she gave her recommendation. The head vet is bringing his wife and three kids to check out the operation and a see if there is a dog up for adoption."

Jace never let a chance slip by to promote the business or forge new partnerships. Jace's unique magic was necessary for the brothers to take Hawkins Ridge in the direction they desired. Logan felt a surge of pride in his heart for everything his youngest brother had achieved.

He nodded in approval, scanning the area of the booths. "Let me know the time and I'll make myself available. Please tell me there's a donut left."

Jace clapped his older brother on the shoulder. "Even better. Dad saved you two biscuits and Ophelia brought ten pounds of jerky. She made the mesquite flavor."

In the past, he would head straight to the booth for the food, but Naomi caught his attention. She was showing a kitten to an older woman. Both were cooing.

"Tell Dad I'll be right there. Do me a favor first? Go stand in front of Fiona so that boy can stop eyeing her."

Jace's head snapped in the direction and broke out in a chuckle. "He's with the vegan farmers and harmless."

"He's looks fourteen and they're smiling at each other."

"You did the same thing when we started at these things."

Logan rolled his eyes. "That's my point. Just tell her I'm here."

"Aye, aye captain."

"I hate you." Logan pushed his brother in the opposite direction and strolled up behind Naomi. The older woman's eyes went wide.

"Are you up for adoption, too?" she teased.

Naomi looked over her shoulder and gave a cheeky grin. "Sorry, he's spoken for."

He pressed a kiss on her temple before wrapping his arms around her waist. "She's right, ma'am. She took pity on this old stray, cleaned me up and made me presentable for public viewing."

Fiona stormed to the table and planted her hands on her hips. Fire lit her eyes. "Oh, my god, Dad. Must you embarrass me? Uncle Jace growled at that cute boy because he said you told him to."

Naomi took a step back. "Please tell me you didn't."

"I didn't tell him to growl. I told him to stand in front of you so the boy couldn't ogle you like a prime rib." He looked between the two glaring women who held his heart, confused. "What?"

The older woman snorted and handed the kitten back to Naomi. "My husband did the same thing with our two daughters. He still does it with our one son-in-law. If it's okay, I'll come past the rescue to pick her up tomorrow? I want to make sure we have enough food and litter for her."

Logan noticed Naomi's face shift with a warm smile. She handed her a business card. "Yes ma'am. Just call us and we'll have her ready."

"Good luck!" The woman gave Logan another shake of her head as she walked away, cackling.

"I missed you two." Logan flashed his best smile.

"Baby, your mother had to stop Thomas from going over there to talk to the boy when he gave her a smoothie." Naomi sat the kitten back into the playpen after slipping a collar on it. "They just said hi. Nothing more. She talks to more boys during school."

"He's older."

Fiona threw up her hands. "He's twelve."

Logan's eyes popped. "He's big for twelve."

"I've seen pictures of you and your brothers. You were about the same size," Naomi added.

"People keep making my point." Logan recognized this was a fight he would lose and approached it from a different angle. "Let's make a deal. I'm okay if he stays on his side of the aisle. Any drinks or food he wants to give you goes through me. Either that or I go talk to him."

Naomi and Fiona shared a look and nodded. "Fine. Just stop Jace from acting weird."

"I don't think that's possible. Can you get your old man the food Pop Pop set aside for me, please?"

"You just made the deal so I could get you food." Fiona narrowed her eyes. "I'm going to want to go four wheeling when we get home."

"I'm going to want to take a nap, but I'm sure I can make time beforehand." Logan watched his daughter walk off, fussing at Jace as he lowered himself into the spare chair. He motioned for Naomi to join him. "Are you mad because I went overprotective of her?"

Naomi shook her head. "I get it. My father did the same thing with me. Besides, she's your daughter. I don't have a say in how you raise her."

"Stop right there. She may be my daughter, but she's also a growing young woman who only had her grandmother to ask about female things." He took her hand in his. "We are building a future together. I want us to get to where you give me your opinion. I'm not asking you to take the place of her mother, but I want her to know she can come to you if she has questions or problems."

"Of course she can come to me. I care for Fiona. But you should have the final say on disciplining her as long as it's within reason." She glanced over his shoulder. "I think you're overreacting about the boy. He just gave her a smoothie and asked her name. That's it."

"Then comes exchanging phone numbers, late night texts and asking me to drive her to a movie theater so they can go on a date. Too soon, sweetheart."

Naomi stared at him for a beat before laughing. "You are hangry. I know you can get growly when you're hungry, but this is a new level."

Logan leaned forward and brushed his lips against her ear. He didn't miss her full body shudder. "That's between you and me. I want her to believe I'll put the fear of God in any boy she brings by." He finished with a kiss to her temple before sitting straight in the chair just as Fiona returned with an aluminum foil packet and a five-pound bag of jerky.

Naomi rose to her feet and patted him on the shoulder. "Fiona and I are going to walk around. Maybe I'll treat her to a smoothie. I placed collars on the kittens that are spoken for."

The two giggled as he glared. Instead of leading her to the other farmer's booth, Naomi guided Fiona towards the popcorn vendor. He tore open the bag of jerky with his teeth and ponder how lucky he was to find a woman his daughter adored and made him think about marriage again.

Chapter 31

"You're even smiling when sweeping up dog fur," Izzy said from the other side of the receptionist's desk. "It's nice to see."

The two were enjoying the break between appointments to tidy up. With Maeve at the Becketts full-time, Naomi had hired a part-time receptionist—a friend of Josie. The woman was a godsend. She kept the place clean and chatted with the waiting owners. Sadly, she had a doctor's appointment in the city that day.

Isabella wasn't the only one to comment on Naomi's smile. Putting the house tragedy to the side, things were going well for her. Business saw an increase in patients, and Naomi could see operating in the black by the end of the year. Personally, she couldn't be happier.

By the end of the farmers' market, all the kittens found their forever homes. A veterinarians group offered to sell the homemade treats Sam and Claire made. More importantly, Naomi drove Fiona to school the past few days. Since she and Logan had that talk about their future, a level of trust blossomed, and one Naomi wouldn't squander.

She ran the sweeper vac over the entrance runner a final time. "I'm not sure if I should be worried that you never saw me smile to the point when it happens, you tease me."

"It's the level of brightness that's worth noting. I think a tall, dark-haired hunk has something to do with it."

"Hunk?" Naomi grinned. "I don't know if I would use that word to describe him. He is handsome."

"Girl, please. The entire Beckett/Garrison clan could model jeans. That includes Fi and Josie." Isabella shoved the dust rag into a drawer and woke up the computer. "Are you two talking about marriage?"

Naomi shrugged and sat the sweeper in a corner. "We're moving faster than I expected. I don't think we're talking about marriage in the next few weeks, but we're having dinner together every night. Everyone has gone out of the way to let me know the house is mine until I move in with Logan and Fi."

"How does Fiona feel?"

"That's a good question. I know she likes me; that's not an issue. She asked me this past weekend if I had plans on moving back into town. I told her not in the foreseeable future." Naomi sat in the chair next to her friend and ran her hand over the bracelet the girl made her. "I worry if anything bad happens between Logan and I, it would devastate her. The last thing I want is to hurt her. She's been through enough already." *Fiona wouldn't be the only one crushed,* Naomi thought.

Isabella turned in her seat. "Agreed, but I don't think that will happen. I've known the Becketts my entire life. I've seen all the boys go through terrible relationships. They chose women that wanted the prize of having the Beckett or Garrison last name. None of them wanted to put in the work on the land, and all thought they'd pop out a kid right away to hold on to them."

"Only Fiona's mother managed that."

Isabella pointed a slender finger at her. "I still believe she tricked Logan, but I don't have proof. Anyway, what I'm trying to say is none of them have dated since their marriages ended. Jace doesn't count since he's never been. They knew the right woman would be one that doesn't care about their name, would have her own thing going, and wouldn't be afraid of hard work. You check every box."

Naomi understood that. They didn't believe in having the workers do everything. Thomas, Josie and Owen were out every day, helping whatever area needed extra hands. Even Fiona helped brush the horses, bathe the dogs and whatever else her family asked her to do. If it was true about their exes not wanting to get their hands dirty, then they didn't care about the family.

"And to think if I had listened to the man whose name I will not say, I would have missed out on love." Naomi thanked the powers that be daily for opening her eyes to the truth.

"Walter."

Naomi chuckled, rising to her feet. "Didn't I just say I didn't want to say his name?"

Izzy shook her head and stood as well. "No, he just pulled into the lot. Considering he's illegally parking in a handicap spot tells me he's not happy."

"What?" Naomi suspected why he was there. Given she hadn't talked to him since the day she moved out of her home, this wouldn't be an apology visit. "Can you text Mike or anyone at the station to swing by?"

Isabella's husband was a deputy and might not be in the area, but if he wasn't available, she'd take anyone just in case this went sideways. She moved closer to the front window to stand as a blocker for Isabella. As expected, Walter stormed in waving papers. The ruddiness of his cheeks said he may have had a nip or two.

"How dare you! Do you think you can sue me? I made you and yet you tossed years of friendship away for what? A few months of living a life with a family that doesn't care about you. You've made a huge mistake today."

Naomi refused to let his words take root in her heart and mind. Everyone at Hawkins Ridge, and some of the towns-people, have shown more kindness to her than Walter ever had. She stood to her full five feet, one inch height, and squared her shoulders.

"Before I ask you to leave, I need to correct your delusion. I am the one that made me and everything I've accomplished. You had nothing to do with it. Yes, I am suing you because my home is being leveled next week, thanks to you and your fraudulent paperwork." Naomi took a step forward, planting her fists on her hips. "People are stopping me with horror stories of you and your little friends. How you've attempted on more than one occasion to ruin businesses if they didn't kowtow to you. Well, guess what? They are still thriving while you're seen as a parasite."

"I don't think parasite is the right word," Izzy added from behind her.

Naomi swallowed a laugh and glared at the man before her. "Now, get out of my business."

"You wouldn't have any patients if it wasn't for me," Walter hissed.

"You're right. People are coming here *because* you're gone. Now, I'm asking again—" Tires screeching drew their attention. A full-size charcoal gray pickup made a U-turn in the middle of the road and turned into the lot.

"This is going to be fun." Izzy bounced on her toes while Naomi prayed for the police to show up.

The tall figure that climbed out from behind the wheel was the one Beckett she didn't want. A moment later, Thomas flung the door open and stalked the short distance to Naomi.

"You good Doc? Isabella?"

Naomi offered a weak grin. "Just trying to take out the trash." Thomas coughed out a laugh before glaring at the other man.

"Oh look, her great white hope," Walter mocked, shaking the papers clutched in his fist. "I bet you're the one that put her up to this. She wouldn't even had considered this if it wasn't for you and that spineless son of yours."

Naomi saw red and positioned herself in front of Thomas. "I have had enough of you and your insults. You're jealous because I made this business into something you couldn't. For some backwards reason, you didn't realize I had a mind of my own. You took advantage of me when I was at a low point in my life and mistook it for weakness and submissiveness. The reason you tried to turn me against the Becketts is because you knew I'd find out the truth about you. But I realized on my own you were a tiny little man who feels big by manipulating women. Thomas, Logan and every man on that property is a better man in their pinky than you'll ever be."

Thomas cut off Walter's attempt to move into Naomi's personal space.

"You roll up on my future daughter-in-law like that and I will shove those papers down your throat. Now, why don't you do us all a favor and leave?"

Another car pulled into the small lot, but this one had lights on the roof. Walter muttered a curse to Izzy when her husband, Mike, hurried out of the cruiser. A few seconds later, he stepped into the small waiting area.

"Someone wants to tell me what's going on?" Mike waved his hand to silence them when everyone talked at once. "Scratch that. Doc Hendrix, we'll start with you."

Naomi filled him in, leaving nothing out. Beside her, Thomas growled as she recounted the mean things Walter said. She patted his arm to calm him.

"In a nutshell, he's mad because of the lawsuit," Naomi finished.

"No, he's mad because your lawyer is seeing if they can press criminal charges against him." Mike held his hand up to silence Walter. "How did you get involved, Thomas?"

Naomi wondered about that herself. The older Beckett shoved his hands into his pockets. "I was headed to the feed store to pick up an order. When I drove past the business, I saw Walter's SUV. Only seeing Naomi and Isabella's cars, I knew they were alone. So I changed course and came to see if they were okay."

Mike gave a nod, then turned his attention to the other man. "I've known you my entire life, Walter, and I know whatever you're going to say is a lie and you'll try to look like the victim. To avoid that and prevent me from giving you a ticket for parking in a handicap spot without a placard I know you don't have, I am asking you to leave."

Walter sputtered for a moment, shooting daggers at Naomi and Thomas before he spun on his heels and stormed out. Naomi leaned into Logan's father when he wrapped his arm around her shoulders. Mike went to Izzy and pulled her in for a quick hug.

Naomi figured suing Walter wouldn't go over well, but the side she'd seen was disturbing. She didn't know his true feelings for her were based on hatred and manipulation. Questions of his true intention swirled in her mind. Did he know John wouldn't be faithful to their vows when he introduced them? Did he help ruin her reputation back home? Was money the only thing he cared about when he sold her the practice? She'd have to be okay, never finding the answer because she didn't want to see him again.

"I think you should close for the rest of the day," Thomas commented, cutting into her thoughts. "You don't know if he's going to come back."

Mike agreed. "That's a good idea,"

Naomi immediately shook her head. "I'm not letting him ruin my business. We have two more appointments. One should be here in fifteen minutes. Canceling isn't an option."

"Then I'm staying." Thomas made a show of pulling out his phone. Naomi gently covered the screen and forced him to meet her eyes.

"Thank you for stopping and standing with me. You have errands to run, and I won't be afraid. If he sees I've taken to closing down, he'll think he won and I won't give him that power."

Thomas blew out a breath. "You're killing me here, Doc. Knowing he may come back, how am I supposed to go about the rest of my day? Let me call Logan. He has to pick up Fi in an hour. He can get Sam or Claire or whoever to finish whatever he's doing."

Holding Isabella's hand, Mike stepped forward before she could stop him. "Thomas, I'll still be in the area and will monitor things. I would suggest since you're only expecting two more patients, keep the door locked. You'll see when they pull into the lot." He turned his full attention to Naomi. "Also, file a restraining order. There are cameras here. Send the footage to your lawyer and let him take care of it. I'll also take a copy and submit it with my report."

She hadn't thought about a restraining order. It made sense, given Walter's actions that day. She nodded. "Fine. I'll download it in between patients. I think keeping the door locked, at least for today and tomorrow, is a good idea."

"Thanks, Mike." Thomas shook the officer's hand. "I know I'll feel better. Logan will still be a wreck."

"Then let me tell him when I get home. He doesn't need to know now. The last thing I want is for him to be late picking up Fiona or worse, bringing her here after school with an upset Walter out there. Izzy and I will be fine."

"Well, too late for that." The vet tech pointed to the window. Naomi looked over her shoulder and sighed. Pulling in behind their patient's owner was an identical truck to Thomas's.

Naomi glared at the patriarch of the Beckett clan. "What did you do?" A sheepish grin expression crossed Thomas's face as he held up his hands.

"We were on the phone when I drove by because he remembered something he wanted me to pick up at the feed store. I may have said a bad word about seeing Walter's car and told him. I swear I didn't know he would drop everything and come down."

She believed him. Though Naomi was sure what went down with Walter would make its way around town in a couple of days. She didn't want to have her conversation with Logan while Mrs. Morgan brought her cat in for its vaccinations.

Naomi shook her head at Thomas and started walking to the desk. "You can't see the dogs for the rest of the day."

Thomas argued. "Tell me, how's that fair? I didn't know he was coming."

"You've known your son for thirty-eight years. I've only known him for three months and I knew he would come if he thought I was in danger." Naomi turned her attention to Mike and Izzy when she noticed Logan in the lot, talking to Mrs. Morgan. His eyes were on the building the entire time. "If you could just take her back to the exam room and Mike, I'll have a copy of the footage ready when you bring back the paperwork. If you can bring back the meat chews the dogs like from the feed store, Thomas, I'll give you ten minutes with them after dinner."

His deep laugh killed the tension in the room. "I love you too, Doc. Consider it done. You want me to stick around while you talk to him?"

Logan held the door open for her patient. His gaze roamed the space until it landed on her. A simple look of concern sent a shot of warmth through her body. Naomi greeted Mrs. Morgan and sent her with Isabella. Thomas pulled Logan to the side while Naomi took the email address from Mike. The two men did the weird handshake half hug greeting before walking out with Thomas.

Logan locked the door once they left before hurrying to pull Naomi into his arms. He nestled his nose in her updo, but stayed quiet. It was then, the events of the last few minutes crashed upon her and she shook with fear, holding him tighter. The woodsy aftershave aroma she loved slowed her racing heart. Being in his arms for a few moments assured her that everything would be okay.

Once her nerves settled, she took a step back and peered into his deep blue eyes. "Are you okay?"

"Better now. I put on a brave face for Thomas. You didn't need to come down."

"I was coming back from the next town over and wanted Dad to pick up shampoo for the dogs. I asked him to grab Fiona after the feed store, so I can hang around until your last patient." He ran his fingers along her jawline. "I love you, Naomi. The thought of Walter here doing lord knows what gutted me. I need to stay, for my peace of mind."

"I love you, too, and glad you're staying. We'll talk after the exam."

"Okay." Logan pressed a kiss to her forehead. "You can also tell me how Dad is being punished. He wants me to talk you into giving him thirty minutes with the dogs."

Naomi did something she hadn't done for the past forty minutes; she laughed. The Becketts had wormed their way into her heart and she loved every single one of them.

CHAPTER 32

Logan couldn't catch his breath until he followed Naomi home and saw her to the door. Grateful wasn't a strong enough word for what his father had done. He didn't want to think about what would have happened if he hadn't stopped and the women hadn't notified Mike.

He sat with Naomi as she found the footage on her simple security camera. It was the one most families used for their homes, but good enough to capture Walter storming into the lobby and threatening her and Isabella. He tilted his chin with pride, as she didn't let Walter intimidate her. He could see she was nervous the way her hands fidgeted, but to those that didn't know her, she held a strong facade. His lips upturned upon hearing his father refer to Naomi as his future daughter-in-law and the quick smile she flashed.

He raked his fingers through his damp hair. Logan needed a moment to himself, and took a quick shower. He'd been thinking about marriage that week. Listening to Fiona gush about how she enjoys riding with Naomi to school. He chuckled when she mentioned the satisfaction she had seeing the single mothers scowl when she climbed out of Naomi's Subaru. He would need to discuss her enjoyment of causing the viper women's pain later.

Logan never gave into the theory of gender roles when raising a family. He didn't think Fiona needed a mother to be complete. Yes, there were female issues he eagerly directed to his mother, but if she wasn't around, he would suck it up and deal with it.

As he slipped a t-shirt over his head, he smiled at the memory last August. A trip to the mall for her first bra. Awkward wouldn't even describe what they both felt walking into the popular lingerie store. Thankfully, the store manager took pity on him and guided them both through the process. Logan soothed their fragile minds by going for ice cream afterwards.

He acknowledged having a person for Fiona to go to, someone younger and not her father, would make it easier for his daughter. It was one reason they were having dinner tonight as a threesome. He knew he should have cooked, but he grabbed their servings from the main house and had the meatloaf, roasted potatoes and veggies warming in the oven. He wanted Naomi to have a quiet night without the questions.

Logan strolled to the front of the house and found Fiona in the den with the seven-week old puppies. The mothers, Rosebud, Tulip, and Bluebell were playing with toys.

"Make sure you wash your hands," he said as he walked past. "Did you do your homework at your grandparents?"

The slap of bare feet followed a few moments later. "Yes, I did my homework. Nana wouldn't let me help with the cats until I did."

"She did the same thing with me and your uncles when we were in school." Logan lined the dog dishes up on the counter. "Grab the food, please."

"What time is Naomi coming over?"

"In about fifteen minutes. Shorty, Mika, and Tam are eating there first."

Before they left Naomi's practice, Thomas sent a text explaining he told Fiona why he picked her up. Logan wanted to be open for her to ask questions before Naomi arrived.

"Did your grandfather tell you what happened this afternoon?"

"He said the Walter guy harassed Naomi at the clinic, and he stepped in to save her." Fiona snipped open the shrink wrap packets. "When he told the story to grandma and Ms. Maeve, they rolled their eyes about the hero part."

Logan howled with laughter. "Knowing your grandfather, the only thing missing from his story was a red cape. I saw the tape of what happened and he's not wrong. He stood with Naomi but it never became physical."

Fiona kept her eyes on the bowls as she dished out the portion for the pups. "Is she okay?"

"It shook her up, but she stood tall against him."

"I'm as tall as she is, unless she has her hair up."

Logan nodded. He wanted to ease into the next part. "I told her I love her today. You know that doesn't mean I don't love you."

"Geez, Dad. I'm not a child. I know it's okay for you to love someone other than me. The two loves are different." She gave him a side look. "Why would you even tell me? I thought you said it a while ago."

Fiona picked up the two bowls and padded her way to the den, leaving Logan to follow her. He sat the bowls in front of the mothers and pugs while Fiona placed the bowl in the puppy enclosure.

"I told you in case you had questions or wanted to talk about feelings you may have about my relationship with Naomi, moving to the next level."

The scandalous look his daughter shot him made him take a step back. "Please don't say 'moving to the next level' again. That's gross."

Logan realized how the comment sounded and quickly clarified his meaning. "What I'm saying is today, Pop-Pop referred to Naomi as his future daughter-in-law. Is that something you'd be okay with?"

"Oh." Fiona leaned against the built-in cabinet that held the extra blankets and pads for the dogs. "I assumed that's where this was going, anyway. I never held the ridiculous dream that you and Mom were getting back together. She's already moved on. I thought you were hoping she would return."

"Yeah, no. I never thought or wanted that." Logan didn't lie to his daughter, but there were some conversations they didn't have. "I guess I just wanted to make sure you were okay if I decided in a few months to ask Naomi to marry me."

"You're making this into a thing, Dad. I told you I like Naomi a lot. I'm cool with you marrying her. Make sure she knows I want to be a bridesmaid."

He wrapped his arm around her slender shoulders and kissed the top of her head. "I'm sure that won't be a problem. Let's finish changing everything out before she gets here."

While the dogs ate, the two made quick work of putting clean pads down and changing out the blankets on the dog beds. By the time they returned to the kitchen, Naomi was letting herself into the house.

"Hi sweetheart," Logan said as he wiped his hands on a towel. Shorty, Mika, and Tam were already greeting their four-legged friends.

"Hi Naomi." Fiona waved and giggled when the dogs converged on her. "Can I take them outside for a bit?"

"Take them out back. We're eating in ten minutes." Logan shook his head as they took off towards the fenced-in yard through the den. "Do you want something to drink?"

"Yes, please." She made her way to the kitchen and wrapped her arms around his waist. "Thank you for today."

He held her tight. "You're welcome. Even though you don't need to thank me. I was worried sick when Dad told me what he saw and had to see for myself you were okay."

"I have to admit, it scared me. Even though I knew Izzy had texted Mike, we didn't know how long it would take him to get there." She rested her chin on his chest, looking into his eyes. "I think she was disappointed Thomas didn't hit him."

The laugh that came from his chest felt good. He kissed her forehead and took a step back. "In school, Izzy was that student that egged fights on and was right up front when they happened. I think it came from growing up with only brothers."

"I was kinda hoping, too."

"If he was there when I arrive, I would have given what you wanted." He flipped the cap off her beer bottle and handed it to her. "Maybe I could drive you and Fiona in the morning, or let you drive my truck."

Naomi shook her head and took a sip of her drink before she answered. "You help me get into the truck as it is. I would have to press myself against the steering wheel in order to drive." She patted his chest. "Thank you, but no. Besides, I am keeping the clinic closed tomorrow."

It took every ounce of willpower not to pump his fist. Instead, he went back to rinsing the dog bowls off and setting them in a sink of soapy hot water.

"Why? I don't want you to be afraid of going to your clinic."

Naomi placed a sheet of paper on the counter and nudged him aside with her hip to take over the dishwashing. Logan dried his hands and picked up the paper.

"What's this? It's from the county."

"Yep. The county wants to buy the land the clinic and house are on. They received word about the damage. I guess from the county DA. It appears they tried to buy the land ten years ago to extend the protected wooded area. Since Walter didn't agree with the purpose, he refused. I believe if the price was right, he would have considered it."

Logan read the letter and scowled when he reached the third paragraph. "They advised him to shore up the foundation when inspectors and surveyors came out. That's when they offered to buy it."

Naomi drained the sink before leaning against the counter next to him, drying her hands. "After I read the letter, I called the preservation office and made an appointment to talk to them tomorrow. I had three patients on the schedule for yearly exams and asked Izzy to call and reschedule."

"Are you thinking about taking them up on their offer?" Logan had ideas which included moving her practice on the property. His gut told him she wouldn't go for that and kept it to himself.

She exhaled and took a seat at the table. "I am. It's been hard seeing the house when I go to the office. After next week, it will be even harder seeing an empty spot. It's just a reminder of what he did to me. I'm finding myself checking every floor in the clinic to see if there are noticeable cracks."

Logan understood that. He wondered how she handled going to the clinic for the past month. Logan wanted to ask before the demolition but was glad she shared her feelings with him.

"I'd be happy to go with you. Just let me know what time."

Fiona took that moment to come inside and flopped in the chair next to Naomi. Her gaze darted between the two, but Logan spoke before she could say anything. "Would you mind giving us a minute, squirt?"

Naomi shook her head, resting her hand on Fiona's arm to stop her from getting up. "She can stay. She'll hear about it tomorrow from someone. I'd rather her hear it from me."

"Please tell me you're not leaving Oak Mountain." Fear flickered in his daughter's eyes. Logan realized that could be a possibility and fought to control his rapid heartbeat. Naomi offered a soft smile.

"No, I'm not leaving town. I'm thinking about selling the land the clinic is on." She turned her attention to Logan. "I've been considering renting a small storefront downtown. I never really enjoyed being in that part of town. Being closer to everything would be easier for my patient and I'd feel more like I'm part of the community."

Fiona kept her eyes on the table. "Would you look for a place that had an apartment above it?"

Logan understood what she was asking. Naomi shook her head. "No. I like it here. You, your father, and family are here. After today, I'm sure your grandfather would lock me in my house if I mention leaving."

"I'd help him, too," Logan added, causing her to give him a flirty smile. She turned her attention back to Fiona.

"As I mentioned the other day, Hawkins Ridge feels like home. Your father and I are working towards a future together. Marriage will not happen next month, but we love one another." Naomi met his eyes as he joined them at the table. "We still have a lot to learn, but I don't see me leaving."

"She's right. We're working towards that step." Logan clasped Naomi's hand. "For now, that means her living across the way, spending as much time together as a family, and making sure her old house is taken care of first. That's when we can move forward."

Fiona nodded. "Good. Now that it's settled, can we eat?

Logan pressed his lips to Naomi's before rising to his feet. "Yep. Grab the plates."

Naomi took care of the silverware while asking Fiona about her day. Logan exhaled a deep breath. An idea of doing something special formed in his head. He pulled his phone from his pocket and tapped a quick text to his mother. Once he received confirmation, he glanced at his two loves talking in hushed tones.

This was the life he wanted when he met Fiona's mother. Now he had a woman he loved more than he thought was possible. His daughter cared for her and they were talking about a future together. Once she rid herself of Walter and the pain he caused her, they could move forward as a family.

Chapter 33

Naomi stood at the end of her walkway and inhaled, focusing on the rays peeking through the branches. The morning activity of the property bustled around her. Some may find the sound chaotic, but she found it settled her.

"Morning Naomi. You're getting a late start," Claire commented as she walked across the grass that separated their houses. "You're not sick, are you?"

Naomi liked the woman a lot. They'd started having evening teas on either porches once or twice a week, and on the weekends went for morning walks before they started their day. She didn't have a chance to update her about what happened yesterday.

Claire, about an inch taller than Naomi, stopped in front of her. Her furrowed brows disappeared behind the frames of her glasses. Naomi offered a genuine smile and shook her head.

"No. I'm fine. It was late when I left Logan's last night, so I haven't told you what happened." Naomi gave an abridged story of everything while she waited for Maeve. Claire's jaw dropped when she finished.

"Unbelievable. But you're okay? He didn't hurt you?" Claire's gaze roamed over Naomi's face. "I'm glad I never met the man."

Like Naomi, Claire was new to Oak Mountain. Her cousin lived in town and recommended her for the job with Logan.

"Believe me, you're better off not knowing him." Naomi looked over her shoulder when the front door opened and Maeve tossed a wave to Claire. "Why don't we talk more later? I'm going to help with the rescue this afternoon."

Before Claire could answer, a larger ATV pulled up beside them. Jace tipped his worn baseball cap to them. Though he wore sunglasses, Naomi could see his eyes never left Claire.

"Morning ladies. I'm heading up to the stables. You want me to take the dogs, Naomi?"

"Caden already picked them up. Thank you for the offer."

"Anytime. You look nice, Claire. Y'all have a good day," Jace offered another grin before pulling off. Maeve had joined their group by then.

"Why don't you put that boy out of his misery and just go on a date with him?" Maeve commented.

Naomi didn't miss the flush of her friend's cheeks, but Claire shook her head, her dark ponytail whishing in the wind.

"Jace is a flirt. The short time I've been here, I heard about his reputation. He's not serious and I can't act like I am. Besides coming from different backgrounds, I'm not his type. I'm short, round, wear glasses, with burns on her arm, who prefers the company of animals over people. I'm not someone the face of Hawkins Ridge wants on their arm." Claire spared one last look in the direction Jace rolled off to. "No, friends is all I can offer him. Good luck today. I'll see you when you get back."

Naomi and Maeve watched Claire pass Logan's home and turn onto the pathway for the clinic. Anyone could see Jace's feelings were true. Anyone but Claire. She hoped her friend wasn't throwing away a chance at happiness because of her past.

"Ready?" Maeve pushed past her daughter and walked towards the main house.

Naomi wanted to have breakfast with the Becketts and tell them about the letter. Maeve suggested Josie may know of storefronts available for rent, or at least the name of a realtor she could trust. She had to wait for Logan to return from taking Fiona to school. Naomi might as well eat.

The two stepped into the mudroom and quickly wiped their feet. Thomas greeted them with a smile.

"Well, this is a treat," he said to Naomi, giving her a hug. Maeve walked past him and went to the tablet on the counter to clock in.

"You act like you haven't seen me in days." The smell of bacon had her stomach growling. "What can I help you with?"

"Nothing, we're bringing everything to the table." Josie said, coming into the kitchen and wrapped her arms around her. "Grab a cup of coffee. Are you okay after yesterday?"

Naomi knew Thomas would tell his family. If he hadn't, Logan would've. She didn't mind. Following her instructions, Naomi pulled two mugs for her and Maeve from the cabinet and poured coffee.

"I'm fine. There is something I wanted to talk to you and Thomas about."

She passed the hot beverage to her mother and headed to the table.

Thomas set a plate near him. "You take my advice on closing for today?"

"No, but I needed to close for another reason." Naomi waited until they'd settled and started passing the cheesy scrambled eggs, smothered potatoes, and bacon around before she spoke. "I got a letter in the mail from the county. They want to buy my land."

She pulled the folded envelope from her pocket and slid it to Thomas. While he read, she gave the abridged version while slathering preserves on her biscuits.

"So Logan is going to go with me to see if it's a reasonable offer. We're then going to stop past my lawyer to give him a copy of the letter, since it shows they told Walter about the foundation years ago."

"Had you thought about selling before this?" Josie asked, setting the paper on the table.

"Honestly, I didn't know what I wanted to do. Seeing the house every day is hard. Once it's gone next week, it will be worse. It just reminds me of everything Walter has done and how stupid I was for listening to him." Naomi hadn't admitted the last part to anyone. Maeve vehemently shook her head.

"You weren't stupid. He manipulated you and your trust. What happened wasn't your fault." Maeve reached for her daughter's hand. "I wouldn't wish what you're going through on my worst enemy, but look at the blessings that have come from it."

Her mother was right. She needed to look for the positive. Naomi believed in karma and things happening for a reason. Her life was over in Oklahoma and she didn't have a path to where she should go. Moving to Oak Mountain was the best decision. Even as hard as Walter tried to keep her from the Becketts, they found a way to each other.

The back door opened with the sound of heavy boots clomping across the floor. Logan appeared a moment later, a cheerful smile brightening his face.

He made his way to her in three long strides and pressed his lips to hers. She could get used to starting the morning like this.

"Morning darlin'. Everyone."

"Good to see you have your priorities," Thomas teased. "There's a plate set for you. Naomi was filling us in on your plans for the morning."

Logan rested his cap on the post of his chair and reached for the platter of eggs after taking a seat. "I noticed a few for rent signs when I took Fi to school."

Naomi explained. "I have no intention of giving up my practice, so I wanted to look for a place in town. It would be better for my patients." She turned her attention to Josie. "That's what I wanted to ask you and Thomas. If you know of a real estate agent, you trust."

Both nodded, but it was Josie that spoke. "We'll have that information before you head out."

Naomi gave her thanks and tucked into her meal. The table fell into a light conversation about what needed to be done that weekend. Warmth flowed through her heart when they included her in their plans.

Finding a second family was not on Naomi's list when she moved to Oak Mountain. She would have laughed at anyone if they told her she'd have another chance at love.

Logan nuzzled her temple when he placed an extra piece of bacon on her plate, giving her a saucy wink.

Maybe she could thank Walter for something after all.

Naomi watched cars zip up and down the city street as she waited for Logan to climb into the truck. The death grip on the brown envelope was her reminder it wasn't a dream.

They'd just left her lawyer, a two-block walk from the municipal office. Now that she had the time to digest everything, she could finally make sense of what had occurred. Logan climbed into the truck and turned the ignition just enough to lower the windows.

"You've been quiet since we left the meeting." Logan gently pried a hand from the envelope and ran his thumb over her palm. "Talk to me."

"I'm still turning everything over in my mind." Naomi turned in her seat to face him and held up the envelope. "That just happened, right? This offer is genuine and what the lawyer said was true."

Naomi had a hard time wrapping her head around the six-figure offer from the county. In addition, her lawyer informed her Walter, and the inspector were facing criminal charges with papers and arrest happening that day. The investigation by the insurance company led to the county to learn Walter had sold the land. His argument that he didn't know about the foundation proven to be a lie. The money would allow Naomi to pay off her business loan and the balance on the house.

Logan held her gaze. "Yes, everything happened and you aren't dreaming. You've had a lot thrown at you in less than two hours. It's normal to let everything sink in before deciding on your next step."

Naomi nodded. "I know. Even though the lawyer has a copy of the offer, I want to look at it again with fresh eyes tomorrow. Unless something raises a red flag, I plan on signing it. I'm ready to move forward, put everything Walter touched behind me."

He leaned across the middle console and pressed his lips to hers. Naomi let loose a contented sigh into the kiss, making him smile.

"I love you, darlin'."

"I love you too, baby." Naomi gave him another quick peck before placing her purse and envelope on the floor. "I wanted to get your opinion on something."

Logan started the truck and backed out of the spot. "Lay it on me."

Naomi mentally tossed around ideas for the past week, but kept it to herself while she worked out the details. If she and Logan were planning a future together, she wanted his opinion.

"The practice is doing well, but I still have slow days, like today. I'm thinking about offering doggie day care or doing a mobile vet once a week. The day care would depend on if I found a rental with a large enough outdoor space. Maybe help at the rescue more."

Logan was quiet as he maneuvered around a double parked delivery truck. It took him a minute to respond.

"The selfish part of me would pick the rescue because we'd spend more time together."

"You're a softy like that," she teased.

Logan chuckled before turning serious. "There are positives about the other options and both would benefit the working families in town. It's why we let staff bring their dogs with them if they want." Logan tapped his chin while they waited for a red light. "Most families don't have the extra money for something like day care. I think either assisting at the rescue or offer mobile services."

The light turned green and Logan made a left onto the ramp for the highway.

"How about I do both?" Naomi fought the urge to bounce in her seat. "Mobile services on weekends or maybe two weekends a month. I can set up a schedule for the rescue and then plan the clinic hours. Izzy wants to spend more time with her children and we could probably figure out something she could do at home so she can work her full hours."

"That, darlin', is an excellent idea." He pressed a soft kiss on their still joined hands. "Why don't we head home? I have a surprise for you."

Home. Naomi liked the sound of that.

Chapter 34

Workers bustled with their daily routines when Logan parked next to his house. He told Claire and Sam before they left, he would be around that afternoon but wanted to do something special for Naomi before he reported in.

The woman beside him had a lot thrown at her in the past twenty-four hours. He wanted to give her a chance to take a mental break and just enjoy being together.

"I thought we could have a picnic for lunch. We'll take the ATV to a part of the property you haven't seen yet," he said as they climbed out.

Naomi hurried to meet him at the back of the truck and threw her arms around his waist. "A picnic sounds perfect."

He pressed his lips to her forehead, melting into her embrace. A loud throat clearing had them slowly pulling apart, their lips in sheepish grins.

"Hi Thomas." Naomi kept her arms around Logan's waist.

"Doc, Son. Celebrating?"

"You could say that. Logan is taking me on a picnic." She tilted her head. "I need to change. Ten minutes?"

"Take as much as you need. I will grab the food and change my shirt."

She stood on her tiptoes and gave him a quick peck. "You can fill your dad in."

Logan watched as she speed walked to her house, disappearing when she closed the door. He felt his father's gaze bore into his temple and turned to meet the twinkle in his eyes.

"You got it bad, son."

"Yep. Not even going to lie or deny it." Logan patted his father's shoulder as he walked past. "I've cared about women in the past and I loved Kaylee to a certain extent. I can honestly say I didn't know love until Naomi."

Thomas fell into step beside him as he headed to the main house. "Having a mature partner who has the same goals makes it easier. Tell me what happened."

Logan filled him in as they stepped into the mudroom. He grabbed one of the Hawkins Ridge T-shirts from the shelf where they kept extras. He finished the tale by the time he slipped on the shirt.

Thomas shook his head. "So Mike told the truth when he said they were thinking about criminal charges. I still don't understand why Walter did it."

Logan shrugged. "The lawyer thinks the deception was only about control. Walter knew Naomi's husband and family before he met her. It could have very well been a way to punish her for taking her ex to court and winning."

"That's exactly what it was," Maeve commented as she stepped into the kitchen. "Walter tried to talk her out of suing John for defamation and said she should just take the divorce settlement and start over. Thank goodness my daughter listened to me. Two weeks after she won, Walter approached her with the offer on the practice. I knew it was a way for her to leave Oklahoma, so I encouraged her to take it."

Logan wrapped an arm around Maeve. "Thank you for giving her the push. I wouldn't have found her if you hadn't."

"Oak Mountain turned out to be a godsend. Naomi found her confidence again. She's building friendships." Maeve flashed a soft smile at Logan. "She's found love. My daughter is being blessed for dealing with four years of trials and pain. Despite my strong desire to coat Walter in salmon and honey and drop in a cluster of bears, I appreciate that his deceitfulness that enabled my baby to blossom."

Logan shuddered before Thomas cleared his throat. "We're all grateful to have you and Doc in our lives. You should get going. Naomi said ten minutes."

Logan gave Maeve a good squeeze, then headed to the fridge to grab the meal of chicken salad sandwiches, cucumber salad, and cookies. He slipped them into a picnic basket sitting on the counter, which held a thermos of iced tea.

"If anyone is looking for us, we'll be back in an hour."

Logan jogged to the ATV next to the clinic and sat the basket in the back. Naomi strolled up as he pulled the blanket out of the storage box from his truck. She kept the black jeans she wore earlier but changed into a long sleeve T-shirt and sneakers.

"Ready?" He held out his hand, and she linked her fingers. "Ready."

Logan guided her to the ATV and thought of what Maeve said. Naomi had indeed blossomed. Her feistiness when they first met attracted him, but getting to see and know the real woman warmed his heart and was eager for their future.

Naomi thought she had seen all of Hawkins Ridge, but when Logan turned to go through a crop of trees past the stables, she knew that wasn't the case.

"We'll pick up the dogs on our way back," he said as they slowed to maneuver through a trail marked for horses and the fleet of ATV.

Less than two minutes later, they cleared the trees and came upon a clearing with a view of the east side of town. Several down trees surrounded a fire pit.

"This is amazing." Naomi climbed out and made her way to the front bumper. "Do you all use this place a lot in the summer?"

Logan stopped beside her and wrapped his arm around her waist. "We do. It's for everyone at Hawkins Ridge to use. There's a drop off about a yard that way." He pointed towards town, then pointed to his right. "There's fencing there, which is for the other farm. The only way you can access it is through our property. The alarm system and Caden are the first defense on this side."

Naomi had questions, but they could wait. She wanted to enjoy this time with Logan. The day's activities caught up with her when she changed her clothes. The reality of putting the damaged property behind her became real. She looked at the offer again before setting it in her mother's room, in case she came home before Naomi could talk to her.

The future of her practice and where she wanted to take it also weighed on her. Giving it up wasn't an option. It warmed her heart when Logan didn't ask or press her to devote more time to his goals. They had a future together. She wouldn't deny that. Their plans for Hawkins Ridge did not involve her clinic. Naomi had to figure out a way her practice supported the family and not give it up.

"What's for lunch?" She asked, bringing herself back to the present.

Logan kissed her temple before retrieving the basket. He rattled off the list as they worked to set up their lunch on a log.

"How are you feeling after today?" Logan asked as he handed her a sandwich.

Naomi sighed. "I'm not sure. Happy that the sale would eliminate my debt. Sad that I never knew the man that I considered a friend. Nervous about taking on a new adventure with my practice." She rested her hand on his thigh. "Thankful I had you with me."

He grasped her hand and brought it to his lips. "I'll always be there for you. Everything you're feeling is valid, and no one would expect you to feel otherwise. I'm glad you're taking the weekend to process it all."

Squirrels darted from under a bush and chased each other up a tree. A soft smile graced Naomi. "I haven't been in Oak Mountain a year and so much has changed in that short time. Most of it for the best." She gave him a flirty wink. "Some for the worst."

"That's a good way to look at it. Had you stayed in Oklahoma, do you think you would have discovered the truth about Walter?"

"That's a good question." Naomi turned to face him better. "I think I would have, but not before he caused insurmountable damage to my career. Even with his efforts to keep me from your family. I think it wasn't so much his dislike for you, but knowing your family would shed light on his actions. The day he saw me packing and learned we were dating, he knew he lost."

"I agree. Walter wanted to be your lifeline and control you. He easily manipulated Kaylee because this wasn't the life she wanted. He misjudged your strength and determination to make Oak Mountain work. Now he has to answer for everything."

"I'm still keeping the lawsuit, even though they are bringing criminal charges."

"Good. Even if you decide to drop it, I would support you." Logan rested his forehead on hers. "I love you. We have a life together in front of us."

"I love you too." She leaned forward to get a quick taste of his lips, but the sound of the walkie talkie interrupted them.

"Logan? You there?"

Naomi recognized Claire's voice and the end of their quiet time together. Logan gave her a quick peck and reached inside the basket to pull out the radio.

"Yep."

"Sorry to bother you, but we got a shelter from two towns over wanting to see if you have time to check out a few animals. They're having an adoption event this weekend and their regular vet is sick."

Naomi perked up. "I can go with you if you want to see them."

The love in Logan's eyes swelled her heart. "Get the information. Tell them I'll be there as soon as I can and Dr. Hendrix will be with me."

Claire's chuckle echoed in the air. "Sure thing."

They cleaned up their mess, and Naomi spared one last look at the view of town. This was her new life. One with a man and the daughter she loved. A second family who treated her as one of their own. The opportunity to live her dreams caring for animals.

Logan linked his fingers with hers and guided her back to the ATV. A life she always meant to have.

CHAPTER 35

The playful yips and yaps from the pack had Logan grinning while he sipped his morning coffee. He wanted to enjoy the rare Friday morning indulgence and get his mind right, so he could be the rock Naomi needed.

Today was the demolition day of her house.

It'd been a week since they left the county office. Naomi took a few days to read everything and talk to her lawyer to see if she missed any fine points. The offer was straightforward, and she signed the contract yesterday. Barring any surprises during their inspection and land survey, she would sign the final sale papers in forty-five days and move her practice in sixty.

To say his woman was nervous was an understatement.

The sound of boots crunching on the packed gravel drew his attention. A soft smile graced his lips as he moved over on the bench to make room for his mother.

"This is a surprise." He gave her a peck on the cheek. "Sorry I didn't show for breakfast."

"I didn't expect you to. It was just your father, Owen, and Sam, so we kept it simple with oatmeal, fruit, and yogurt. Has Fiona forgiven you?"

Logan snorted. "She still didn't understand why she had to go to school. I get she wanted to be with Naomi for today, and we appreciate it. But, she had finals."

"She loves her," Josie simply stated. "She already sees her as a stepmother."

"I know. Naomi tries to hide how happy she is about that, but I see the glow when they're outside with the dogs or when they do the dishes together." Logan rested his forearms on his thighs. "They're good together."

"When are you going to make it official?"

Logan took a gulp of his coffee to buy time. He wanted to ask her the day they left the lawyers when she mentioned spending more time with the rescue. It wasn't the right time, and he didn't have a ring. They've only known each other for a short time. Yes, having her yards away and seeing her every day it felt longer. He didn't doubt Naomi was the woman he wanted to spend the rest of his life with. The reason he hadn't…

"I want her to get past Walter and what he did," he answered. "Today will make him part of her past. Once the land is out of her name and she moves her practice into a location *she* wants, then we can take the next step in our future."

Josie nodded. "That makes sense."

They sat in silence for a minute, watching the pack find their spots in the early sun beam to rest. Logan gave his mother a side glance and chuckled at the look on her face. "What else is on your mind, Mom?"

"You know there are times you're not my favorite."

"None of us are your favorite. You claim you love us equally."

"True." Josie linked her arm with his. "I know your father talked to you about fully taking over in a year. Owen has put his procedures in a binder. That means Sam will take a step back as well. Is Claire up to taking his role? Do you have an idea how many new employees we will need to expand the sanctuary and product line? We also think you and Naomi should take over the main house when you get married."

Logan pulled off his cap and tugged the ends of his hair. "I haven't talked to everyone, but I know Caden put together a plan for the therapy dog training. Jace understands he has to leave the fire department unless it's a genuine emergency and find someone to help with the marketing and social media. Noah …" He shook his head, grinning. "He wants to do a lot and we need to reel him in."

Josie joined her son in laughter. "Owen said Noah has a lot of ideas because he doesn't have a woman to direct his energy. And Claire?"

"Claire is ready. She's come out of her shell since she's been here. Naomi is good for her as well. I worry Jace will scare her off. If he truly cares for her, I will do what I can to make that happen. If he sees her as a challenge and gets bored when he wins it, that won't be good for either of them."

"I agree." Josie ran her hands down a mastiff who came to say hi. "I think his feelings are real. Your brother isn't used to women not falling all over themselves to get his attention. Before either of them can pursue their obvious attraction, both need to get out of their heads others are judging them. For Jace, by their looks, or in Claire's case, her scars."

Logan agreed. Jace was smart and had the business brain of the family. People didn't see that. They saw the good looks, friendly personality and women falling in his lap. Only his family saw the big heart, hard worker and loyalty. Naomi, spending time with Claire, helped them both to build a friendship outside of a family member.

He checked his watch when two employees stepped into the dog run area. The pack hurried over to greet their friends. Logan held his hand out to help his mother stand.

"Are you riding with Naomi and I to watch the demolition? The realtor wants to show her two places afterwards."

Josie nodded. "I'm going to let the fact you didn't answer about moving into the main house go for now. Hawkins Ridge is changing. Your father, Owen, and I are ready to pass it on."

Since childhood, Logan and his brothers understood they would take over the family property one day. As much as he wanted to wait, they all knew the time was now to make the move. It was the next generation he worried about.

The only grandchild now was Fiona. His brothers wanted families, but were they running out of time? Logan shook his head and split off from his mother when he stopped in front of Naomi's house, agreeing to meet at his truck in twenty minutes.

For today, Logan's only focus was being there for Naomi as they took a step towards their future.

The warmth of Logan's hand grounded Naomi as she watched the dozer make the initial swing into the house she thought would be her new beginning. She, Logan, Maeve, Josie and

Thomas stood outside his truck in the lot across the street. The contractor took care to protect the clinic from potential damage. It took four weeks for the insurance company to get permits, have the land surveyed, hire a licensed contractor, and move the rest of her belongings into storage.

In her heart, it wasn't enough time to reconcile the betrayal, but she was getting better.

Naomi turned to Logan as the front loader attacked her roof. "Can we go?"

He pressed his lips to the crown of her head. "Of course."

Naomi normally would take the front seat, but she wanted to sit in the back with Maeve and Josie. Logan and Thomas helped them in before climbing in the front. Silence filled the cab as he drove toward town.

Naomi didn't think she could do any of this without the love and support of Logan and his family. She wondered if it was still just her and Maeve, if she would have just packed up and moved again. Dread course through her at the thought. Naomi believed everything happened for a reason. Now wasn't the time to wallow in self-pity and second guessing. It was time to move forward with the man driving the car and the family that came to stand beside her when she needed it.

"Thank you for being there. I'm sorry for leaving. I thought I had it in me to see the entire thing." Naomi shrugged. "I just want to be done with everything. Going to the clinic on Tuesday is going to be hard."

The contractor wanted the weekend to level the property and estimated a week the clear the debris. For safety reasons, she wanted as much cleared before she allowed her patients back on the property.

"You don't need to apologize, darlin'." Logan reached through the opening in the front seat and gave her knee a squeeze. "I'm proud of you for trying."

Thomas nodded. "No one would expect you to pop open a bottle of champagne while doing a jig, Doc."

Maeve clutched her hand. "You said it yourself. You are moving past the hurt. Seeing some of it told you it was okay to stay on that path for a new life. Walter tried to keep you the same person you were in Oklahoma. But remember, you are strong and worthy of every goodness. After today, he doesn't get another minute of your time. You have love, a new supportive tribe, and an opportunity to do what you love on your own terms."

Josie nodded from her other side, wrapping an arm around her shoulder. Deep down, their words and love healed her soul. Naomi wasn't the woman who moved to Oak Mountain eight months ago. She was a survivor. She could handle going to the clinic for two months.

Like a freight train, a thought slammed into Naomi's head and took root. "Can we stop at the coffee shop? I just had an idea." She nodded to herself, hope blossoming in her chest. "I want to toss this around with you all."

Logan met her gaze in the rearview mirror, his lips up-turned. "Anything you want."

Naomi blew him a kiss as she worked the logistics in her mind. Thomas began talking about having a cookout the next day. If it worked, she could put the past behind her.

Ten minutes later, Logan parked in front of the shop. It was a block from where they were supposed to meet the realtor in forty-five minutes. Everyone piled out and gathered on the sidewalk to have a quick chat with a man the Becketts knew. Logan held her hand while they exchanged pleasantries before making their way inside. After placing their orders for coffee and a pastry assortment, they found a table near the window and settled in.

"What's working in that mind of yours, Doc?" Thomas never one to beat around the bush.

Naomi took a deep breath and spoke. "I don't want to go back to the clinic." She held up her hand when it looked like everyone would say something. The server delivered their coffees and plate of bite-size danishes. After offering thanks, she continued.

"I also don't want to close while I wait for the sale to finalize with the county. I would risk losing patients if they started going to the vet a town over. So, I was thinking about having my customers come to the clinic at Hawkins Ridge, and those that don't want to make the trip, I would use the screening van you have once a week to go out to them." She turned her attention to Thomas. "This means I pay rent and we draw up a contract."

"You are family and don't need to pay rent."

Naomi shook her head. "I'm not a Beckett yet. When Logan and I get married and I take the name, then we can talk—"

"I thought it was too early to bring up marriage," Logan said from the side of her. "You know where I stand."

"What part of working towards a future wasn't clear?" She rolled her eyes. "I love you and thought it was a drawn out conclusion. I figured a proposal would be soon." Naomi ignored Maeve and Josie's cheese eating grins and barreled forward.

"So, yes, Thomas and Josie, I would like something in writing if we agree with this idea. I would like to call my patients scheduled for next week and send out an email for the rest. Isabella is closer to Hawkins Ridge than the other location, so I'm sure she would be on board. I'd also need to take an inventory of what I would need." Naomi snagged two packets of sugar for her coffee and tore off the top. "What do you think?"

"You thought of all that in the last fifteen minutes?" Thomas met Logan's gaze. "You didn't talk about this ahead of time?"

His son shook his head. "This is new to me as well. We talked about helping part time at the sanctuary and doing the mobile van once or twice a month on the weekend." Logan kissed Naomi's temple. "I think it's a good idea. Primarily, we use the clinic for the pack and new rescues. You won't even need the van if it's a simple exam or vaccination. You can use your car and write off the mileage, or the small truck."

"She'd need to update her practice insurance for house calls. We can also offer free bags of treats if patients agree to come to the property." Josie tapped her chin before turning her comment to Thomas. "She's right about putting something in writing. This is her business. After what she just went through, it makes sense she would want to do this on her own terms."

Naomi wanted to keep her business separate when she and Logan were married, but now wasn't the time to bring it up. Thomas held up his hands in a surrender pose, a cheese Danish pinched in his fingers.

"I'm not saying it's not a good idea. It is. I'm just wrapping my head around charging you, but I get why you need to do it." The elder Beckett nodded. "Let's iron out the details when we get back."

"Seriously?" Naomi held Logan's gaze. "You're okay with me being there, in your space more?"

"Of course. If I could spend every minute of the day with you, I would." He rested his cheek on the crown of her head. "I love you. It's an excellent idea and one that will work."

Naomi melted into his embrace and gave a mental fist pump. It was time to move out of the past and work towards a successful future.

Chapter 36

Loud laughter, ribbing and undeniable happiness filled the Beckett's enormous kitchen and eating area. Logan took a moment to take in the scene.

He cared for every person who shared dinner with them. Even Harold Smith, who looked at Maeve with hearts in his eyes.

Shaking his head, he stepped into the walk-in pantry in search of popcorn kernels. He had an overnight movie marathon planned with his two favorite girls and the dogs. It was a Friday night he could get used to. Thomas strolled in just as he located the container.

"I'll bring this back tomorrow."

His father offered a dismissive wave and reached for the canister of shortbread cookies. "Take it. We're not planning on popcorn tonight."

"What are you doing?"

After grabbing the pretzels, Thomas grinned. "It's couples' game night. The last time we played, Owen and Sam won. Your mother and I need to redeem ourselves, even though Maeve and Harold are talking a lot of smack."

"Just as long as you stay away from the moonshine, you should have fun."

Logan and Caden got a hold of one of Harold's special brews after Logan's divorce was final. Three sips and he and his brother saw stars.

"Maeve's been good for him. You know he made his creations for himself, family and a few close friends. But now he only has a taste or two a month. He's back to focusing on his crops. His kids see the difference in him."

"That's good news. He fell hard and fast for Maeve."

Thomas held his son with a look. "I could say the same for you."

He couldn't stop the curve that graced his lips if he tried. Logan glanced and Naomi laughing with her mother and Harold. "I know I have. I'm sure the feeling is mutual."

He walked past his father and stopped at the island to pocket a lemon for Naomi's tea. He met her gaze, a silent request for them to get their night started.

"Doc is a strong woman. I'm glad you found her. She's good for this family." Thomas turned his attention to Caden, Jace and Noah as they stepped out of the cat sanctuary. "Now we just need to find women for them."

"I think Jace has found his. Noah will be more open now that Jace is becoming a homebody." Logan studied the middle Beckett brother. "I'm not sure there's a woman in Oak Mountain for Caden."

Thomas snorted. "Of course there isn't. You and Jace found women not from here. Your brother won't know what hit him when that woman comes to town.

Logan agreed and motioned for Fiona that it was time to go. Everyone said their goodbyes and made plans for breakfast to dole out the weekend chores. He held the back door open for

Naomi as they followed his brothers out. Fiona darted past them, making her way to their house.

"I'm going to change and get everything ready," she yelled, flinging the screen door open.

"Hold it." Logan's voice had Fiona skidding to a stop. He held out the container for her to take. "See if the pads for the pups need to be changed and let them out back first."

Fiona agreed. Tulip, Rosebud, and Bluebell darted out before the screen slammed shut.

Naomi wrapped her arms around Logan's waist. "She reminds me of Jace some days."

"And I take that as a compliment." the youngest Beckett tipped an invisible cap.

Logan shook his head and peered down at the love of his life.

"I'm proud of you for standing your ground with Dad." He gave her lips a quick peck. "See you in an hour?"

"Yep. I'll bring the jerky and homemade Chex Mix." She waved to the men as she strolled across the gravel road.

He turned to find his brothers smirking. Logan didn't have time for teasing. He needed to change into comfortable clothes, but wanted to touch base first.

"Save the teasing for later," he admonished.

"Why would you assume we'd give you a hard time?" Noah said, taking a seat on the bench in the yard. "I just wanted to say how impressive Naomi was with Thomas."

It'd been a few hours since their discussion at the coffee shop. True to Naomi's word, she came home and wrote a simple agreement. Ironing out the rent amount took the bulk of dinner. Both dug in, his father firm on a penny a month.

Eventually Thomas cave and they agreed on an eighth of what she would pay to rent a storefront in town.

"Remind me to bring her to my negotiations," Jace added when he squatted to pet Tulip.

Logan agreed before turning serious. "I just wanted to let you know Mom talked to me this morning. They're serious about taking a giant step into the shadows and giving us the reins."

He went into detail about his conversation, including her request for him and Naomi to move into the main house after marriage. Caden sat in a lounge chair, resting his arms on his thighs, and met each brother's gaze.

"Considering everything we want to do, we need to establish priorities. Like when *are* you popping the question?"

He rolled his eyes. "Soon. Today was the first time she mentioned us getting married. I knew we had the same end goal, but hearing her say it moved up my timetable."

"That makes sense." Caden grinned. "I got a call from Mike before dinner and said Izzy's excited about working here."

"I think her and Claire will get along," Logan smiled, thinking about their tattooed friend. "Back to what Caden said about priorities."

Noah nodded. "I think Jace shoring up partnerships with other sanctuaries and finding a replacement for Pops has to be at the top of the list."

"Agree." Logan turned his attention to his youngest brother. "We need you here full time. I know you want to be on call with the station for disasters, which is cool, but we can't expand without new contracts."

"I already told the station I needed to focus on what's happening here," Jace assured them. "Claire did some valuable research on local pet stores and organic markets. I started making calls today and setting up virtual introductions."

Logan needed Jace to stay focus. He remembered what Josie said about being seen past their outward appearance and kept quiet. Caden must have read his mind and spoke.

"I'm just going to say it. Claire is becoming like family. She's friends with Naomi and will take over for Sam. I think you two would be good together, but if this is a game, you need to stop. There's nothing wrong with being friends."

Jace linked his fingers behind his head. "I thought being friends first was a ridiculous idea, but you were right." He held Logan's attention. "I need to show her I'm more than the reputation her cousin told her I had. I'm willing to bide my time and chip at her walls if it means she'll give me a chance."

Well, I'll be. Jace is growing up, Logan thought. "Good enough. We'll do what we can to help."

Jace gave a nod of thanks. Noah held the end of a rope toy for Rosebud before sharing. "Just so you know, Pops and Sam are moving out of the main house before winter hits. He asked Ophelia to keep an eye out for anyone looking to take his place. He's confident we'll have everything up and running by next spring."

"Do they want to move off property?" Jace gave a quick glance to the main house. Noah shook his head.

"They want to get a modular because Thomas and Josie will probably take over Logan's place. Maeve and Harold are moving quick so that's only a matter of time."

His future mother-in-law and the moonshine farmer made each other laugh. The three older couples were thick as thieves and planned to do a lot of traveling together. Things were changing for everyone.

They stood as a group, the same way they had as kids. Logan had faith in his brothers. "Then let's show them we're ready to take over."

They grunted in approval and broke off, headed in different directions. Logan didn't doubt they were ready to step up. They each had different paths to make Hawkins Ridge their own.

Now it was time to get ready for a night with his new family.

Epilogue

*F*ive *months later*

Claire

"I now pronounce you husband and wife," Harold's voice boomed in the tent, as Logan wrapped his arm around Naomi and planted a hard kiss on her lips. No one knew the farmer went to theology school and held a license to perform weddings.

Claire wiped at her tears as the dogs barked when the crowd erupted in applause. Logan proposed two weeks after Naomi moved her practice to the property. Neither wanted a long engagement. Josie and Maeve planned the wedding in the short time and pulled it off without a hitch.

Fiona bounced with excitement when she met her uncle Caden so they could walk out of the first tent. Claire moved her flowers to her other arm as she met Jace at the end of the aisle. She linked her arm in his and tried to ignore the guest's eyes on her and the fruity smell of the man who haunted her dreams.

The Becketts erected two tents near the greenhouse for the wedding. A small one for the ceremony and a larger one for the reception. Jace guided Claire to the empty tiny home off to the side used for workers. Today, it was for the wedding party, parents and the couple's dogs.

"Are you okay?" Jace whispered when they stepped across the threshold. "Do you need something to drink?"

She shook her head, worried the small flowers in her updo would fall out. "I'm just happy for them."

Jace followed her eyes to the whispering couple. A warm smile graced his lips. "They look good together. I thought Logan wouldn't have another relationship until after Fiona went off to college. Definitely not with a woman who had a connection to Walter."

Claire nodded, taking a seat on a wooden straight-back chair. Jace leaned against the wall and crossed his legs at the ankles. "Having Walter out of the picture is a wedding gift for them."

The scoundrel made a plea deal with the district attorney for probation and a hefty fine. Since she sold the property to the county, Naomi had settled for less in her lawsuit. Walter and his wife lost their home to pay the money owed and moved two towns over in disgrace.

Isabella strolled over with Noah in tow and parked herself next to Claire. The two became friends since the move of Naomi's practice. Claire envied the colorful, outgoing woman in a good way. She made her laugh more and open up a little.

"How long do we have to wait for pictures?" Izzy looked around the room. "I'm ready to eat more than the finger foods they have out for us."

"The photographer is coming," Noah nodded to the window. "Do you want something to tide you over? The last thing I want is to turn you over to Mike with an empty stomach."

"You joke, but he knows how important keeping me well fed is." Izzy peered around him. "How about a brownie bite and two of the cream cheese pinwheels?"

"You want something, Buttercup?" Jace asked as he pushed himself off the wall. He'd taken to calling her the pet name after she wore a scrub top with the flowers on them.

"Water is fine." Heat rose to Claire's cheeks when her stomach chose that moment to growl.

"What do you want to eat? You know what, never mind, I'll bring something back."

Claire tucked her chin to her chest. She didn't want Jace to think she was one of those women that didn't eat in front of men. Why, she didn't know. They were friends. He'd stopped flirting with her, and though she was a little disappointed, she told herself it was okay. As she told Naomi, flirting was part of Jace's charm. He meant nothing by it. Izzy leaned closer and nudged Claire's arm.

"Please tell me you're not embarrassed to eat in front of him. Let me tell you, Jace likes a woman with a healthy appetite."

Claire gawked. "It had nothing to do with that. I was too nervous to eat earlier. I just pictured me tripping on the runner as I was walking down the aisle. Now I just thought I would wait until they served the late lunch. Besides, Jace and I are just friends."

"Really?" Izzy shook her head and patted Claire on the arm. "Keep telling yourself that. I've known Jace my entire life. The few female friends he's had, not once has he given them a pet name. Calling me Icky Izzy in second grade doesn't count."

Claire coughed out a laugh. That was something she could see him doing. Before she could comment, the photographer began gathering everyone just as Jace and Noah returned with small plates of appetizers. Isabella took her plate and shoved a pinwheel in her mouth as she stood.

"Nibble on these while we walk outside." Jace plucked a stuffed mushroom cap and held it in front of her lips. Confused, Claire opened her mouth for him to feed her. "If you were hungry, why didn't you say something? Do you have food in the house? We can go shopping this evening."

The earthy flavor of the appetizer lodged in her throat momentarily before she could swallow. "Why do you think I don't have food? Why would you even care?"

"Your stomach growled."

Claire rolled her eyes. "I didn't eat breakfast because I was nervous. I have food. Even if I didn't, I can buy my own."

"I didn't like hearing that sound. To answer your other question, Of course I care, why wouldn't I?" He held the door for her to step out into the autumn sun first. Claire squinted for a moment while her glasses darkened.

"I don't know. You confuse me sometimes."

Claire snagged a brownie bite and popped it in her mouth. Jace held her elbow, bringing her to a stop. The photographer had the wedding party stand to the side while she positioned Logan and Naomi for their couple photo. Claire sucked in a breath when Jace bent and held her gaze.

"I'm going to make this clear so there's no more confusion. I like you. For some unknown reason, you think that my compliments, the expression of how I feel, is a joke. I'm not kidding, Buttercup. I like everything about you. The way you talk to the dogs before you give them their medicine. How you nibble your lower lip when you measure out the cat's food. The way you twirl your hair around your finger when you're reading an email. How you wear your red rimmed glasses every Monday because you want to start the week off in a positive mood." Jace took a step closer. "The way your cheeks turn pink when I wink at you. So why I care is because I want more than what we have."

Despite being aware that her mouth was open, Claire couldn't remember how to close it. Jace was serious. Did he stop flirting so she could get to know him better? When he stopped was when she opened herself up to seeing him as a friend. Now came the question did she want more? She felt at ease and content with him in the friend zone. Too much was at stake if things didn't work out, including her job, a place to live, and her friends.

"I don't know what—"

"Don't say anything," Jace interrupted. "I'll give you until the new year to wrap your head around what I said. Just know that I have an answer for every argument you can think of as to why we wouldn't be good together. Now let's go get our picture taken so we can eat a decent meal."

Words failed Claire as she stood there, wide-eyed and unable to speak, only able to communicate through a slight nod of her head.

Claire realized she needed to do some thinking.

The End

Afterword

Thank you for reading Claire's Forever Love. This is the second book of the Hawkins Ridge Animal Sanctuary series. Each brother will have their own chance at finding their forever love.

The Asher House, an organization based in Oregon, partially inspired the idea of the sanctuary. What Lee Asher and his staff are doing is amazing. If you have not seen their videos on YouTube or social media and you love animals, check them out.

I have a soft spot for all animals and I'm embarrassed by the rabbit hole I go down watching animal videos on Instagram. If you are interested in sharing your home with a furry friend, please visit your local shelter. So many dogs, cats and a variety of other friends are desperately looking for homes. If you don't have the space, consider volunteering your time. They are always looking for people to take the animals on walks or simply just sit with them. Too busy? Consider donating food, blankets or toys. Something to let the underpaid and overworked staff know they are not alone in their love of animals.

Yes, I did name Balty, Oriole and Cammie after my love of the Orioles. Thanks to the MLB ticket, I was able to see every Oriole game in the 2024 season here in Albuquerque. Keeping fingers crossed for the 2025 season.

Want to keep up with what's going on in the series and be the first to see cover reveals and sneak snippets? Sign up for my monthly newsletter. or follow me on Instagram at @rubyjameswrites.

Acknowledgements

There are so many I want to thank. First, my husband Paul. I wouldn't be able to follow my dream without your love and encouragement. I am thankful every day for agreeing to meet you for that glass of wine.

To Becky, thank you for being there for me and letting me use Vader as a character. Duke is already on the pages of the next book. I am still waiting to hit the lottery so we can buy the small island, set up our sanctuary and stop adulting.

To my amazing beta readers, Joyce and Nancy. You are the best and your feedback helped make this story better.

To my mother. The woman who taught me how to be a strong black woman. She is the muse for several mothers and grandmothers in my stories. I wouldn't know how to love and be myself if it wasn't for her. I miss her every day.

To my father, thank you for letting me be me and encouraging me to follow my heart. I miss you.

My LERA (Land of Enchantment Romance Authors) group. Present and past members have been nothing but encouraging. All of this, every book, is because my group of fellow writers talked me off the ledge when I wanted to give up. You've all made me a better writer. Thank you.

Melody Jeffries, my cover artist and friend. Your smiling face will always pop into my mind whenever I hear the Friends theme song. Your artistic vision for my covers is appreciated. I hope you're falling in love with green chiles.

Kate Marope, thank you for believing in my first attempt at publishing. You are making me a better writer and I appreciate you and all your directions.

To my ARC team. Thank you for being my first 'fans.' It means more than I could ever express.

Most importantly, thank you to <u>every</u> reader who has purchased or borrowed one of my books. I am thankful for helping me make my dream a reality,

Also by

Point Harbor Sweet Romance
From Illustrating To Love
Maybe More Than Friends
Ronan's Queen
Seasoned New Beginnings
Point Harbor Box Set
**Hawkins Ridge Animal Rescue—Sweet and Clean
Small-Town Romance**
Sheltering Naomi
Claires' Forever Love (Jace and Claire–January 2025)
Rescuing Sienna's Heart (Noah and Sienna–Spring 2025)
Blair's Sanctuary (Caden and Blair–Summer 2025)

About the Author

Ruby James is the pseudonym of a middle-aged woman living in the Land of Enchantment (New Mexico). Having grown up in the Washington, DC, area, she made the move to Albuquerque in 2006 alongside her future husband. With a background in healthcare, A bohemian woman who adores classic rock, Marvel, bacon, and coffee. She and her husband share their home with the Queen of the Castle, a tuxedo cat named Random.

9 798992 517200